A CAR TO DIE FOR

A CAR TO DIE FOR

BY

JOHN WING JR

Library and Archives Canada Cataloguing in Publication

Title: A car to die for / John Wing Jr

Names: Wing, John, Jr, 1959- author.

Description: Translation of: Bienvenue en Afrique.

Identifiers: Canadiana (print) 20210169095
                 Canadiana (ebook) 2021016915X

ISBN 9781771615723 (softcover) ISBN 9781771615730 (PDF)
ISBN 9781771615747 (EPUB) ISBN 9781771615754 (Kindle)

Subjects: LCSH: Economic development—Africa. | LCSH: Africa—
Economic conditions. | LCSH: Africa—Foreign economic relations—Asia.
| LCSH: Asia—Foreign economic relations—Africa.

Classification: LCC PS8595.I5953 C37 2021
                   DDC C813/.54—dc23

Published by Mosaic Press, Oakville, Ontario, Canada, 2021.

MOSAIC PRESS, Publishers
www.Mosaic-Press.com
Copyright © John Wing Jr 2021

Printed and bound in Canada.

Cover Design by Rahim Piracha

MOSAIC PRESS
1252 Speers Road, Units 1 & 2, Oakville, Ontario, L6L 5N9
(905) 825-2130 • info@mosaic-press.com • www.mosaic-press.com

Everyone must feel the temptation to leave their life behind. Don't forget that in fact no one ever does...you take it with you.

Diana Phipps

A CAR TO DIE FOR

SATURDAY

The drive to the office took five minutes, eight with traffic. And there was never any traffic on Saturday mornings. Clarence was pretty sure he was the only lawyer in town who saw clients on Saturday. Though Elder wasn't a large town, with roughly eighty thousand people, it contained at least a hundred lawyers, probably more. How all of them made a living was a mystery to him. He scraped out an existence on bank loans, bitching at clients to pay their accounts, and the occasional settlement, though he hated civil work. All the money possibilities made the clients drool with anticipation but most often it was years before you got anything, if you did. Ten days ago he had received his share of the largest settlement he'd ever been a part of. Eighty grand was the lawyer's cut, and it took two solid years to get it. By that time, of course, he owed virtually every cent of it and it was already gone. But as he liked to say, he was almost solvent again, and his banker was happy, so the five minute ride today wasn't as frightening and unpleasant as it sometimes was.

Seeing people on Saturday was good business, since most people worked and sometimes couldn't get to their lawyer's office during regular hours. It was odd that no other lawyers he knew had thought of that. And he didn't have to stay long today either, since there was only one appointment, at 9:30. *We're going to make a dent in the paperwork today*, he thought. *Go hard until the client arrives. And it's Nate Erdmann, so it's probably nothing more than a codicil for his will.* Nate was a man who changed his mind a lot, and since he'd filed his last will and testament two years earlier, he'd added fourteen codicils. He had four children and each of them had been disinherited and then reinstated at least once. Clarence couldn't remember who was in or out at the moment, but the will was two inches thick.

He parked in the lot behind his office, an old blue clapboard house across from the Elder town library. They were both open for business on Saturday morning. He got out of his Mercury, and paused to check his reflection in the driver's window. A mildly vain man, Clarence was now forty-five and beginning to show signs of wear. His hair was a sprinkled grey and he had the beginnings of a paunch that, left alone to collect interest, would soon be a fat bank account. *I should walk more*, he thought, as he strolled the twelve steps to his door.

He'd been a lawyer for twenty years, most of it here in Elder, a quiet lake town 2 hours northeast of Detroit. He'd come from Marquette in 1958, trying to get some distance from his hometown, lured by the promise of - what else? – money. The oil and chemical refineries paid fantastic wages to almost 20,000 people then, as now, 17 years later. In '58 he was sure he wouldn't stay long, and now it was already 1975, and he was established. He knew he would never go back to the Upper Peninsula, and in truth he didn't want to for a variety of reasons. He walked up the steps, past the sign that said Clarence Keaton, Attorney-At-Law. His offices took up the second floor. He had rented the first floor to a physician for a while, but he was now gone and the first floor was unoccupied. His secretary was working on finding a new tenant.

Most Saturdays started with a pot of coffee and several cigarettes. He had two motions and a discovery to prepare for cases coming to court the next week, and had written one line of the first one when he heard the door open downstairs and a voice calling him.

"Mr. Keaton?"

Clarence went halfway down the stairs and invited the man up. He was in his early fifties, wiry and strong looking, maybe five-seven or eight, and there was an other-worldliness about him; an ease within the space he occupied, a force field surrounding him for a couple of feet.

He didn't smile or frown, seeing everything without actually appearing to look at anything. Clarence knew before he sat down that he'd been in prison.

"My name is James Elliot," he said. "I need a lawyer."

"Of course, Mr. Elliot. For what reason?"

"Do you mind if I smoke, Mr. Keaton?"

"Please do." They both lit up. "Coffee?" Clarence asked.

"Yes, please. Black." Clarence got two cups ready and surreptitiously checked his watch. Okay, only 8:15. Erdmann wouldn't be late, but he was never early, either, so it was possible to get this guy done in time. He brought the coffee over to Elliot and sat down behind his desk, moving the glass ashtray where they both could reach it.

"What is it I can do for you, Mr. Elliot?"

"Well, I'm going to be arrested today."

"I see. For a criminal offense, I take it?"

"Burglary."

"One burglary?"

"Oh, I doubt that. I think it will be in the range of ten or fifteen charges." Clarence made a note of that.

"What do you do for a living, Mr. Elliot?"

"I'm a burglar, Mr. Keaton." Clarence laughed, in spite of himself. Laughing at the client wasn't normal procedure, but it was funny to hear a professional lay it out so clearly. Elliot was not fazed in any way. He started to grin a little, then thought better of it.

"Forgive me, Mr. Elliot," said Clarence. "You seem a bit old to be a second-story man."

"That's possibly true," Elliot admitted, shrugging. "But ability is nothing without opportunity."

"Aha," said Clarence, "A renaissance man."

"What do you mean, Mr. Keaton?" Elliot asked.

"A burglar who reads Napoleon." said Clarence. "Can't say I've seen one before this."

"And you've been a lawyer for twenty years," said Elliot with another tiny smile.

"Indeed," Clarence replied, brushing off the question of how Elliot would know that and stealing another glance at his watch. "So, you're going to be arrested and charged today. Do you have bail money?"

"They won't give me bail."

"You've been convicted before, then?"

"Yes, sir, and I escaped once."

That stopped Clarence. Someone who admitted they were a professional criminal was rare enough, but someone who'd successfully busted out of prison, and stated it like they were saying they'd installed a new doorknob was thin air indeed. His mentor in the law, Benjamin Yawkey, had drilled that into him. "Son, nine hundred and ninety-nine out of a thousand criminal clients are full of shit, and they're paying you to defend how full of shit they are. Never act surprised." One who told the truth was surprising, and made it a special Saturday.

"From which penitentiary did you escape?" Clarence asked, unable to control his curiosity.

"Southern Michigan."

"Well now, I would say that's quite an achievement."

"To the layman, I suppose," Elliot grinned again. "Law enforcement viewed it as something else entirely."

"That's not unusual. So you'll need me for arraignment and trial?"

"That's correct, sir."

"The retainer will be five thousand dollars," Clarence said, hoping a professional wouldn't balk. Elliot stood up and took out his wallet.

"I can give you a thousand in cash now, and I have a car I won't need while I'm in jail."

"I'm afraid I don't need a car either, Mr. Elliot."

"I thought perhaps you could sell it for the rest of your fee. Assuming we go to trial and I'm convicted. . I'm fifty-one, Mr. Keaton, and this'll be my fourth stretch. I don't anticipate getting out again."

"I'm not the worst lawyer in the world. I might get you off."

"I know you're good. You come highly recommended."

"If you don't mind me asking, by whom?"

"Tony Ferrera." That surprised Clarence, though he took pains not to show it. Tony Ferrera had gone down for ten years for armed robbery, and hadn't been notably grateful when verdict and sentence were read. But, you never can tell about people.

"I'm not sure the car selling idea will be enough," said Clarence, recovering from the idea that an asshole like Ferrera would actually throw him some business. "What kind of car is it?"

"A 1954 Studebaker Starlight coupe."

Really? Clarence had a brief moment or two of reverie, time-traveling back to his twenties, a place he rarely went anymore. He loved cars, then. And the Studebaker Starlight was something he once envisioned himself driving. Hell, *owning*. As a criminal lawyer in a smallish town, he had to drive something solid and respectable, like the Merc. Appearances were important, and indulgences were dangerous. *Business is business, and Christmas is bullshit*, as Ben Yawkey used to say. He snapped out of the dream, which seemed much longer than the two or three seconds it lasted.

"Where is the car now, Mr. Elliot?"

"It's downstairs in your parking lot." Clarence rose from his seat.

"Let's go down and take a look at it."

The car was parked on the far side of Clarence's Mercury, which was much larger and made it invisible unless you were right next to it. It was a pale red, with the distinctive front grille and sleek lines, and of course the silver hawk hood ornament. It was in perfect condition and took Clarence's breath away. He resisted the urge to say *they don't make them like this anymore*, which was true, since the car was over 20 years old and the company had been out of business since the late sixties. He presented the fantasy of keeping the car to himself for a moment, in lieu of the rest of his fee. *Why not?*

"I suspect it's worth at least eight thousand," said Elliot quietly, breaking the silence, "of which you might lay aside eight hundred to a thousand for my commissary account at whatever escape-proof pen they send me to." Clarence nodded.

"That's no problem. But there might be a small glitch. It's not a stolen car, is it?"

"I thought you might inquire along that line." Elliot opened the passenger door, reached into the glovebox and came out with the registration and the title certificate, handing them over. The title assignment section was neatly filled out.

"I bought it in 1960, from a little old lady who rarely drove it. It was collecting dust in her garage."

"How did it come to your attention?" Clarence was breaking a rule by asking a question he might not know the answer to, but his curiosity got the better of him.

"Her garage had a skylight, Mr. Keaton," Elliot replied. "I noticed it there one summer evening."

"What were you doing on the roof of her garage, Mr. Elliot?" You could never tell with clients. Even the stories that sounded true were often bullshit.

"I wasn't," said Elliot. "I was on the roof of the place next door. The take from that place fenced for enough to buy the car and keep it in storage while I was in the can." Clarence started to laugh.

"I'll take the case," he said, shaking his head. What an odd Saturday. They went back upstairs and Clarence filled out the buyer's section of the title, after which Elliot handed him the keys. It was getting close to when Erdmann was supposed to show up but Clarence had a few more questions.

"While I appreciate the prompt payment, Mr. Elliot..."

"I think you can start calling me Jim, Mr. Keaton."

"All right, Jim. While I appreciate it, is there anything about the car, or possibly inside it, that I might need to know about?" Elliot's face registered a small twinge that lasted only a moment or two. It could even have been called a twinkle, but Clarence noticed.

"Mr. Keaton, I love the car. Truly. I've had it a while and have often considered it my only friend. By selling it to someone who will also love it, and take care of it, you would be doing me a favor. I suspect if the police get hold of it, they'll impound it and I don't want that to happen. So it's yours now, all legal and above board once you take that form to the DMV and pay the transfer title fee. There's nothing in it as far as I know that I'm going to need, although I will caution you that it rusts easily in winter, so I wouldn't drive it during the cold months, the salted-road months, and I wouldn't park it on the street, either. There are a lot of people who might try to steal it."

"That's not unusual," said Clarence. He resisted the urge to suggest that Elliot call him by his first name, too. Clients respected you more when you were Mister. It came with the title 'Attorney'. That was another bromide from Ben Yawkey. "They gotta respect you, son. So stand up tall. You are *Mister* Keaton. Even if you're not sure what the hell is going on, you hold your tremors and goddamn *act* like you do. Don't ever let them see you surprised." Nothing ever flustered Mr. Yawkey. The client could say, "My wife has been jerking off our dog." And Ben would nod soberly and say, "That's not unusual," or "They all do." Clarence smiled, remembering it, and heard a siren getting close. He looked at Elliot.

"Is that for us?"

"For me, yes sir. I called this morning and told them I would surrender at my lawyer's office at 9:30."

"How did you know I would be in the office on a Saturday?" Clarence asked, beginning to get the feeling he was in the dark about something. Elliot shrugged.

"I asked around. Shall we?" Clarence glanced out the window to see the cops were getting out of their cars. Three cars for one burglar. What assholes. Then he saw Nate Erdmann walking around from the parking lot. Oh, *shit.*

Nate saw the cops pull up as he was turning toward the path to the front door. Initially he wasn't alarmed, until one of the uniforms called out to him.

"Freeze, Elliot! You're under arrest! Nate immediately stopped dead and raised his hands, turning to the group of four uniformed men and a man and woman in plainclothes.

"My name is Erdmann," he said, as the male detective walked up to him.

"Could I see some identification, sir? Nate produced his wallet, at which point, the front door of the house opened and Clarence came out with Elliot behind him. The other five cops drew their guns, which looked and was ridiculous. Clarence raised his hands.

"Gentlemen: I represent James Elliot. This is he and his wish is to surrender right now." Turning, Clarence saw that his client was now lying on the ground, on his stomach, with his hands behind his head. *Man, does this guy know the drill*, he thought. The two detectives and two of the uniforms came up, cuffed Elliot and took him to one of the patrol cars. As he left the porch, their eyes met, and Clarence put a finger to his lips, even though he was fairly sure Elliot knew that drill as well. The two patrol cars took off. The detectives stayed. Clarence turned to Nate Erdmann.

"Please go on upstairs and make yourself at home, Nate," he said. "There's coffee on the sideboard. I'll be a moment or two." Nate huffed a little but did as he was told. Clarence turned to the detectives, Ross and Merwin by name. Big Mike Ross was a veteran of the Elder PD, probably at least twenty-five years on the job. Six feet tall, thick as a plank road, black hair in a military buzz, graying at the edges now. His latest partner was Louise Merwin, Elder's first female detective. A big-shouldered brunette who put up a no-nonsense, all-business front, although some, Clarence included, knew it was just that. Clarence had represented her in her divorce two years earlier from an abusive husband and had seen her softer side firsthand. She liked him, he thought, and understood he had a job to do, as did she. Mike didn't like Clarence, and had held a grudge for a at least a decade over a single case. The Thrasher case. Clarence's cross-examination of Mike was one of the big moments of that trial and Mike was made to look a fool. Privately, and sometimes not so privately, Mike Ross believed that if it hadn't been for that goddamn testimony in that goddamn case and that goddamn fucking lawyer, he'd be the chief of police in Elder now. He was his usual blunt self.

"Did he give you anything, Keaton?"

"I'm sorry, Detective Ross? He retained me to represent him."

"He's guilty as hell, and you know it."

"If memory serves, Mike, it's your job to prove that."

"This guy is going for the whole hog. We've got plenty on him."

"Well, I certainly hope it was all legally obtained. Please don't try and question my client until I'm present, all right?"

"We don't take orders from you, asshole."

"Come on, Mike," Louise touched his arm. "Let's get back. We got the guy." She nodded to Clarence as Mike turned and went to the car.

Clarence waited on the porch until they pulled away, which Mike noticed, and gave him the finger out the car window. Some cops had real class.

Upstairs, Nate was in something of a pique. Clarence sat down and lit a cigarette, hoping for a moment or two before Nate told him what new vengeful notation he wanted to add to his will. He'd barely blown out the first lungful when Nate spoke up.

"What in the holy blue hell was that downstairs? I'm not comfortable being accosted by the police, I'll have you know."

"I apologize, Nate. The man showed up out of nowhere an hour ago. You were the only client on the sheet today. What can I do for you?"

"I want to change my will," Nate said. Successfully concealing his shock, Clarence opened his notebook and grabbed his pen.

"Tell me how."

Nate had a check for two hundred dollars ready and handed it over when they were done. Clarence assured him that his second-born son would be out of the will (for the third time) by Monday morning. After Nate left, Clarence tried to do a little paperwork. He wrote out one of the motions, doing his best, even though he was sure both motions were going to be denied. The discovery was most likely going to show his client was incontrovertibly guilty of sexual assault. But, you could never be sure. Cops and prosecutors often got very sloppy when they were sure they had someone open-and-shut. He wrote out the second motion, then went over the discovery stuff on his side. Then he sat for a while looking across the street at the Library, wondering why the hell he'd ever become a lawyer in the first place. Librarians were on his envy list today. Easy salary, spend the day with books, and your biggest worry was books lost or not returned. You rescued books and introduced people to reading. He should have gone into that. Of course Librarians were mostly women, but he would have fit in. Maybe his mother would have agreed to that profession. She certainly didn't agree to any of the ones he aspired to.

Maybe I could be a judge, he thought, perhaps for the hundredth time. It was something lawyers often did. And there was a guaranteed salary and expenses and a nice chair, above it all. The only difficulty was the judging part. He certainly judged everyone he knew or met, but there were no real consequences to that. Having to send people to prison? No thank you. Plus you had to be elected here. And running for office wasn't something he could envision. Ever.

He shook his head to break the reverie. It was a good day, twelve hundred dollars earned, a cool car, and the rest of the day off. No need to spoil it with ancient thoughts. He looked around the office and decided he'd been there long enough. When he got to the parking lot and saw the Studebaker, he realized there was more to do. He couldn't leave it here, or take it home. He opened the Starlight's trunk and found a zippered leather bag about three feet long. It was heavy, and he feared the worst as he unzipped it. But it was just tools. Drills and bits, a pry bar, a pinch bar, a small crowbar, a wire hanger, wrenches, screwdrivers, et cetera. Burglar's tools. He put them in the trunk of his Mercury. A cursory eyeball search found nothing else in the Studebaker, save some receipts in the glove box and what appeared to be an extra set of keys. *Okay,* he thought, *now where do I put it?* Elliot's warning about someone stealing it was clearly code. And although it was pretty obvious code, Clarence took it seriously. If he was going to get the fee by selling it, he had to be sure it was safe. Looking at it, though, he wondered if he actually could sell it. It was so beautiful. He was contriving some elaborate hiding scenarios when he realized he had a perfect place within a hundred feet of where he was standing.

When he'd bought the house, eight years earlier, he'd been very pleased with the large backyard, fenced on three sides that, once he'd gotten rid of the lawn and installed gravel would serve as a perfect hidden lot for himself, his secretary, and the clients. Then the real estate woman pointed out a little perk. Behind the back fence, not visible because two large oaks were flanking it and the fence itself was overgrown with ivy and other bushes, was a small garage that appeared to belong to the house behind his, but was actually on his property. There was a gate in the fence, that, because of the ivy, couldn't be discerned. Clarence walked out to the street and looked around. Nothing stirring, no traffic, and no one walking. He went back to the fence and opened the gate wide, walked through and opened the garage. He hadn't been inside it for close to two years, and the smell hit him hard. *Along the road to musty death,* he thought. Spider webs were all over the place, floor to ceiling, and he wondered how they could all make a living in such a tiny enclosed space. Like this town, he thought. A quick look and some moving of small items emptied a space large enough for the car. He went back to the lot, fired up the Starlight, glorying in the sound of that V-8, the perfect meshing of the gears, and drove it into the garage, covered it with an old tarp, shut the doors and locked them, then rejiggered the gate to look like there was no gate. He rewarded himself on a job well done with a cigarette as he walked back to his Merc.

When he got there he saw a plastic bag slung on the driver's door handle. It had two big lake trout in it and two gold-eyes, packed in ice. That would be Eddie Two Crows. Clarence acted for the Odawa tribe a lot, as well as other men and women in the Council Of Three Fires. There were two reservations within a thirty mile radius, and cops were always harassing them, as though their lives weren't shitty enough. Eddie was a Tribal Council member who had first hired Clarence to defend him over a small criminal matter over ten years before. Clarence had readily agreed to act for Eddie for a fee of year round fresh fish and game to eat. The Odawa council paid him a small annual retainer, but mostly his services were bartered. He had a gorgeous winter coat that one of the ladies had made for him, and he ate rabbit, fish, wild turkey, some deer, the odd moose, and once or twice a year, bear steaks. Every two or three weeks, Eddie would drop off some fresh kill. But he normally came inside. He must have seen the police cars. Maybe he was holding some pot or something. Natives avoided contact with the cops . Clarence smiled as he got in his car, laying the bag carefully on the passenger seat. Twelve hundred dollars in his pocket, on a Saturday, no less; and fresh fish for dinner. He drove home to put the fish away.

Home was 428 George Street, across from the Parish Hall of a Catholic church, Saint Mary Magdalene, or as Clarence referred to it, 'Our Lady of the Whorehouse'. His apartment was in a house, a sort of faux-Victorian monstrosity that was built for a wealthy couple who disagreed over the style, so it looked like two ugly houses mashed into one. The couple had long since died and it was owned by a widow named Elaine Turner, who was called 'Shorty' by everyone. She was sharp-tongued and something of a bore, but he liked her because she never held back an opinion and didn't give a rat's ass who it might offend or shock. That kind of personal honesty was something he greatly admired, and envied. He rented the second floor of her ugly house, which had plenty of room, privacy and relatively low rent because he helped her with chores, oversaw the hiring of workmen as needed, and kept an eye on her finances for her, making sure she wasn't being cheated by bankers or accountants, something she was occasionally suspicious about. He also took her to the movies virtually every Sunday. The four o'clock show at the local Odeon, which had recently expanded to two screens. His apartment had a private entrance and he didn't see Shorty as he zipped upstairs, put the bag of fish in his freezer an changed his clothes. Attired in a more relaxed way, he headed to the golf club for his regular Saturday afternoon drink. Or two.

On the way, He stopped at the new police headquarters-city jail-courthouse complex to make sure Elliot was being treated properly. It was only three blocks from the golf club, which was magically convenient during the week. He hoped they hadn't questioned Elliot yet.

Even though he was a professional, that was worrisome. You told people time and again: Don't say anything other than 'I have nothing to say' OR 'I want to see my attorney', but clients managed to do that perhaps one or two times out of a thousand. Cops knew how to pry words loose, and people who'd been arrested were so susceptible. They wanted *so* much to explain what happened and why they were innocent, and they all thought they were smarter than cops, who happened to do this sort of thing for a living. And, of course, once you *started* talking it was almost impossible to stop until they had you on tape saying you sank the goddamn Titanic and all your lawyer could do at that point would be to plead you guilty of being criminally stupid. Don't talk, and they have to use the evidence to convict you, and that evidence is often a bit thin.

Clarence had always admired the Brinks robbers. There were eleven of them, and it took the cops six years, eleven months and twenty days to get a single one of them to talk. The statute of limitations had eleven days left on it when one of them broke, and the others continued to say nothing throughout their trial. Clarence respected professionals, and he knew that when you had something to tell people, it was extraordinarily difficult to restrain the urge to spill it.

The Elder City Jail was a depressing place, gray walls and black linoleum floors. Sergeant Al Donohue was pulling the weekend desk duty.

"Hi, Al," Clarence began.

"Counselor," Al replied, seemingly uninterested.

"I'm here to see my client, James Elliot."

"Right, the burglar."

"*Alleged* burglar is, I believe, the correct phrase," Clarence said, trying to appear stern. Sergeant Donohue wasn't impressed.

"Ross says they've got him cold."

"I guess we shouldn't even have a trial, then," Clarence intoned. Donohue looked up .

"Well, Mike said they had him cold. They've been in interrogation for two hours, so I bet he's signed a full confession by now."

"I specifically told them not to question my client without me present!" Clarence didn't raise his voice often in the jail, but it seemed appropriate. Donohue shrugged and indicated the hallway.

"You know where it is."

"Goddamn right I do." He headed down the hall, expecting the worst. He reached the first interrogation room and found Louise Merwin watching through the one way mirror. Through the glass he saw Elliot sitting at the table, still cuffed, and Mike Ross standing over him, clearly agitated.

"I said not to question him without me, Louise. I *said* that."

"Not to me you didn't." She smiled a little. Clarence failed to see the humor.

"Has he confessed?"

"Oh, he's said a lot of things."

"Shit," said Clarence. *Shit, shit, shit.*

"He said he wanted to see his attorney. He wanted his phone call. He wanted a coffee. He said, 'I don't know' about a hundred times, and he said 'Why don't you go fuck yourself' once, to Mike." Clarence relaxed, a bit. He was still in dangerous territory.

"I should get in there. How are things going for you, Louise?"

"Fine, thanks, Clarence. Greg is respecting the restraining order you got. So far." Louise's ex-husband had been having a hard time with closure regarding his now-dissolved marriage. Clarence nodded and put his hand on the door to go in. She stopped him.

"You know, that offer I made still stands."

"You were serious about that, Louise? You'd date a lawyer?"

"Why not? You gotta try everything once, right?" Clarence laughed.

"I'm working. I'll get back to you." He opened the door and strode in, trying to look stern and strong. Mike Ross was in the middle of one of his loud Cop-proclamations.

"...well I KNOW you did it, you son of a bitch!"

Clarence took as deep a breath as he could, careful not to trigger a coughing jag.

"This illegal interrogation is over, Detective."

"Illegal, my ass," Ross snarled at him.

"My client has asked for his attorney, has he not? To continue to question him after that request is illegal."

"Fine. You gonna bring me up on charges, Keaton?"

"It wouldn't be the first time, would it Detective Ross?" That shut the big fellow right up. Louise came in and handed Elliot a cup of coffee, which he accepted with cuffed hands.

"Why is my client still in handcuffs?"

That's procedure, Mr. Keaton. You know that." It was Louise who answered.

"Procedure, yes, I see. Has he been booked yet?" Clarence was asking a question to which he knew the answer.

"No, he hasn't."

"Isn't that also PROCEDURE, detectives? Or is your goddamn evidence so thin you decided you'd better beat a confession out of him first?"

"We didn't beat him, you asshole," said Mike Ross, "There isn't a mark on the guy."

"I intend to inform the judge and the Police review board that you questioned my client for two hours without his lawyer, in direct violation of the law, and anything he said will be unusable in court because…"

"Oh, shut the fuck up, Keaton," interrupted Ross. "Louise, book this piece of shit."

Detective Merwin helped Elliot up and escorted him out and down the hall. Clarence caught his eye for a moment and winked. Elliot responded with a barely perceptible nod. Detective Ross wasn't finished, though.

"Keaton, this guy has stolen millions in cash and jewelry. You should see his sheet. Why would you defend a scumbag like him?"

"Because everyone deserves a defense, Mike. Even the scumbags. I'll be back after he's been processed to confer with him. If you start questioning him again, I'll stick the entire review board up your ass, and I'm not kidding." Clarence turned and walked out swiftly, though not in a hurry, and halfway down the hall he was pretty sure he could still hear Detective Ross seething.

Booking usually took about an hour, so Clarence repaired to the golf club, a four minute walk. He ordered a beer and found his friend Simon Roche at his usual table. Simon was a gambler. He lived by his wits, playing high-stakes golf in the summer, and cards – bridge and poker – in the winter. He bet the horses. He bet football. He'd bet on anything. He lived with his widowed sister in her house, paid no rent, drove his dead brother-in-law's car, had few expenses at all other than the thousand dollar a year membership to the golf club, which he strongly resented and felt was too high. Clarence found him funny and admired anyone who could actually live that way. Simon was also honest to a fault, and didn't give a shit what people thought of him, which Clarence also admired.

It was Saturday afternoon, so Simon had already played a round of golf and was into his third or fourth scotch while perusing the racing form. A large man, alcohol seemed to never affect him, until about the eleventh or twelfth snort, after which he might get a strange look in his eye and pass out, collapsing to the floor like an emptied sack of laundry. He saw Clarence coming and motioned him over.

"Counselor. Sit yourself down. I've been wondering what became of you."

"You see me here most days," Clarence replied, smiling.

"Yeah, but a lot earlier than this." Simon pointed to the racing form. "Look, man. Cat Burglar in the fourth at Lawrence Park. He's fourteen to one. We have about 20 minutes to get a bet down."

"Cat Burglar, eh? How have the horses been treating you lately?"

"Horses treat you like the weather. Some days good, some days it rains."

The serendipitous name of the horse felt strange to Clarence, and where once he might have immediately laid out his money, today he hesitated. A twelve hundred dollar Saturday early in the month wasn't enough to make him feel flush. One of the things growing up with his mother taught him was caution. She could take a sip of her third beer and suddenly turn into a dragon. He was always on the lookout for dragons.

"So, you want a piece of this? I'm going to the phone," said Simon.

"Not today, Simon. But good luck." Simon drained his drink, sucking the ice noisily for a moment to make sure all the alcohol was inside him, then headed off to the payphone in the back of the bar. There were two other payphones by the locker room down the hall, but this one was strictly for calling the bookies. Clarence poured a beer from the pitcher on the table and took a sip, finding it calming and delicious. He looked around the room. On an early fall Saturday it would hold forty or fifty men, mostly professionals; doctors, lawyers, teachers, engineers and such. He saw Bob Flacco, his main competition in town for criminal work, decked out in impeccably fitted and pressed golf clothes. Bob always cut a dashing figure. They exchanged nods. They'd faced each other once in a civil suit, but hadn't become friends, even though he liked Bob and admired his abilities. There was a wariness in both of them that precluded it. For Flacco it was just the general you don't fraternize with the competition. For Clarence it was something else.

"Got it down. Two hundred on the nose," said Simon, returning. "Could be a red-letter day." He sat down and poured himself a beer. "So we're rooting hard for Cat Burglar, right Clare?"

"Yeah, you bet, Cat Burglar....oh shit." Clarence realized most of his beer was gone and a glance at his watch told him most of the hour was gone, too. He got up, stubbing out a smoke. "Gotta run, Sime. Hope the burglar wins." He was almost out the door when Bob Flacco called to him.

"Clarence!" He turned. Bob gestured toward the table where Simon was sitting. "Your briefcase, Counselor." Clarence knew his face was red as he walked back and retrieved the case.

"Thanks, Bob," he said as he passed him. Bob smiled.

He briskly walked the three blocks to the jail. James Elliot was waiting in the conference room when he got there. Louise was with him. When Clarence walked in, she rose, nodded to him, and left. Clarence pulled a legal pad from his briefcase and sat down.

"She likes you," Elliot said.

"Louise? How do you know that?"

"She complimented me on retaining you. Said I couldn't do better in the whole town."

"That was sweet of her."

"I think she wants to fuck you as well."

"You're just full of pleasant information, aren't you?" Clarence replied. Elliot looked at him quizzically.

"You're not married anymore. You should go for it. I would."

"Fucking someone you're generally in an adversarial position with professionally is not a good idea, not that it's any of your – Excuse me? Did you just say I wasn't married anymore?"

There it was again; that twinge in Elliot's eyes. It wasn't longer than a second, but it was the same thing he'd seen at the office. And he was beginning to get a sense of it. It clearly meant *How much of this should I tell?* Twenty years of clients lying to you produced some odd instincts, and while he wasn't a man who generally trusted his own instincts, he made an exception here.

"I asked around....about you..." Elliot ventured.

"Sorry, not buying. The people around here who know that wouldn't know you or talk to you about me. Try again." Elliot smiled slightly.

"I'm sorry, Mr. Keaton. I shouldn't lie. Call it an occupational hazard. I did a little research on you. And you're right, the people around here don't seem to know anything about you, other than you're a good lawyer."

"Okay, you researched me. Why?"

"Well...in my business you have to case things, check them out, to be sure. And I like doing it. The guys who don't do their research get caught."

Clarence refrained from stating the obvious, that even the researchers get caught, as Elliot had, more than once. Elliot continued.

"So I went to the library and ascertained when you arrived here. The newspaper article said you came from a town in the U.P. Marquette, right?"

"That's right," Clarence said, nodding.

"And you'd been a lawyer there for three years. I thought it was odd that you'd spend three years establishing a practice and then just up and move. So I called a guy I know up there and asked him to check out the news stories for those years."

Clarence was almost not listening, since this was something he had long tried to convince himself would never occur.

"He found your wedding announcement, from 1955, and the death notice for your wife in 1957. Car accident."

"And you thought it prudent to let me know you knew this. Why?" As he said it, he could see the notice in The Mining Journal. *Rosalie Keaton, nee Walsh, died Sunday in a one car accident on 550 just east of Wetmore Landing. She leaves her husband, Clarence...* Her parents put it in the paper. They were both dead now. And her brother Frank was no doubt in prison somewhere. His eyes met Elliot's and he snapped back to where he was. *This is business. Get in the game.* Elliot hadn't responded. He was just staring at him.

"All right, Jim," Clarence said," Why is this relevant to me defending you?"

"It's not, Mr. Keaton. I'm sorry. I get a little obsessive about research. I don't trust people easily. I needed to know I could trust you."

"All right, from here on out, let's make this about you and your case, not me. What did you tell Mike Ross?"

"Nothing," Elliot replied, "I tried to irritate him enough to get him to tell me a few things."

"And did he?"

"A little. Someone saw me leaving one of the houses. A kid."

"A child who lived in the home?"

"Yeah. Eleven or twelve years old, I think."

"Whose house?" Clarence was making notes.

"Not sure. A large blue house on the lake. It had a turret."

"A turret? At the end of a winding lane?"

"Yes, that's it."

"Shit, that's the mayor's house."

"How can someone live in that kind of house on a municipal salary?"

Something didn't smell right. Clarence's nose twitched. He stared at his client, trying to sense what it was, because it really felt like he was being played.

"So, you check me out to the extent that you know more than anyone in this town knows about me, but you aren't aware of who owns a house you took a big score from? That's horseshit, James. I can't defend you if you keep lying to me, unless your goal is to go right to prison and make me look like an idiot." He took out his cigarettes and shook two out of the pack. The no smoking rule had only recently been put into effect in the jail, so he figured if someone came in he would say he forgot when the inmate asked for one. Elliot took the smoke and Clarence lit both of them. Each of them took a deep drag.

"What's it going to be, Jim? You either trust me, or you'll need a new lawyer. I could recommend Bob Flacco."

"I thought he was too flashy. Bit of a dandy. No, I wanted you. Look, Mr. Keaton, my life is essentially over. I just want this to be painless and I want my car to go to a good place, not rust up and die in some junkyard. I won't lie to you anymore." Clarence knew the last sentence was most likely a lie, but he let it go. Elliot continued. "I knew it was the Mayor's house. But I didn't know he had a kid. I cased the place for a week and never saw any children."

"The Mayor has two children," Clarence said.

"Well, I never saw them."

"They have a cottage on Houghton Lake. His wife and boys spend most of the summer there. The boys are fifteen and ten."

"It must have been the ten year old." Elliot shook his head in frustration.

"He called your name?" Clarence asked.

"No, just a 'hey there!' or something like that. No name. It was muffled."

"Okay." Clarence stood up, putting the legal pad back into his briefcase and closing it.

"You'll be arraigned Monday morning," he said, "I'll be there."

"Okay."

"In the interim, sit tight and don't say a word." Elliot started to say something but Clarence stopped him. "I know you know that so forgive me. It's a thrill to say it to someone who's actually going to do it." Clarence knocked on the door and Louise came in. Clarence turned and tossed his almost full pack of Camels to Elliot. He turned to Louise.

"See that my client gets some matches." She nodded, then leaned and whispered in his ear.

"Can I call you?"

"Sure," he whispered back, hoping it wouldn't be another attempt to date him. Looking at his watch as he left the building, he noted it was almost four o'clock and a long day for the only lawyer working in Elder. He got in the Merc and went home.

Shorty Turner was watering the small garden she kept at the side of the house when he drove up. She met him at the driver's door when he got out.

"I suppose you thought I'd forgotten!" Clarence had no idea what she meant, but he stayed cool. It could be anything.

"Forgotten what, Shorty?"

"That you were going to take me to the movies today! But no, I didn't forget. I'm not one of those older people who can't remember anything, you know!"

"I didn't think you were. I had a client get arrested and I had to go to the jail and see him."

"Oh, really? So you weren't at the club getting drunk?"

"No. I had one beer with Simon."

"Let me smell your breath, mister." He leaned down and she took a long sniff.

"Hmmm, smells like you had a bunch of cigarettes. How many today?"

"A thousand would be my guess. I lose count. I can't remember like you can."

"Have you got an extra one for me?"

"Shorty, the doctor said you weren't allowed anymore."

"Fuck him. He also said my husband was the picture of health two days before he dropped dead." Clarence opened a new pack and gave her one. They walked over to the porch to sit and smoke. Shorty clearly enjoyed every second of each drag.

"Just because you gave me a smoke doesn't mean you're off the hook about forgetting the movie, you know," she said.

"I thought we were going on Sunday," said Clarence. "That's when we usually go." The look on her face told him all he needed to know.

"It's not Sunday?" she said. Clarence shook his head. "Damn," she snorted, blowing out a cloud of smoke. "When you don't work anymore, every day seems like Sunday, doesn't it?"

"I suppose," said Clarence. Shorty flicked the smoke expertly into the gutter, a distance of a least twenty feet, and got up to go.

"See you tomorrow, then," she said, and went inside. When she was gone and out of earshot, Clarence very quietly said, *you're welcome*, before flicking his own cigarette into the street and heading upstairs to his place.

MONDAY

He and Shorty did go to the movies on Sunday. *One Flew Over The Cuckoo's Nest*. Clarence liked it, although he disagreed with Shorty about McMurphy. She said he pretended to be insane for so long that he became insane. Clarence didn't think so, but he eventually gave in to Shorty's argument, since it meant a more pleasant ride home.

Monday morning appeared and the first cigarette of the day was smoked at 6:35 a.m. Nothing ever tasted as good as that first one. In the Merc by seven and at his desk ten minutes later, Clarence reviewed the book for the week. It looked okay. A couple of busy days with three or four clients coming in, and a couple of court days, including today. Not bad. When Paula, his secretary, came in at five to eight, he had already finished the two motions and was making notes for the discovery.

Paula Atherton, a tall, spare black woman, was thirty-nine years old. She had been married and divorced before she was thirty and now lived alone in her parents' old house on the north side of town.

The black side. Her parents were dead, and she'd been an only child. The house was paid for, and she was quite comfortable on a legal secretary's salary, thank you very much. She used her height and her blackness to intimidate people a little bit, since she occasionally had to show people that she ran this office, and if they wanted access to Mr. Keaton they were going to have to go through her and no one else. But what set her apart for Clarence had been her intelligence, her quick-study ability to grasp or anticipate what he wanted, and her sense of humor. She had been his secretary for eleven years, and Clarence had never once regretted the decision to hire her, although her sharp tongue was irritating once in a while. She put her head in the office door to say good morning before going to her desk in the foyer at the top of the stairs.

"Morning, Slim," Clarence said, "Can you call the clerk and find out when Elliot is being arraigned this morning?"

"Elliot?" she asked.

"Sorry, Jim Elliot – *James* Elliot. New guy. Came in Saturday morning."

"And he's already in jail? Charming."

"Don't judge. He paid a thousand retainer in cash. Here." He handed her the wad. "Oh, and Nate paid me two hundred by cheque to change his will." He handed her the cheque as well. She was riffling through the cash.

"There's only nine hundred and sixty-five here," she said.

"I took Shorty to the movies. I bought Chinese food. Sue me."

"I wonder if Flacco would take a small claims case like this," she said, grinning.

"I doubt it," said Clarence. "But you could certainly call him. Maybe he has an opening in his secretarial pool."

"I'll find out," she said.

"Before you do, deposit that stuff in the office account, get the mail, oh, here." He handed her the notes from the meeting with Nate Erdmann. "Type up this codicil to Nate's will, and find out when James Elliot is being arraigned this morning. And have some coffee. Oh, and put Elliot in the client file. He's fifty-one years old, and he's a professional."

"Baseball player?"

"Burglar."

"Well, at least he paid something." She turned to leave, then turned back. "Oh yes, the massage people called again on Friday after you left. They upped the offer to three hundred and twenty-five dollars a month."

"Paula, I can't rent the first floor to a goddamn massage parlor, ok?"

"The clients would certainly come upstairs more relaxed," Paula said, almost seriously. She left him stewing at his desk. Three twenty-five was a decent offer. The ground floor of the house had been vacant now for two months, since the lawyer who'd been in residence there had been disbarred. Clarence wanted another lawyer, or a doctor. Not a massage parlor, which was like saying there was a brothel downstairs. But the money would certainly help. *I wonder if they'd throw in free massages for us...?* He banished from his mind and finished the discovery notes. When he finished, the clock said 8:20. Would Hallberg be in the office yet? He decided to chance it. Hallberg answered on the first ring.

"Hallberg Insurance."

"It's Clarence Keaton."

"Of course it is," said Jessie Hallberg, "Who the hell else would call me this early? Whaddaya need? You have an accident?"

"Not today, Jessie. I need to insure another car."

"You bought a new car?"

"No."

"A used car? How many times have I told you, Clarence..."

"Jessie, I need a favor."

"What? I mean, you got it, whatever."

"I need you to shut up for a second so I can tell you what I actually need. Okay?"

"Okay. Shoot."

"I got another car, sort of by accident."

"So it was an accident?"

"No, goddamnit! What did I say?"

"Sorry. Shutting up now."

"I got another car, by...by *chance*, all right. I'll probably end up selling it, but in the meantime I need it insured."

"Okay. What kind of car is it?"

"A Studebaker Starlight."

"No shit? What year?"

"1954."

"Mint condition?"

"I'd say so."

"What's the VIN?"

"Damn, I don't know. I'll get it for you."

"No rush. So you're probably gonna sell it?"

"That's the plan."

"So I should insure it as a collectible valuable on your home policy....except...wait a minute, you don't own a home and so we don't have a policy on that…we have car insurance on the Mercury and your whole life policy. Okay, I'll add it to the Merc and make it a collectible, too. Shit, that'll be a lot of work."

"Well, what if I pay you? Would that help?"

"I guess. Okay, I'll make some calls and see what it might bring at auction."

"Okay, thanks," said Clarence. Then he remembered Elliot's warning. "Oh, and Jess?"

"Yeah?"

"Don't mention my name or that it's me you're doing it for."

"What, are you hiding assets for a divorce or something?"

"Sure, whatever. Just don't put my name on anything yet."

"No problem. I'll call with more info when I have it."

"Great, thanks Jess." As he hung up, Paula called out to him.

"Elliot's arraignment is at 9:30." Perfect. Get it in, make both motions and the discovery, and then the day would be done. Could be an easy one. He put everything in the briefcase and headed out, pausing at Paula's desk.

"Might be back before lunch, might not."

"Sure, leave me here, alone, penniless," she replied. It was a subtle reference to the raise she'd been angling for the last couple of months. He'd been putting her off.

"Get the mail. Thanks." He zipped down the stairs and was heading to the courthouse within two minutes.

Once there, he had a few minutes alone with Elliot before the arraignment and was surprised by his client's suggestion that they just plead guilty and get it over with. Clarence was forceful in his disagreement. We plead not guilty and we get to see their evidence. If they have you cold, *then* we make a deal. We don't just hand it to them. No, sir. Finally Elliot agreed, deciding that the city jail would be preferable to the penitentiary, at least for a while. A.D.A. Antoinette Gallo, normally a most formidable foe, seemed surprised at the plea, but recovered and said they would be ready for the discovery hearing, which was set for Thursday morning. Elliot went back to the cells, and Clarence dashed over to Courtroom four, where he made a motion to exclude certain evidence collected in a case of armed robbery, as it was, in his opinion, obtained illegally. The Judge was not swayed by this opinion and his motion was denied. Then on to Courtroom two where he made a motion to exclude a Psychiatrist's report in a civil suit, and though the Judge seemed to waver for a moment, giving him hope, that one was also denied. And finally Clarence went to the smallest Courtoom in the building, Room eleven, for the sexual assault discovery.

He was seriously worried about this one. Jamie Highfield was the son of one of Elder's more prominent wealth-makers, Justin Highfield, a man who owned two lumber companies, two construction companies, a small oil company, and twenty-odd gas stations. Jamie worked for his father in some capacity, although like many a rich man's male progeny, he was that special combination of privilege, playboy and asshole. He drove a fast car, fucked a lot of girls, and felt that regular laws didn't really apply to him. His father, a sober and careful man, had already bought him out of a couple of legal scrapes, thanks also to the crafty legal maneuverings of Clarence Keaton. Justin had a falling out with his regular attorney fifteen years ago and had hired the young and ambitious Mr. Keaton to act for him in the purchasing of several gas stations. Clarence did a pretty good job, and had eventually wormed his way into the position of family lawyer for the Highfields. Securing Justin as a client in his second year in Elder was a coup, and the annual retainer was a great blessing, though as often as not, it went entirely to office expenses and taxes. But still. Losing Justin would be a major blow to Clarence's bottom line, and he knew it. And this case was scary.

Jamie Highfield had gone to a party on the lake and started flirting with a girl there who, it turned out, was only fifteen years old. She also happened to be the daughter of a local Methodist minister. Her first attempt at rebellion with liquor and flirting landed her in Jamie's Corvette, and she must have realized early on that she was in over her head, when he parked in a deserted area and tried to fuck her. That was her claim. And it was most likely true, though it might be difficult to prove. Jamie swore up and down that he only offered her a ride home. She suggested they have sex, he said, and before things had really gotten started, she was crying rape. That tale was laid out for Clarence in the office three weeks earlier. It sounded like bullshit then. Clarence started to suggest that they plead to a lesser charge, maybe get off with probation, when Jamie said something frightening.

"Ask her if I'm circumcised." His father nodded in agreement.

"You're not serious," said Clarence.

"I'm serious, Mr. Keaton. Ask her."

"I can't, Jamie."

"Why not?" Young Highfield was entirely used to getting his own way.

"It's too risky. What if she answers correctly? She has a fifty percent chance of that. And if she answers incorrectly, what are we going to do to prove it; have you stand and pull your cock out in front of the jury? It's not a plausible strategy. It's too risky."

"Mr. Keaton, she never saw my dick. I swear. I'll take the risk." He was so sure it unnerved Clarence. He wondered about it the rest of that day. What if the kid was innocent? Only a complete fool or an innocent person would be willing to take a chance like that. Innocent clients were actually so rare that they only appeared on TV lawyer shows. All the clients were innocent on TV. The cops were *always* charging the wrong person. An innocent client in real life made the job harder. Now I *have* to get him off. God help me.

Of course there was always the possibility that Justin would pay off the girl and her family, but on this one they ran into an honest man in her father, who refused all emoluments offered if he would convince his daughter to drop the charges. So here they were, in the discovery hearing, with the pressure squarely on the sometimes less-than-formidable Keaton shoulders. Justin made it quite clear that getting Jamie out of this utterly unscathed was the only outcome that would satisfy him, and the unspoken implication that the job of Highfield empire lawyer would also be on the line. It was a special Monday for that reason. A nervous, two-pack Monday.

A.D.A. Gallo was ready with the evidence files. She was the number three prosecutor on the county totem pole and was usually someone who knew her business. She laid out the discovery in a brisk manner and the Judge quickly ruled that it would go to trial. So far it had been kept out of the papers, because both families wanted it that way, but if it got out, and these things normally did, it would hurt Jamie's case, not to mention his reputation, such as it was. But Clarence wasn't disheartened after seeing the prosecution's case. Aside from some party people testifying it would essentially be the girl's word on trial. So it wouldn't be any fun, doing what he would have to do. He hoped the girl *was* lying, which would make it much easier to trip her up and destroy her version of the events. People who lied were the best to cross examine, if you knew they were lying.

He ruminated on all this driving back to the office, though it was a good day. He got back just after two p.m. and was going to look at the mail and do some business things for an hour or so and then head for a restorative couple of hours drinking at the club. He found the day's mail piled on his desk and started going through it. There were thirty-two pieces, and one of them included a cheque for $250, on an account that owed at least ten times that. It dampened his strangely sunny mood considerably. What a shit business the law was. People were desperate for help when they needed you, but once you fixed their problem, they couldn't remember who you were or why they owed you. You had to dun them for money constantly, which was an aspect of the job Clarence despised above all others. High retainers alleviated the problem a little, but even then, everyone assumed you must be fine financially, because hey you're a lawyer! They're *all* dishonest and rich, right? He silently cursed his mother for forcing him into a business he hated. The fact that he was quite skilled at it and her choice was perspicacious in that regard he always conveniently left out of the cursing process. Paula's voice was heard.

"No, sir! You cannot just walk in there! Hey!" And his office door opened and George Barnet, his honor, Mayor of Elder for fifteen years walked in like a train leaving a station in a hurry. He was a substantial man, perhaps not as tall as some, certainly wider than most. He had been Mayor for so long not so much due to his political skill, but more that no one else really wanted the job. The only child of rich parents who had died relatively young, he naturally assumed his wealth and municipal position made his opinion important on all topics. He didn't have many friends, and this was the first time he'd ever set foot in Clarence's office.

Clarence stood up and indicated one of the client chairs. When the mayor had taken his seat, Clarence went to the door. Paula was just outside, mouthing the word '*Sorry*'. He held his hand up to show her it was fine, then turned back to the Mayor, who was now standing and leaning over his desk, looking at the pile of mail and the papers. Clarence kept his anger in check, lining his voice with cashmere.

"Excuse me, Mr. Mayor. Is there something of yours on my desk, by chance?" Barnet stood and turned, indicating the photo, prominently displayed on the desk, to make it seem as though that had been what held his interest.

"Mr. Keaton," he said, turning to shake Clarence's hand, as they both retreated to their respective chairs.

"What is it I can do for you today, George?"

Barnet indicated the photograph, a black and white of a handsome man from a long ago time.

"Is that your father, Mr. Keaton?"

"No, sir. It's Earl Rogers."

"I'm not familiar with him."

"California attorney, died over fifty years ago. When Clarence Darrow was charged with bribing a juror, he hired Earl to defend him."

"Hmmm, I would have thought you'd have a picture of Darrow."

"A guy who bribed jurors? That wouldn't look too good."

"Darrow was *guilty* of bribing the juror?"

"Of course he was. It's almost impossible to get charged with bribery unless you actually bribe someone." He wanted to add, *But of course you would know that,* but he stopped himself in time, swallowing the phrase.

"Did Darrow go to jail?"

"No, he didn't. Earl won an acquittal. Damn good lawyer, he was. Excuse me, George, but what's your business here today?"

Barnet squirmed a little in his seat, as if what he was about to say would sound better if he were sitting on his left ass cheek instead of his right one.

"Mr. Keaton, my house was robbed a few nights ago."

"I see."

"They've arrested someone for it. And I hear you're defending him." He looked up straight into Clarence's eyes as he said the second part, like a bad poker player trying to show strength when he was bluffing. Clarence spoke slowly in reply.

"Well George, if I were defending a client charged with robbing your house, I hope you understand that I couldn't discuss it with you."

"Yes, of course, I mean I do understand, but…"

"Ever," Clarence stood up, "Nice of you to come in, your honor." Barnet stood but didn't make a move to go. Instead, he stepped closer to the desk.

"Look Keaton, some very valuable and important things were stolen in that robbery, and I need them back. I need them back right now!"

"Well, you're asking the wrong person, George. You need to speak to the police about that."

"The police haven't recovered a single fucking thing! I know Elliot gave the haul to you!"

"You don't know that at all, sir. The statement is lunatic and wrong."

"Keaton, do I have to remind you that I'm the Mayor of this town? I can make your life go away. Did you know that? I can destroy your business and your reputation."

"The only thing that would destroy *my* reputation, *sir*, would be to talk with you any further. There's the door. Good day."

"I'll give you a day or two to think about this, Keaton, but that's all. Do you hear me? I need that shit back, and if I don't get it, there will be a heavy price. I hope you understand what I'm saying to you."

"I understand that you've come into my office without an appointment, asked me to break attorney-client privilege, to break the law, and when I refuse to do so, you threaten me. If memory serves, Mister Mayor, that's criminal solicitation and blackmail."

"Yeah? Sue me, shyster. I'll give you forty-eight hours." And with that, Barnet turned and stalked out, down the hall and down the stairs, every heavy step recorded. Paula came in as the downstairs door slammed shut. She was walking slowly, measuring her steps, not sure of her boss's mood.

"What's his problem?" she asked.

"He thought I could help him, but when it turned out I couldn't, he got a little upset." Clarence lit a smoke and indicated what she was holding in one hand. "Is that the afternoon mail?"

"Oh, yes it is," she said, "And there were two cheques. Two!"

"My God, we're rich, aren't we?"

"We are. Mrs. Ripley paid in full, $2000, and Mrs. Dalton sent the last instalment, $750."

"Adding the twelve hundred we got over the weekend..."

"The *almost* twelve hundred..."

"Right, wow, we might make expenses this month! Hell, I'll go out on a limb and say we will."

"I could use a raise," Paula said quietly.

"What? Already? Why I gave you one last...last..."

"Year. Last year."

"One good month – one good beginning of a month, doesn't mean I should go crazy and....okay, I'll think about it."

"Thanks, boss."

"Dammit, Paula, you're ruining the wonderful mood I had going after the Mayor yelled at me and said he'd destroy my career."
"Sorry. It's just that your good moods are infrequent, so I have to take advantage when I can."

"Yeah, yeah. Anything else today?"

"Not on my book. I have a date later."

"All right then, go home and get ready. We'll discuss the raise tomorrow. Or possibly Wednesday."

"Really? It's not even three thirty. Thanks boss."

"You're welcome. Go." She walked out and he heard her sprucing up her desk and then leave. When he heard the downstairs door, he picked up the phone and dialed a Lansing number. It picked up right away.

"Pappas Tailors."

"Hey, Benny."

"Hey yourself! What's the good word down in one-horse Elder?"

"It's a little busy, you know, for a lazy ass like me, but we're getting along." Clarence loved talking to Benny. He was always so upbeat.

"You gonna be able to get up here and see me soon?" Benny asked. "Business is slow and I need one of your big three-suit orders."

"Not sure I need three suits just at the moment, man, but I wouldn't go to anyone else. You know that."

"You wouldn't dare go to anyone else," said Benny. "Benjamin Pappas is the finest men's tailor in all of Michigan. He also gives – hang on, somebody just came in."

Unless you counted Simon Roche, who was more than an acquaintance, Clarence didn't have any real friends in Elder. Benny was his friend. He came back on the line.

"Hey man, you should come up anyway. It'd be good to see you."

"I'll try next weekend, ok?"

"Great! You need some shirts?" Clarence laughed at that.

"Sure I could. Three, same as before. White, off-white, and light blue."

"French cuffs. Pappas remembers everything. All right, brother. Fight the good one."

Putting the phone down, Clarence was sad just for a moment. *I need a drink*, he thought. He briefly considered the bottle of scotch in his desk drawer, then Paula's voice startled him.

"Boss?" He jumped involuntarily, his pack of smokes flying out of his hand.

"Paula? What's the trouble?" She picked up his cigarette pack and the two that managed to fly out and returned them to his desk. He lit one, just a hair shakily. He didn't like to think anyone heard his private phone calls.

"There's a car across the street with a young guy sitting in it and he's been smoking cigarettes, so there are a whole bunch of butts on the street in front of the driver's door."

"Okay," Clarence replied. "And what's important about that?"

"I think he's watching our door."

"That's interesting. Why would anyone be watching us?"

"I drove around the block and parked and walked back through the back lot and up the back stairs so he wouldn't see me and think I was warning you." She was clearly pleased with her courage and good-sense-sneakiness.

"I left my medals in my other pants," he said. She smiled. Another reason he liked her was she never took anything he said too personally.

"Well, I thought you should know. He didn't follow me. See if he follows you."

"What kind of car was it?" he asked.

"What? How would I know that?"

"It might be easier for me to spot it when it followed me. Okay then, what color was it?"

"Blue, or teal green maybe. It had two headlights."

"Most do. Okay, Girl Friday, good work. I'll keep an eye out. Thanks." Paula smiled and nodded. She would bring this up tomorrow when they discussed her raise. She went down the hall and then the back stairs. Clarence finished his smoke and stabbed it to death in the glass ashtray. A momentary pause, possibly to be sure one's actions would be the right ones, then he grabbed his jacket and briefcase and headed downstairs. He made sure the back door was locked and then went out the front. He had a surreptitious look through an upstairs window before he left and the car was a blue Chevy, a Bel-Air that looked to be no more than a year or two old. He didn't look at the car as he walked around to the parking lot and he almost didn't look at it as he pulled out and made a left to head for the club. But within in a few blocks he saw it again, a hundred yards or so behind him.

He pulled into the golf club parking lot and repaired to the men's bar downstairs. It was only four o'clock, but it was half full for happy hour and he spotted Simon at their regular table, and a seat open. Simon bought him a beer.

"Man, you should have been on Cat Burglar today, Clare. He came flying in at fourteen to one. I made my nut for two months on one horse!"

"Your nut? Only if you don't gamble any of that, right?"

"Oh," Simon smiled, "that's right. You are as ever the bearer of gloom, Clarence."

"At least I'm consistent," said Clarence.

"True. What do you think of a four horse parlay tomorrow?"

"I think," Clarence smiled, "That you might lose your two-month nut on that."

"The Roche parlay occasionally wins big, man. Plus I'm on a streak!"

"Streaks go both ways, my friend."

"You gotta respect a streak, Clarence. You don't respect it, it turns on you." Clarence pulled a twenty out of his pocket and handed it to Simon.

"Put that on the parlay tomorrow for me."

"All right! You get it. I knew you were getting it. Another beer?"

"Yeah, one more."

He stayed until seven thirty, eating dinner and having a third and then a fourth beer, but spacing them out to every forty-five minutes or so, and finishing the last one at least forty minutes before he left. They talked baseball and football, and people drifted in and away from the

29

table so there was always a group of three or more. People giving their tips to Simon, or their betting strategies for the football season, which had just started, or the baseball season, which was winding down. It was pleasant in the way that men can be pleasant, when there's nothing personal on the line and no one needs anything from anyone. Clarence had to be disciplined about his drinking, but the conversation and the camaraderie was relaxing enough that he came close to letting his guard down a couple of times. If he'd been reckless about his alcohol intake, he might have. But he stood up at seven-thirty, sober or at least close enough to drive, and bade his acquaintances good night. He was out of the parking lot and at the first of three traffic lights on the way home when he noticed the Bel-Air again.

He parked in Shorty's driveway a few minutes later and headed upstairs, turning the lights on in his living room and then going into the bathroom in the dark and watching the street from there. The Bel-Air had pulled into the parking lot of the Parish hall across the street. There were a couple of other cars already there so it didn't look odd, plus it afforded whoever was driving a perfect view of Clarence's place. The guy got out and walked up the street to the variety store payphone and made a call, then came back and got back inside and sat there.

Clarence turned on the TV, then went into the kitchen and made coffee. He wanted another beer, but that was a bad idea for what he was planning. The TV was on WXYZ Detroit, but he kept the sound off. He just wanted the reflect light and images to convince the guy across the street that he was there. It was dark now, and he sat and smoked two cigarettes, considering his options. Someone was following him, and the question was why. After a bit, he decided they figured he would lead them to something. The mayor was pissed enough this afternoon to threaten him about whatever Elliot stole from his house. But Elliot was a professional. He would only take jewelry or cash. He made a mental note to very carefully ask Elliot about that. So it was most likely something he stole that somebody wanted back and they weren't willing to wait for the cops to find it and/or return it. A wife's most prized ring or necklace, maybe. But would they follow him for that? Doubtful. The car? Elliot had all the paperwork, but what if he'd lied about who owned it? He started to laugh, and began to berate himself. *Of course he lied, you moron. They ALL lie.* Elliot had checked him out as well. *Could this have something to do with me?* No, that's silly. It's the car. The Studebaker. There was something inside it that was getting some people nuts enough to start paying guys to follow a lawyer.

It was 9:30 when he turned off the TV and the light and went to his bedroom. That light would also be visible in his front window, so he brushed his teeth, undressed, got into bed and turned off the light. After ten minutes by his watch, he got out of bed and crawled to the living room, where he'd left a fresh set of dark clothes. He dressed quickly, crawled to the window and confirmed that the guy was still there. *Okay, pal.* He put on a blue Detroit Tigers baseball cap, grabbed a flashlight and his keys, and slithered back into his bedroom and opened the window.

One of the really odd featured of the house was a fire escape in the back that wasn't visible from the street. It was a bit rickety and he'd never had occasion to use it before, but necessity knows no law. He climbed out, stepping very carefully, trying not to make any noise. If he woke Shorty, whose bedroom window he would have to pass going down, she would turn on all the lights and the guy would know something was up. He managed to pass her window without her noticing although she was up, reading in bed. He got to the ground and went through the backyard and through a small alleyway that led to the driveway of a house on Logan street, one street behind George. He waited for a bit at the edge of the garage to make sure no one in the house, or the neighbor's on the left, was standing by any of their windows, and then he fast-walked down the driveway and turned right onto Logan for the walk to the office, which would take about twenty to twenty-five minutes. *I could use the exercise,* he thought.

He'd gone about halfway when he realized that he hadn't brought the keys to the Studebaker with him. *Oh, for Christ's sake, Clarence. How can you BE so goddamn stupid?* It was his mother's voice. No matter how old he got, her voice was never more than a single mistake away. He headed back and had gone about two blocks when he realized he actually had no idea where those keys were. He couldn't remember if he'd locked the car when he hid it in the garage, but he probably did. And to drive it he would also need the keys. But all the way back to Shorty's he racked his brain and couldn't come up with a spot where he would most likely find them. His only hope was that they were just sitting on a counter in his kitchen or in the ceramic bowl by his door. He encouraged himself that they *were* there. Of course they were.

He snuck back up the driveway and across Shorty's yard, once again stepping carefully to go up the fire escape. But as he passed Shorty's window, she saw him. Not his face, but she screamed. He raced up the steps and dove in the open window, thankfully he hadn't been stupid enough to close that, tore off his clothes, put on a bathrobe and slippers, and went downstairs and knocked on her door.

"Shorty! You all right?" She came to the door, out of breath.

"Oh my God! Did…did you see him?"

"See who?"

"A man, a pervert! A peeping Tom at my goddamn window!"

"No, I didn't see him. You sure?" He regretted saying it immediately.

"Am I sure?? The son of a bitch was peeping in my goddamn window trying to see me naked! Of course I'm fucking sure! I'm not senile, you know."

"I know, Shorty, I'm sorry." But he was thinking, *You weren't naked. I saw you. Plus the guy could just as easily have been trying to see me naked.* Then he heard a siren. Getting really close. Oh, Jesus, Shorty, you didn't…

"Wow," she said. "The cops got here quick." And they had. A car pulled in and two patrolmen got out. While they were questioning Shorty, Clarence stole a glance across the street and saw the Bel-Air pulling out of the lot and driving away. He answered a couple of cop-queries, saying he'd been asleep and heard nothing until Shorty screamed, and seen nothing. One of the cops mentioned that there'd been other reports of a prowler in the neighborhood in the last few weeks. *Great news.* He went back upstairs and did a search of countertops and other resting places where one might normally find keys, but found nothing. He lit a smoke and took a folding chair from his closet and settled it by the window so he could keep watch. About a half hour after the cops left, the bel-Air came back, and this time parked on the street where both the front and the side of the house were visible. When he saw that, Clarence realized he could have left when the cops were still talking to Shorty and the guy was gone. *Shit, fuck, piss.* Maybe being hopped up on adrenaline made you dumber. Now it was almost eleven thirty. *Screw it,* he thought, and went to bed. Plan foiled because of stupidity. He fell asleep wondering both where those damn keys were and why anyone would ever hire a dope like him.

TUESDAY

When he woke up, he had a headache which felt just like a hangover, though he'd been very strict with his booze intake the previous evening. Then he realized it was a stupid headache; a regretful, how-could-I-have-been-so-goddamn-dumb headache. He took a shower, had aspirin with tobacco for breakfast, and the headache had dissipated by the time he climbed into the Merc for the grueling eight minute jaunt to the office. The Bel-Air was not in sight as he headed down George Street, but he did notice a gray Cadillac pull away from the curb as he left. Five minutes later, he saw it again, two cars back. He parked in the gravel lot behind his place and walked to the front door without even a glance at the hidden gate behind him. He saw the Caddy pull into the Library lot across the street, but he didn't waste more than a second look. He unlocked his door and went upstairs.

Coffee poured, cigarette lit and first drag taken, he scanned every surface in his office for the keys to the Studebaker. Nothing. Then he went through every drawer. Nothing. *Goddamnit.* Maybe Paula knew where they were. It was magical thinking Tuesday. He gave up the search for the moment and opened his book. There wasn't much on the docket, thank goodness. One court appearance for a DUI and he was fairly sure he could get the client off, since it was a cop he'd dealt with before who'd usually get flustered on the stand. And a client at three, provided the DUI didn't go long, and they never did. He decided to go and get the mail before Paula came in, anxious to find the large cheque that would signal a great month, or the two large ones that would make it the best month ever. As he got to the door, he found Sergeant Louise Merwin, Elder police detective, on his porch. She was quite subdued and appeared to be wearing a lot of makeup.

"Mr. Keaton," she said very quietly, indicating it was a personal visit. When it was cop business, she always called him 'Counselor'.

"Come on up, Louise," he said. "You want a coffee?"

"Yes, please."

When Clarence brought her the coffee he noticed that the makeup was covering some nasty bruises on her cheek and over one eye. He felt a little sick about that. The restraining order wasn't working. Her ex-husband, Greg Merwin, was a welder. Her success as a police officer had clearly been a problem for him, and when they were married, he liked nothing better than to drink to excess and then scream at her and eventually beat her. She stood it for a year or two longer than the one day it should have taken, and had finally divorced him, Clarence appearing on her behalf. Some of what had come out was pretty bad, but there were other things that were horrible that hadn't come up in court. At first, Greg wouldn't agree to the divorce, but Clarence had shown him the proof they had of some of his actions, and told him quite plainly if he didn't agree to it, those things would come out and he'd go to jail. He'd finally agreed, with great reluctance, but since the divorce had become final, he'd grown bold again and begun to harass Louise and their daughter, Amy, who was now fifteen. Hence the restraining order.

"Jesus," said Clarence, looking at her face, "We have to have him arrested. We can charge him with assault."

"My word against his," Louise said. "He came to the house, got in somehow, and was waiting for me. I guess I'm lucky he didn't kill me. Thank God Amy was staying over at a friend's house."

"You didn't have your gun?" asked Clarence. Elder detectives, almost to a person, carried Ruger .357 police specials.

"I keep it in the car," she said. "I don't want a gun in the house. He's just as likely to get it and shoot me. Hell the only time I've ever drawn my gun on the job was the other day when we were here for Elliot."

"And that was mostly peer pressure," Clarence replied, making her laugh until she winced in pain.

"He's been calling me, too," she said.

"Calling you?"

"At night. He knows my shift hours, so he waits till I've been home about an hour and then he calls."

"What does he say?"

"He says he's going to kill me." Her voice got tinier. "He says he's going to come over some night and strangle me, or beat me to death. He says I should choose."

"Well you don't have a choice anymore," said Clarence, a deep anger rising in his chest. "You have to charge him."

"I don't want to charge him. I tried that the first time and he was out in five hours. I need him to leave me alone. Maybe you know somebody who could sort of…persuade him, maybe."

"Louise, you're a cop. *You* know more people who could do that than I do. And I don't arrange things like that. Why don't you talk to the guy downstairs in the Cadillac?" He regretted saying it, but it was in his head, formed as a complete sentence, and came shooting out of his big mouth so fast he couldn't stop it.

"I can't ask Mike or any of my colleagues…" she said it like *colleagues* was a joke. "…for help, Mr. Keaton. They don't even like working with me and they all resent that I made detective. Either I'm a dyke or a whore, and sometimes both. They don't think I'm qualified and if I ask for their help protecting me from my husband, because I'm afraid of him? Forget it."

"Ex-husband," Clarence said. He had been feeling sorry for himself at the beginning of the day, and this reminded him that many others had it worse, and there was almost no way to tell, since everyone put up some kind of front.

"Hey," he asked, "how did Greg get in?"

"He still has a spare set of keys."

Something went off in Clarence's brain when she said that. *Spare keys…spare keys.* Through the general fog, his mind was attempting to alert him to something. Louise went on.

"I don't know what I'll do if he comes over again." Clarence got out a new yellow legal pad, purchased in bulk from an office supply company for five dollars per fifty pads, and began to make a list. He wrote LOUISE'S LIST in block letters at the top.

"I'm going to list a few things you should do, Louise. First of all, call Luther the Lock Man, I'm writing his number down here, and have all the locks changed. Every lock in the house. See if he can put locks on all the windows as well, okay? He's over on Mandarin Road…"

"I know where it is," she said.

"You keep the gun in the car and the car in the garage, right? Okay, have the locks changed on the garage, too, and all the garage windows."

"Okay. Sounds like it'll run into some money."

"Tell Luther I sent you. He owes me a favor. You'll get a discount. Make the house really, really hard to get into, right?"

"Right."

"And I wouldn't normally advise this, but you might consider getting another gun. One that would stop somebody Greg's size."

"An elephant gun?"

"I would get a shotgun. A 12-gauge pump. And I would get some practice in with it. Loading it fast and shooting it. You don't have to do that, but I'm suggesting it as an option. He's threatened to kill you. You might have to defend yourself at some point, because new locks will certainly give you some time but they probably won't keep him out forever."

"Jesus, really?"

"He's obsessed. He'll eventually find a way. Go see Luther. Today. Right now."

"Okay, but only if you tell me something."

"What?"

"Who's the guy in the Cadillac?"

It was one of the reasons he admired Louise. Nothing escaped her notice. He shouldn't have mentioned the guy, but he had, and though he spent some time after steering the conversation elsewhere, she put it where she could find it – something *he* should have done with those goddamn keys – and when she was ready, she brought it back up. She saw the look on his face and tried to help him.

"You were speaking of the man in the grey Cadillac parked in the lot across the street, right?"

"Yes, I was. How did you know that?"

"It's not even eight yet. The Library doesn't open until ten. What the hell is he doing there if not watching someone? You noticed him so he's probably watching you."

"Yeah, since yesterday afternoon. A guy in a Bel-Air, and then this morning, the new guy in the Caddy."

"Wow, round the clock. Wonder what they're hoping you'll lead them to? Must be good. Round the clock is pretty expensive. They follow you, too?"

"Yep."

"Do they know you know?"

"Not completely sure, but I would venture most likely not."

"Okay. I'll ask around and see if I can figure out who's paying for it."

"Thanks Louise. But do that after you go see Luther. Get the locks changed today. Tell him I said if he does it today, it'll wipe the slate. Call me if there's any problem."

"You call me, too. Now we've promised to call each other. Wow."

"In some Indonesian countries we'd have to get married." They both laughed, and she winced again. She asked to use his bathroom and he showed her where it was. She fixed her face a little and left, though it seemed to take her a while to get downstairs and open the door. Finally he heard it close and he sat at his desk, wondering about who was following him and why and where those goddamn keys were. The what was Paula and the when was anticipating her imminent arrival. He decided not to wait for Louise to find out who was following him.

The door opened downstairs and Paula came in. He looked at his watch, and noted that it was 8:15, so she was fifteen minutes later than she should have been and a half hour later than normal. He debated whether to say something or not, but when she came in she was noticeably not well. So he mentioned that instead.

"You all right, Slim?" She shook her head slightly, then grimaced in pain. He realized the symptom meant she was hung over. Something that happened to him regularly, even more than he cared to admit. The hunched shoulders, the slow movement, the pain of nodding. Her voice confirmed it.

"I had a tough night."

"The date went not so well? Or did it go too well?"

"We had dinner and went to a jazz club. He wanted to go. And my ex was playing drums." Paula's last long term boyfriend had been a musician. A mercurial sort, their relationship was marked with blow-ups and reconciliations, and Paula had finally ended it three months earlier. "So he comes over and acts like an asshole and pisses off my date, who forgets that HE wanted to go to the goddamn jazz club in the first place. So we had an argument and I took a cab home."

"I see." Clarence wanted to ask how she got drunk enough to be hungover, but he decided to wait. If she wanted to tell him –

"So I go home and have a drink, and the phone rings and it's my ex and the son of a bitch makes me break up with him *again*. Third time. And it takes two hours and I have the bottle out the whole time, and I woke up on the couch wearing my date clothes. I need to ask you a question."

"Shoot."

"Why are men such assholes?"

"Practice. And when you're good at something, you want to keep it in shape." She laughed just a little, and smiled at him.

"I wish they were more like you, boss."

"You mean smart, good looking, full of anxiety, but austere and professional?"

"No, white."

Clarence laughed out loud, a burst of sound that aggravated her headache but made her happy all the same. She loved making him laugh.

"I'll go and get the mail," he said, "And you watch from the window. There's a grey Cadillac across the street. If a guy gets out of it and follows me, you run down and get the license plate number for me, okay?"

"No problem."

He left the office, pausing on the porch to exaggeratedly light a smoke, but he didn't even glance at the Caddy as he headed up the street to make a left for the post office. Once there, he collected the meager pile of letters from his box. The blazing inefficiency of the Postal service infuriated him. He paid a monthly, robbery-high fee for the box, and they were supposed to fill it with whatever mail came in *as it came in*. But whoever did the sorting was so lazy that Clarence had to visit the box two or three times a day to get everything, and even then stuff would carry over. He knew he received between thirty and fifty pieces of mail per day, everything from cheques to requests for money from his alma mater, or the Trial Lawyers Association, requests he forwarded directly to his wastebasket. He hated having to pay for such crap service, and he regularly stopped at the counter to tell them so, provided there wasn't a line of people waiting. Today he just scooped the pile and headed back, sorting through it. No cheques. *Christ*, he thought, was he ever going to be paid for his work? He reminded himself that it had been a decent month so far, and he wasn't up to his buttcrack in debt as he sometimes was, so he should be grateful, an emotion he found difficult to master.

Arriving back, again not even giving the side-eye to the Cadillac, he went upstairs to find Paula in slightly better shape, and assumed whatever painkiller or hangover cure she had taken was starting to kick in. She followed him into the office with her pad and pen. He handed her the mail in the resigned way that signaled no cheques and mostly bullshit. She sat down as he did, and waited till he lit his cigarette before beginning.

"He waited until you turned the corner then he got out and followed. He's wearing a tan jacket and jeans."

"And you went down and got the plate?"

"I didn't go down; I looked out the window with my little binoculars. Here it is." She handed him a piece of paper. "And I need a raise."

"How old was the guy?"

"Young. Mid-twenties. Kind of cute, too."

"You have a thing for bad boys."

"So do you," she replied.

"What?" His tone surprised them both.

"Well, you defend them, don't you?" she said. "I just take them to bed and let them ruin my life."

"Right." He laughed a little.

"Hallberg called about the car. Your car okay, boss?"

"Yeah, it's fine. I'll call him back. How long do I have until court?" He looked at his watch as he asked her and they both said "forty minutes" simultaneously. Paula got up and went to the door, but he called her back.

"Listen, I seem to have misplaced a set of keys around here. Could you do a search for them later?"

"Sure. You lose your car keys?"

"No, I didn't. I *misplaced* a different set of keys. And I need them. If you could have a look for them, that would be *helpful*. Okay?

"Got it," she said, thinking *Geez, he's in a pissy mood.*

"And search my desk last. I don't want you to be distracted by the bottle of Scotch in the left hand bottom drawer."

"Right hand bottom, boss," she said as she walked out, feeling his eyes bore a hole in her shoulder all the way to her desk.

So she knows about the Scotch, he thought, *I wonder what else she knows about....spare keys, dammit, spare KEYS.* He called Hallberg, who answered immediately.

"Hallberg Insurance, Jessie speaking."

"It's Clarence."

"Hey man, I got what you wanted. The car is insured for fifteen thousand."

"That much, really? Seems like a lot."

"I found three auctions of that model and year in just the last ten months, and they all went for around that price."

"Okay then, thanks Jessie. I need to come in and sign the papers?"

"Sure. Anytime today. It's another sixteen dollars a month."

"Sixteen? Well, I hope you're making some profit on that."

"Some of that is administrative costs, you know. Only fifteen-fifty or so is actual profit for me. I'll see you later today."

"I'll be there," said Clarence. Hanging up, he saw the license plate of the Caddy that Paula got for him. He called Morrissey at the DMV.

Tim Morrissey was the number three man at the local DMV and he and Clarence sometimes played bridge together. Some years earlier, Clarence had handled an insurance problem for him, and then twice gotten his son acquitted of shoplifting charges, which made Tim so grateful that he would occasionally cut red tape for Clarence and give him information about cars and their owners, provided Clarence used the marker infrequently. Tim was quite willing to find a name and address for the grey Cadillac's plate number. Clarence thanked him and headed to court, noting in the rearview that the Caddy followed.

The drunken driving case in courtroom three that morning would normally look to be open and shut and Clarence, with a reasonable client, would have pled it down to a fine and driving probation, but the client, Otto Joyce, a referral from Simon Roche, swore he was innocent, and Clarence knew the arresting officer was an idiot who could get flustered on the stand, so he had a plan of attack that, if the fates were kind, might bring a good result. Judge Lang was presiding, and he was a little thick, even for a judge, but Clarence thought he could handle him as well. He had before. You just needed to get on his good side.

A.D.A. Gallo put the officer, one Brian Dillon, on the stand and led him through the bare facts as he saw them. Mr. Joyce had blown 0.11 on the breathalyzer, and was obviously intoxicated beyond any reasonable standard, put him away, take his license, blah blah blah, and et cetera. Miss Gallo finished, seeming quite pleased, and Clarence rose to cross-examine.

"Officer Dillon, you stated that my client registered a point one-one on the breath test, is that correct?"

"Yes, sir."

"I see. And the current law states that zero point eleven is not, strictly speaking, under the influence. Is that correct?"

"Yes, sir, but there were other factors."

"Other factors, Officer? Could you please explain that to the court?"

Officer Dillon spoke as though he'd memorized the speech directly from the supplemental manual, like a drone.

"If a person blows above point zero five and below point fifteen, the person is not strictly considered to be impaired, but the officer may take into account other factors."

"Thank you, Officer Dillon," Clarence smiled, hoping to throw him off just a little. "Could you tell us the other factors that you noticed with regard to my client?"

"His face was somewhat red, sir."

"What time of day was it when you stopped my client, Officer?"

"Ten-thirty at night," Dillon replied, after checking his notebook.

"And his face was red? You could tell that in the darkness?"

"I shined my flashlight in his face. It looked red to me."

"I see. Where was it you pulled him over, exactly, Officer?"

"The street, you mean?"

"Yes." Another notebook consultation provided the answer.

"On Cobden Street."

"Where on Cobden Street, Officer Dillon?"

"Ah…the east side, I believe. Just before London Road."

"So the east side….and you were near the corner?"

"Yes, sir."

"And is there a light on that corner, Officer? A traffic light?"

"Yes sir, there is a light."

"In fact there are four lights, are there not? Two on London Road and two on Cobden?"

"That's right. Yes."

"Were any of those lights red while you were talking with my client?"

"Well…it's possible, I suppose."

"Possible? So it's possible that two red traffic lights were shining on my client's face when you came up to the car?"

"Yes, sir, it is possible." Dillon was getting a little pissed off. "When I brought him into the station some other officers noticed that his face was red, too."

"Others? Are they in the courtroom today ready to testify?" Clarence glanced around the almost empty courtroom for emphasis.

"No, sir. But they did think his face was red."

"So a group of people who are unable to testify thought his face was red. I'll make a note of it, Officer, thank you. Were there other factors in your decision to railroad my client?"

"Objection, your honor, to the term railroad." Toni Gallo found her voice as Clarence knew she would. It was better to force an objection than to be surprised by one.

"Tone down the rhetoric, Mr. Keaton, if you would," said the Judge.

"I apologize, your honor. Officer Dillon, please tell us the other factors that led you to arrest my client."

"He was stuttering."

"Stuttering? Is this a general affliction of people who drink?"

"Objection. Asking for a medical opinion." *Shit. Nice one, Toni.*

"Sustained."

"All right, we'll pass over that, Officer. Other factors?"

"He was sweating. Which is a sign of alcohol consumption."

"Is that your medical opinion, Officer, which you are allowed to give, but I'm not allowed to ask for?" This got a small laugh from all the other participants, with the exception of Officer Dillon, who, remarkably for a policeman, had no sense of humor.

"He was walking a little funny, too," said Dillon, with a touch of defiance.

"You gave him a field sobriety test?"

"Not exactly."

"So your answer would be 'No', then?"

"When I walked him to the patrol car, he seemed to be a little unsteady. That's all I meant."

"Thank you for the clarification, Officer. So he had a red face, in your opinion, his speech was stuttered but not slurred…"

Judge Lang smiled a little at that one. He was a James Bond fan, and also liked his martinis shaken and not stirred. Clarence was well aware of it, naturally. Even the tiniest advantage in a courtroom could sway a case.

"…he was sweating and a little unsteady on his feet, correct?"

"Yes, sir."

"And those were the factors that led you to arrest my client, despite the fact that his breathalyzer was not over the legal limit, correct?"

"Correct," through slightly clenched teeth, "those were the other factors."

"Could I direct your attention to the defense table, Officer?" Dillon looked over and Clarence continued. "This is the man you arrested, Officer?"

"It is, sir. Yes."

"Would you say his face is red right now, Officer Dillon?"

Dillon looked and nodded.

"Yes, sir, I would say that."

"And is he sweating?"

Dillon had to squint a little, and he nodded again.

"Yes, he does appear to be sweating."

"Thank you, officer. I have no further questions."

A.D.A. Gallo had a few questions on re-direct, trying to lock down the facts again, since Officer Dillon was her whole case. When she was done, the prosecution rested and Judge Lang instructed Clarence to call his first witness. Clarence called his client, Otto Joyce, to the stand. As he made his way to be sworn in, it was noticed by everyone in the courtroom that Mr. Joyce was limping. Clarence had a sip of water and looked at his watch. He figured to be on his way home in about ten minutes when Miss Gallo would drop the charge. Or Judge Lang would dismiss it. He stood and addressed his witness.

"Mr. Joyce, you appeared to be limping a little when you came to the stand. Why is that?"

"I have a bad knee. An old football injury. It acts up s-s-sometimes. I favor it when I walk."

"You also have a stutter, sir?"

"Objection. Leading." *Oh, for Christ's sake, Toni.*

"Sustained. Ask it properly, Mr. Keaton."

"Of course, your honor. I apologize. Mr. Joyce, do you have a speech impediment of any kind?"

"Yes, sir, I have a stutter. I've had it since I was a kid. It never w-went away completely. And it's worse when I'm stressed." In their rehearsal of the testimony, Joyce had said it was worse when he was nervous, but Clarence told him to say *stressed*. Nervousness could connote guilt, which was not the idea. Clarence was very pleased Mr. Joyce had remembered.

"It seems to me, Mr. Joyce, that your face is clearly a bit red and you're sweating. Is that normal for you?"

"I'm afraid so. Irish heritage and I'm a little overweight."

Now Clarence moved in for the kill. What a shame the courtroom was empty and no one would see him win this one.

"And have you had anything to drink today, sir?" he asked, the triumph sugary on his tongue.

"Not really, just three vodka stingers and two beers."

It was 10:40 a.m. The courtroom was instantly filled with the sound of people sneezing. Judge Lang's left hand went straight to his mouth, clamping it to choke off the sound. His eyes were closed and he was shaking. Miss Gallo had her head down on the table and was slapping the wood with her hand, as her shoulders rocked with laughter. Clarence stared at his client, his mouth opening and closing, as "*The defense rests*", a phrase he now wasn't going to say, echoed in his head. To the small cacophony, he managed to choke out "No further questions, your honor", and sat down. Judge Lang managed to ask Miss Gallo if she had any questions for this idiot, and she waved her hand to say no without even looking up. The Judge told Mr. Joyce he could step down, and then called a recess, so he could go and laugh his ass off in chambers.

Clarence sat with his client at the defense table and explained that he would be convicted. Joyce was not pleased at all.

"You said you could get me off!"

"Yes, but that was before you had five goddamn drinks before ten in the morning."

"What the hell does that have to do with it?"

"Look, it's your first offense, so it'll probably only be a fine and probation. And if you go to AA, it might only be the fine."

"AA?" said Joyce, "I don't need to go to AA! I'm not a fuckin' drunk, Mr. Keaton. I was nervous before court and had a couple to get steady."

Clarence almost said "That's not unusual." But he couldn't get it out of his mouth. He settled for, "No doubt you're right. Calm down and I'll talk to Miss Gallo."

Toni quickly agreed to the standard fine and a six month driving probation, and said she'd inform the judge and send the paperwork. He thanked her for her leniency and she said she owed him at least that for the laughs. He went back and placated Joyce as best he could. He knew he'd get bad word of mouth from this jerk-off, and probably not even get the balance paid. He was glad he'd asked for and received a large retainer. He remembered Ben Yawkey's words as he left the courtroom. "Son, *never* underestimate how dumb your client is. Sometimes the only smart thing he's ever done is hire you."

As he headed to his car in the courtroom parking lot, he debated whether to have lunch at the club and decided it wasn't a good idea. The food there was generally inedible. He had once gone for breakfast, ordered raisin bran, figuring they couldn't screw that up, and the cereal was so old the raisins were as hard as birdshot. Plus, the temptation to have a drink would be unbearable. It was almost noon, which had been his mother's usual starting time. Alcoholism didn't run in her family, it galloped. She was the baby of seven girls and three boys, nine of whom survived into adulthood, and five of those were unrepentant drunks. Five out of nine. Count her mother, and it was six out of eleven. And when they got a few inside them, their inherent anger and meanness came snaking out. He'd known at ten years of age that there were things he must never tell her, and that talking to her after three o'clock in the afternoon was like putting your face into a circular saw. The entire time he was in high school, he never entered the house until his father got home. He would hide in the garage or just wait until six when the old man arrived. And it wasn't because his father could protect him. He couldn't. It was that with two of them in the house, there was always the chance she'd start in on the old man first.

She insisted he apply to law school, and when he was accepted, which shocked him, she insisted he go. After getting his Bachelor's degree, he had screwed up what little courage he possessed and informed them that he wanted to be an actor. He asked if they would support him for a year or possibly two until he could make a living at it. He wanted to write as well, but he didn't tell them that. His father wasn't pleased about it, but would have gone along. His mother not only refused, she verbally tore strips off him for over an hour. In clear and deadly language, she informed him that he would go to law school and be a lawyer. And that's what happened. For many years he'd blamed her, but after she died, he realized that it was his own lack of courage. He certainly could have gone to New York, or Hollywood, for that matter. They couldn't have stopped him. He decided not to defy her.

When she met Rosalie, because Clarence brought her by to say hello before their third date, his mother pulled him into her bedroom and told him to marry this girl, and quick. He was twenty-five years old and Rosalie only twenty, but he knew she was right. He would never find anyone like Rosalie. The fact that he didn't exactly love her wasn't something he told his mother, or even himself. It was 1955, for Christ's sake. He had assured himself it would all be okay. After Rosalie died, he stopped believing it would ever be okay. Life was a series of inescapable doom traps, and for each one you slipped through, another was waiting just down the road.

In his private places, he could admit things to himself about those years. How his mother may have been right about acting as a profession. And it was because of his mother and her stiletto tongue that he had developed the habit of not revealing personal things. Which became stronger as he grew into himself and eventually ingrained as a part of his personality. And for a lawyer, this was beneficial. He wasn't even tempted to tell people things about his clients, because it was his nature now. Another reason not to have a drink at lunchtime. Knowing the family history, he had developed some rules. He never drank before the workday was done. Well, hardly ever. He never drank on Sunday, the rationale being that an alcoholic drank every day, so if there was a day of the week he didn't, he couldn't be one. He was tall and hefty enough to be able to hold a decent amount without it showing, and rarely went beyond that. Beyond was, like his mother, a loosening of his tongue and a short bridge to the deep veins of anger within him. Such things were too dangerous, so he had a hard limit in public. He'd had one too many that goddamn night 18 years earlier and said too much. There were no harder lessons to learn. Once in a great while he would medicate alone in his apartment and rave to the walls, but in public he maintained it like a Marine.

Driving back to the office, he saw the Cadillac three cars behind. And he thought about Louise, and wondered if there was something else he could do for her. Then the phrase she'd used came back....*spare keys*, and he had a revelation. The spare keys! In the glovebox of the Studebaker there was a set of spare keys! He'd seen them. They were there. Then he wondered if he'd locked the Studebaker before he put the tarp on it. He couldn't remember locking it, and if he hadn't, he could get the spare keys. All he had to do was find a way to get into the garage without anyone noticing. Or did that matter? Were they following him because of the car? He was so lost in thought he almost ran a red light and realized he'd driven almost all the way to the office without paying a damn bit of attention to what he was doing. Thanks be to God for muscle memory.

Once inside, he was enjoying a coffee and a smoke when Paula came in.

"Morrissey called from the DMV, and that place in Marquette where your father stays called."

"Mill Creek," he replied. "What do they want? I sent the check."

"They asked you to call back," she said. "And here's the name and address of the cute guy who's following you. And I didn't find any keys."

"Thanks for trying. I might know where they are after all."

"I found some old combs, a couple of lighters, and a dirty magazine. But no keys."

Clarence didn't ask about the dirty magazine. He'd left it for her to find. A couple of months earlier, he noticed she was getting a little too curious about his life outside the office, so he put the magazine under a couple of law books in his desk. He knew she went through his desk occasionally, looking for notes or files he would toss in there. When she never mentioned the magazine, he chastised himself for doubting her. Next to smoking, second-guessing himself was his favorite addiction.

"Okay, thanks for looking. We have a client due at three, right? A new client?"

"Correction, we *had* a client due. He called and canceled."

"What was the name?"

"Hay. Charles Hay. I think it was an insurance thing."

"Okay. Did he reschedule?"

"No, he said he'd call back."

"Fine. Go get the afternoon mail and I'll make the calls." She left with a snappy salute.

Charles Hay was rich. Not as rich as Justin Highfield, but who was? Another rich client would always be welcome. Hay owned a lumber company and probably took a percentage of most of the construction work in Elder. He'd never hired Clarence for anything before. This was shaping up to be a stellar week, provided he called back. He lit a smoke with a rare moment of satisfaction and called Mill Creek.

It was the nicest Old Folks Home in Marquette and the monthly bill was commensurate with that reputation. Jameson Auckland Keaton, known to all as Jay, now eighty, had been there for two years. In his working life, he'd been a car dealer, and later, when the dealership went under, he'd done a bunch of bookkeeping for old businesses in Marquette. He retired at age seventy-three, and within a year, his wife died of liver failure at age seventy-one. Jay stayed in their small house five more years, until a series of small strokes made him too infirm to live alone anymore. Clarence had come up and moved him to Mill Creek. He wasn't happy about going, and escaped four times in the first few months, until they put him in a lockdown ward. Three months after his incarceration there, he busted out again. They found him in a bar a half mile from the home, bumming smokes. He had been evacuated during a fire alarm and noticed that the fire doors were deactivated during the procedure. A week later, he set a small fire in the metal wastebasket in his bathroom, right under the smoke detector and stationed himself by the most remote fire door in the place. When the alarm went off, he went straight out the door. When they did the count afterward, they noticed he was gone. Since the fire started in his room, it wasn't too difficult to figure out. They might not have found him, but the owner of the bar called the cops a couple of hours after he got there, and they brought him back. His mind was still sharp and his physical faculties were all good. The strokes had affected his ability to speak and process thoughts in order. His doctor had warned Clarence that he could easily set fire to his home while making dinner, or leave a cigarette burning. So they moved him, over his garbled objections.

Clarence had gone to visit a few times, and the difficulty Jay had in communicating hadn't really changed their relationship, since they were never inclined to have intimate conversations. In the beginning he'd resolved to go up once a month, but the drive was 350 miles. Five and a half hours, and the only other option was taking a small commuter plane, which frightened him so much he never even considered it. He would phone sometimes, but the conversations were like trying to listen to a radio show that was 80% static. You got a few words, but that was all. He'd been slack of late, not visiting for the last three months.

Mr. Crocker, who ran the place as though he would never be an inmate, came on the line a short time after his secretary put Clarence on hold.

"Mr. Keaton, thanks you for returning my call so promptly," he began.

"What's the trouble, Mr. Crocker?" he asked, praying it was something trivial. More clothing, or a new TV for the room. Something that could be handled with money.

"I'm afraid, sir, that your father has not been too well, of late. He seems to be in something of a downward spiral. Another small stroke the other night, and he is confined to his bed. The doctor is afraid..."

"...that he's going to die?" This conversation had been inevitable and close for two years, but Clarence was surprised he didn't feel much emotion – yet. Crocker continued.

"He is not expected to live more than a couple of weeks, Mr. Keaton."

"Is he able to communicate at all?"

"Very little, I'm afraid. It's difficult to make out what he's saying. Although, he did appear to ask for you this morning. He pointed to your photo." Hearing this made Clarence shut his eyes tightly and clench his teeth.

"All right, Mr. Crocker. I'll be there as soon as I can."

"We're doing everything we can for him, of course," said Crocker, in that kindly-officious voice he must have cultivated when he got into the business of shepherding the elderly to their final beds.

"I'll call when I arrive. Thank you for letting me know."

"Of course, Mr. Keaton, very good." He rang off.

Clarence had other relatives, on his mother's side, somewhere, not that he cared. But Jay was the last of his family and Clarence was his only child. There wasn't a choice. An eleven hour round trip. *Fabulous.* He heard someone come in and head up the stairs. Assuming it was Paula, he called out.

"Any checks?"

"No, sir," a familiar voice answered, and then the doorway was filled with the slightly imposing physical bulk of Eddie Two Crows, Odawa Elder, six-one, patent-leather-black hair in a ponytail, the grave-eagle face that was quick to smile if he knew you, and never smiled if he did not. He sat down and lit a cigarette.

"Sorry to come in without an appointment," he said, blowing the smoke out in a plume, "But you didn't look busy."

"Never a problem, Eddie, I'm not. What can I do for you?"

"Kid from the rez got busted for pot. Going down now to bail him out."

"What's his name?" Clarence got out his legal pad.

"Jimmy Akens. Folks call him Bird."

"Age?"

"Seventeen."

"How much did he have on him?"

"Not sure. Probably not more than a quarter ounce."

"Where did they bust him?"

"He was on a boat in Tobico Marsh. Cop came to the shore and waved him in. When he got there, he asked him if he had any pot. Jimmy showed him the little bag. Cop took him in."

"Was he dressed like a cop?"

"Not according to Jimmy. They do this a lot." Which was true. The local police routinely busted the native kids for pot with plainclothes officers. And for what? To lock up kids for getting high? It was unbelievable. Clarence didn't smoke pot very often, and he'd never purchased any, but really, arresting teenagers for using a plant that grew wild where they lived? There wasn't enough stupid-on-stupid crime in the city?

"The marsh has been weird lately."

"Weird how?" Clarence asked.

"Lots of people. I saw two or three guys the other day making a damn movie. Don't know what they were filming."

"Really? They had a camera?"

"Looked like it. On a tripod. Real professional looking."

"You talk to them?"

"No, I was fishing and I hooked one right after I saw them. Hey, did you get the fish I left the other day?"

"Yes, thanks, four nice ones. They're in my freezer. Why didn't you come in?" Something kept his mind on *They're in my freezer* for a couple of extra seconds.

"Saw some cops, decided you were a little too busy." They both smiled. Eddie was one of Clarence's few friends. Now and again they would hang out, drink a little, maybe even get high, and it was always so calm, so letting-the-world-take-you, a feeling Clarence had never known before. Nothing flustered Eddie, and his wife, Kiwi, always made Clarence feel at home, which was odd, because he'd never really felt at home anywhere. Sometimes, when he was cross-examining someone who was lying, and he was leading that person into a corner from which the only answer was going to trip him up, he would feel a warmth, a proximity to happiness, but it was always a fleeting thing, since one couldn't lose one's concentration or rhythm while doing it. One day, with Eddie and Kiwi at their house on the reservation, after getting high and watching the sun set, he sat down to a meal of fresh venison and other treats and felt it for the first time outside a courtroom, and understood that it was family. It was happy people who loved each other, gathering and being together. Something he had never really known.

"What kind of car was that, by the way?" Eddie's voice scrambled his reverie.

"What? Oh, the car. The one parked by mine on Saturday? 1954 Studebaker Starlight."

"Nice car. Yours?"

"No, the client's."

While wishing he could tell Eddie the truth, Clarence got what seemed like a marvelous idea.

"Eddie, did you drive here in the truck?"

"Yep."

"Could you do me a favor?"

"Depends on what it is, but probably."

"Could you drive your truck out of my lot, park it one or two streets over, and then get back into the parking lot without anyone seeing you?"

"Sure. I'm Indian. No one sees me."

"I'll meet you down there in fifteen, ok?"

"You got it." Eddie got up and left. Clarence glanced out the window to see that the watcher noticed Eddie leave. He looked at the name and address Paula had given him. *Ray Kubiak, 1121 Moore Rd. #15.* That was on the outskirts of town. Trailer parks, mostly, a few farms. This guy didn't own a farm.

Paula came in with the mail, which contained no cheques, of course.

"Hey," he said. "Go home."

"What? It's not even three o'clock."

"We got anything else today?"

"Not really. I could do some paperwork."

"Do it tomorrow. Go home, open a bottle of wine and have a nice evening."

"Okay, boss. You're sure?"

"I'm sure. Get going." She left, and he watched from the window of the back bathroom as she got in her car and left. Within a minute of her leaving, Eddie appeared, almost from nowhere. Clarence turned out the lights, went downstairs and out, locking the front door behind him and around to the lot, whistling, twirling his key ring.

"Okay," he said, handing Eddie his car keys. "Take my car and go bail Jimmy out. It should take about an hour, right?"

"Give or take. Why do you want me to take your car?"

"There's a guy in a Cadillac in the Library lot across the street. He's been following me. I need to do something without being watched."

"As soon as he sees me get out of the car, he'll know, and he'll come back."

"Probably, but I won't be here."

"Right. Okay. And bring Jimmy back here when I'm done?"

"Sure. Leave the car. Put the keys in the grass by the post over there, go get your truck and you're gone, okay? Call Paula tomorrow with the court date for Jimmy. I'll be there."

"Cool. Thanks Clarence."

"Thank *you*, Eddie. Best to Kiwi."

Eddie got into the Merc, started her and drove off. Clarence watched from cover and saw the Cadillac follow. Perfect. It was still broad daylight, but another quick check of the surroundings showed no one with their eyes on his place. He walked to the back of the lot, opened the unseen gate, went through and closed it carefully behind him, then into the shed, also closing the door. He turned on the lights and removed the tarp. The car still looked beautiful, gleaming red with all the trimmings. He wished he could just drive it, and he tried the driver's door, praying he'd forgotten to lock it. He had. *Every once in a while*, he thought, *forgetfulness and stupidity bails you out.* He opened his briefcase and set it on the passenger seat, then reached over and opened the glovebox. On top of a pile of papers, he saw keys, but knew immediately that they weren't car keys. They were safety deposit box keys. Another mystery. He put them and all the papers into the briefcase. He crawled into the back seat and put his hands between the cushions and pulled out what appeared to be a Ziploc bag full of pebbles. He put it in the briefcase. This was a finding expedition and he could check everything out later at his apartment. He reached under the two front seats and felt around, and, wonder of wonders, under the driver's seat, he pulled out a gun, a little .32 caliber Beretta. He checked the clip and found it full, so he ejected the chambered shell, pushed it back into the clip, and put both in the case. Then he popped the trunk open with the button in the glovebox and gave that a once over. He lifted the spare tire cover and ran his hands through the middle space, finding a small box that was empty and nothing else. Lifting the tire itself, he collected a thickly stuffed manila envelope. And that was it. He closed the briefcase, then the trunk, then the doors. He thought about locking the doors, but decided he'd better wait and find the keys first. He put the tarp back on and checked his watch. If Kubiak wasn't back yet he was on his way. He turned out the light and locked the garage from the inside. Then he slipped out the side door and locked it with the big padlock, as quietly as he could.

He looked through the ivy to see if anyone was in his parking lot or passing by. He couldn't see the Library lot from here so he decided to play it safe and headed out through the back of the property behind his. Then he walked a couple of blocks over and went to the post office, getting there just before they closed. He checked his box again and was really pissed off to find twenty pieces of mail that goddamn well should have been there when Paula had come ninety minutes before. Fucking government workers.

He walked back to the office and was surprised that the Cadillac wasn't in the Library lot. He went into the office and dropped the mail on Paula's desk, pausing to go through some of the paperwork there. The massage parlor who wanted to rent the space downstairs had upped their offer to four hundred dollars a month. *Right across from the Library*, he thought. *Read a book, get a massage, sue somebody.* They'd be open Saturday mornings as well. Maybe he could get a massage after seeing clients—he stopped fantasizing when he saw the Merc pull into his lot from the little side window by Paula's desk. He turned out all the lights and went to the front window. Sure enough, the Caddy pulled up and parked right in front of the house. He watched Kubiak get out, pull out a notebook and make some notations. Then, amazingly, he got impatient and started to walk around to the parking lot. Clarence went into his office and retrieved a baseball bat, an Al Kaline 1958 special, and went down the stairs and out the front door as quietly as he could. He walked around to the lot and found Kubiak engrossed in trying to break into the Merc. He sidled up close without being noticed and introduced himself.

"Hello, Ray," he said. Kubiak jumped and banged his hand on the side mirror of the Merc.

"OW! SHIT! OW!" he cried out.

"What can I do for you, Ray? You need a lawyer?" Clarence took a short step forward and brought the bat up, both hands ready to swing it, though he really hoped that wouldn't be necessary.

"My fucking hand, man! Jesus!" Then he stopped, eyeing the bat. "How the fuck do you know my name?"

"I know your address, too, you little prick." He raised the bat just a bit. "You want to explain why you're following me?"

"Kiss my ass," said Ray, shaking his bruised hand. Clarence noted that his heart was beating at an alarming rate. Having a heart attack at this moment would be embarrassing, he thought. Was he really prepared to hit this asshole with a baseball bat? He tried to appear quietly menacing while desperately trying to recall lines from movies that might intimidate.

"This can go easy, Ray, or it can go hard. Your choice." God, it sounded ludicrous coming out of his mouth. Ray just stared at him.

"Come on, man," he said. "Come get it. You'd better kill me with the first swing."

"The cops are on their way." He didn't imagine anything could sound so lame. Ray laughed this time.

"The cops hate you more than they even know about me. Why don't you fuck off and die?"

Clarence raised the bat to striking height and came toward Ray in three quick steps. Ray sidestepped him easily and Clarence almost smashed the window of his own car. Ray moved several steps away and gave Clarence the finger as he jogged a bit and disappeared around the corner of the house. A moment or two later, Clarence heard the Caddy start up and drive off. As it did, he buckled a little, leaning on the car. He was breathing so hard it was two or three minutes before he felt right. His heart finally started to slow down, and as it did, he wondered what the hell was going on. He was a lawyer. He helped people. He helped people who rarely paid him. He wasn't a thug. He went upstairs and retrieved the briefcase, locked up, found the keys where Eddie left them, and headed home.

When he got there, he packed a small bag and called Paula. She wasn't absolutely sober, but she was alert.

"What's up, boss?"

"What's the book say for tomorrow?" Paula had an amazing memory, which came in handy.

"Two clients coming in the afternoon," she said.

"No court?"

"No court, but Thursday is ALL court."

"Okay, call both of them and reschedule for late Thursday afternoon or Friday morning. Or even Saturday. I won't be in tomorrow."

"Everything okay?"

"Sure. I have to go see my father."

"You can fly up early tomorrow, and come back on the late afternoon flight. Kalitta Air. I'll call them."

"No," he said, with a finality that made her stop. "I'm not flying. I'll be back tomorrow night."

"Okay," she said. "Drive safe."

"I'll call you from the road. Oh, call Eddie Two Crows and find out when the kid is being arraigned."

"Got it. What's the kid's name?"

"Ask Eddie. See you in a day or two." He resisted the urge to tell her she'd better go in even if he wasn't there, because he knew she would. She didn't ask where he was going because she knew. He only went two places out of town anyway. Marquette to see his father, or the occasional weekend in Lansing. He hung up, filled a large thermos with coffee, smoked two cigarettes, then put the bag and the briefcase in the car. He took a quick visual tour of the neighborhood to confirm that the night follower hadn't clocked in yet, and then got in the car and left. If the traffic was light, and he only stopped once, he'd be in Marquette by midnight. He gassed up the Merc on the edge of town and hit the road.

WEDNESDAY

The drive was decidedly un-scenic in the dark. It was straight shot up I-75 to M-2 at St Ignace and then left onto the M-41 at Rapid River to the M-28 just south of town. He didn't mind the drive, generally. It was flat, and the further you went, the fewer cars and trucks to deal with. He hit the outskirts of Marquette a little after midnight and stopped at the Superior Motel on 28. It was a bungalow motel where you drove your car right up to the door of your room. He bought a soda and some sort of death-sandwich from the vending machines near the lobby and went into his room. He was always struck by the smell of older motel rooms. Mustiness, certainly, but there was also the depressing tinge of mildewed hope. He ate the sandwich and opened the briefcase on the bed. As he sifted through the contents, he got frightened and had to get up to shut the curtains and put a chair under the doorknob, despite the door already being double locked. *You're being paranoid.*

The bag of pebbles had mostly diamonds in it. He didn't have a practiced eye, but he knew good quality jewels and these were A-1.

What the hell is going on? Of course Elliot wouldn't want to have them on him, but surely there was a better hiding place than a car he was virtually giving away? He wondered what he should do. They were almost certainly stolen. Was he being set up? He puzzled on that for close to three smokes, and decided to put the bag in his safety deposit box at First National bank. That was the best place. As soon as he got back… no, tomorrow he'd get back too late. Thursday then. Except he had court all day, so it might have to be Friday. Another 60 hours with stolen diamonds in his possession didn't seem very healthy. The gun was even more problematic, since he knew that professional second story men *never* carried them, which suggested something else that worried him. What if the car wasn't Elliot's to give? No, he had the pink slip. But now the damn thing was registered in Clarence's name. The gun wouldn't be registered to him, if it was registered at all. He knew he should get rid of it, and right away. He had never owned a handgun, though he wasn't unfamiliar with firearms in general. His father had taken him out to the range when he was young, and they'd gone hunting a few times. At fourteen, he'd shot a duck and cried so piteously afterward that his father never took him again. Clarence discovered young that shooting at targets was easy, but killing something that had been alive two seconds ago was horrible. Jay Keaton had at first been proud of his son's obvious ability and shooting eye, but he never suggested they go hunting or to the range again. Thinking about it now, more than thirty years later could still bring up the indelible image of the dead duck in Clarence's mind. He tried to erase it, with no success. Every time he thought of it now it would remain on the periphery of his thoughts for a few days. He put the gun and the jewels back in the case and got out the big envelope. He hadn't looked at more than one or two documents from it when he dozed off, lying on a double King motel bed with a briefcase full of diamonds and a .32 Beretta within a foot of where he was unconscious.

He woke up, quickly alert since he hadn't had a drink for the previous twenty-four hours, something of a mid-week record. It was 6:28 a.m. Wednesday morning. He collected the sleep-spread of documents and put them back in the envelope and then into the briefcase. A quick shower, a shave, and one cigarette, and it was time to go. He considered not checking out since his father might be at death's door, but then he figured he'd just come back and check in again if he had to stay over. So he settled the bill and left. He was two blocks away when he saw a sign for Quarry Pond. It was a deep reservoir and he knew it would be perfect. He'd gone swimming there as a kid. He stopped the car a half block away and strolled to the water's edge. He tossed a couple of small rocks in while taking a good look around. No one was about, it being barely seven o'clock. The fourth rock he heaved a long way out into what he figured was deepest part of the pond. The splash was larger since it wasn't really a rock, but a gun. Then he threw the clip in as well. He walked back to his car and drove to Mill Creek Home For The Aged.

He parked outside the pleasant looking structure, all happy greens and pale reds and blues, soothing colors for the usually cranky inmates. He walked to the desk, gave his name, and asked for Mr. Crocker. After no more than a minute or two, Crocker appeared, holding a file. They walked across the main exercise area to the hospital wing, passing a group of elderly people attempting to play badminton in front of an audience of wheelchair-bound people who looked like they had no idea what they were watching. Clarence tried to space his sight out, so that he focused on nothing in particular and everything was slightly obscured other than the ground in front of him. To focus on anything else was too depressing. They walked into the hospital building and down a hall where he smelled rubbing alcohol, which had frightened him since he was a child, since smelling it always meant you were about to get a needle. At the end of the sterile white hall, also dotted with empty-eyed wheelchair riders, they entered a room where his father lay on a bed. As they walked in, Clarence realized with a shudder that Crocker had been talking to him the whole way over and he hadn't registered a single word.

"...and *our* physician felt that he should be made comfortable for the time he had left..." Crocker sounded like the soft drone of an expensive vacuum cleaner. Clarence just nodded and stared at his father, allowing his eyes to focus properly at last. The old man looked awful, of course. No one in this place looked good. Jay's hair, white in a couple of spots but still mostly iron-grey, was pillow-shaped into a Bozo the Clown do. His glasses were on the white metal bedside table, which Clarence noticed had wheels. His eyes were closed and his hands, resting on his lower chest as though he were already in a coffin, were mottled with age, every vein looking like it was at full capacity. Clarence could find neither word nor emotion, and all he thought was, *he looks the same as always.*

"I'll leave you two alone, Mr. Keaton," said Crocker. Drop by and see me before you leave, all right?"

"Yes, of course," Clarence mumbled, watching his father snore. Crocker left the room. As soon as he was gone, Jay Keaton opened his eyes, glancing sideways at the door as if to ensure Crocker was gone, then registering on his son.

"C-L," he said, his voice a tiny frog-sound. Clarence smiled at the nickname no one else had ever used.

"Hey, Pa."

"Wha dja ing me?"

Clarence understood. *What'd you bring me?* was what he said. He also knew what his father meant. He held up his hand to signal Jay to wait a moment, then went to the door of the room and looked down the hall each way, seeing just people waiting to die in wheelchairs, and way down there, a nurse's station. No one was on patrol, and twenty feet from his father's room was a door that led to an outside patio. He sidled over to it, looked out, and the patio was deserted. It wasn't a cold day, a little autumnal chill was all. He went back into the room and found a collapsible wheelchair in the corner. He opened it and brought it to his father's bedside. He found two thick blankets and set one down to line the chair, then hoisted his father up, out of bed, and into the chair. Jay didn't weigh much more than a high school girl now. Clarence put his suit jacket over his father's shoulders and covered his legs with the second blanket. All set. When he went and checked the hallway again, his father spoke, clearly a little irritated.

"Wha r ee ooing?" He gestured to the door feebly. *What're you doing?* More than four decades of hearing that voice made it easier to understand than someone who'd only known Jay a year or two.

"I just don't want the nurse to catch us, Pa," he said.

"Shicantopis…" he grunted. *She can't stop us.* Clarence was about to say that she could, but decided arguing with his father wouldn't be the thing to do.

He wheeled Jay over to the door, noticing as they got there that it was a coded door with a little numbered keypad. *Shit.* He was about to turn around and risk going past the nurse when Jay reached out and punched four numbers very quickly, then looked at him and nodded. Clarence pushed and the door opened. He coughed a little to mute the sound of it opening as he wheeled Jay onto the patio, found a chair for himself, and pulled out the Camels, placing one to his father's dry, purplish lips and lighting it up, as well as one for himself.

The satisfaction that his old man received from the first drag was astounding, and almost orgasmic. He quivered with pleasure as the first lungful went down and held it for just a moment before blowing it out in a cloud. Then he coughed, just once, and smiled, sitting up straight and focusing on the view of the parking lot and the road.

"Where's your car?" he asked. It was the first coherent sentence his father had spoken to him in a long time. They both took drags off their smokes.

"My car's in the lot, Pa. There, the green Mercury." Jay nodded and pointed to the road.

"The way….the way…out of here," he said. "Just get on….get on that road….and…and keep going."

"Yes, Pa, that's right." Jay cocked his head in the direction of the road, and raised his eyebrows, and Clarence realized he wanted to go right now. He'd been rehearsing the first two lines so they'd come out clearly. *He's been waiting for me to come.* He'd memorized the door code by watching and listening from his room. His mind was still perfectly intact in there. It was just that the gears didn't work very well anymore. The old man tossed the cigarette and indicated he wanted another. Clarence obliged and watched his father's fingers tremble as he smoked. The second one, Clarence knew, was never quite as good as the first, but Jay was smoking it slowly, enjoying it so he'd be able to remember what it felt like.

Clarence was trying to think of something to say, knowing that on the drive back he'd think of a thousand things and berate himself, but he was barren of reasonable conversation topics. *You want a big funeral?* occurred to him, but he rejected it. *I love you* floated up several times and finally he said it. Jay seemed surprised by it. It wasn't something they'd spent a lifetime saying to each other. He puffed his smoke and stared into his son's eyes. Clarence tried to remember even one truly intimate moment they might have shared, and could not.

"C-L…" his father managed. "C-L….I dmibes. Mi-erry ess" *I did my best, my very best.* And he had. The fact that it hadn't been enough didn't matter anymore.

"I know you did, Pa. I know." He was going to cry, and he really didn't want to cry in front of the old man. He knew the next word would bring it on. Jay was looking at him, his brown and red-veined eyes boring a hole in his face. He opened his mouth and nothing came out. He tried a second time, and failed. Then he smiled, and shrugged. Clarence smiled back and was going to say something but the door opened and the nurse appeared with Mr. Crocker. Jay felt the retribution coming and flicked the smoke away so quickly they never actually saw it. It nestled in an ankle high tuft of grass and looked like a distant fire in a hidden canyon.

"Mister Keaton," said Crocker, trying to make his studiedly calming voice reach a level of sternness. "Our residents are not normally allowed to smoke. And *no one* gave permission for your father to go outside." Jay looked up at his end of life jailer and said something that neither Crocker nor the nurse understood. It was garbled, but Clarence got it and tried to cover it with his own apology.

"It's my fault, Mr. Crocker," he said, "Dad wanted a moment outside and I couldn't refuse him."

"Mr. Keaton, please. He can't communicate anything but gibberish, so how did you know what he wanted?" The tone was sneering.

"I know his voice and can understand him a good deal of the time."

"Can you? Can you indeed?" Again with the snarky tone. *All right, Mister. You asked for this.*

"I can. For instance, he spoke to you just now."

"Really? And what did he say?"

"He told you to go fuck yourself." Clarence rose and walked away, leaving the warden of this prison for the elderly with his mouth in a perfect 'O'.

Clarence stayed for lunch, which Jay barely touched, and then said goodbye to his father for what he knew would be the final time. The old man was quite weary after their little outing and couldn't keep his eyes open. He would open them for a moment, but they would close again so fast it was impossible to see if anything registered. He tried to speak once or twice but the garble was stronger now. It was as though he'd saved it all up for those few moments they had. He'd said what he wanted to say. His father wasn't a sentimental man, and had never wasted time on goodbyes or 'I love you'. Clarence held his hand, every vein showing, and whispered a few things. Nothing revelatory; nothing the old man didn't already know. He wanted to cry, but he didn't want that to be the last sound his father took from him into wherever he was going. Jay squeezed his hand twice, which was most likely the only language he still possessed. The decline was a cliff fall from the three hours before when Clarence arrived. Finally Clarence stood up and waited at the end of the bed for a bit, but he had to go. His father would die alone in this room. In a few years he would do the same in a room exactly like it, just as alone. He had a long drive ahead, and knew he should get started, but he lingered, trying to fix the image in his mind. His father groaned and rolled over a little, his left hand reaching blindly for and finding the metal rod that prevented him from falling out of bed. It looked like he was trying to hold on to something while the next world pulled at him inexorably. Death is a mother insisting *it's time to go* to a child who still wants to play. He would never forget the veiny hand holding the silver-steel rail.

Clarence stopped at Crocker's secretary's desk and informed her that Mallon's Mortuary would be handling the body. Then he headed over to Seamus Mallon's building, finding his old high school acquaintance in his office. A short chat, some written down information, and a check changing hands finished that chore. Getting back in the Merc, he thought, *the way out of here…just get on that road and keep going.* Good advice. He grabbed a burger and a coke to go at Mickey's Diner, a favorite place from the old days, and hit the road, planning to go straight home, but he came to a red light at Hampton avenue, and he impulsively turned right and headed to Division and finally to Pioneer road where he stopped and parked outside the Old Catholic Cemetery. Some late daisies were standing perkily by the side of the road as he walked to the entrance, and he picked them and carried on into the graveyard. A quarter of a mile to the right of the entrance was a large sycamore tree and underneath it was a large granite marker that said WALSH. Nearby, just off to the side of her parents' markers, was Rosalie. *Rosalie Walsh Keaton 1935-1957 Dear Heart.*

Clarence looked around, reassuring himself he was alone as he placed the daisies on the marker.

"Hi, Rosie," he said, his voice choking a little. "I brought daisies." She'd always liked daisies. He wondered if he would ever grow so old that he might forget knowing her. Forget the way her hair smelled after a shower, the way her hands touched his face when she kissed him, the things she said, the sound, the goddamn *lilt* of her voice. Was remembering it all a penance? Was there really any penance for it? Was her ghost here, screaming at him, calling him an asshole? He wanted to say he was sorry, even though he'd said it many times here in this very spot. He hadn't come in five years. But he was tired of apologizing. Words ran through him, but failed to reach his mouth, which was closed, anyway. *You said it wouldn't matter. You said you'd love me no matter what.*

He made the sign of the cross and kissed his knuckles, which was something she always did, and then got back in the car and headed back to Elder. He didn't have a thought that registered until he got to Mackinaw City, and realized he had to take the 1-75 turn-off. He stopped at the first exit and gassed up, took a leak, and called Paula collect. It was just after four p.m. and she answered on the first ring. It thrilled him that she wouldn't even take an hour off on a day when the boss was not expected. It brightened everything.

"It's me," he said, concealing his pride in her work ethic. "What's the scoop today?"

"Okay, the clients were handled with a deft touch, if I do say so myself. Nobody got too angry, and they all agreed to the rescheduling."

"Excellent, next."

"The mail delivered one check, for four hundred and fifty smackers, from Kelso the plumber, now paid in full."

"About time, too. The office pipes should burst any day now so we can give it right back to him. I should have been a goddamn plumber."

"Who would I work for then?"

"A rich plumber. Next."

"A traffic court thing came in and someone called about suing a Chemical company. Wanted your opinion, said they'd call again tomorrow."

"Fine. Is that it?"

"No, the cops called. Mike Ross; wanted to talk to you. ADA Gallo as well. As soon as you can, they said. And the Mayor called three times."

"Three times?"

"I think he was checking where you are. I told him you were out of the office today and I had no idea where your sorry ass was."

"I like it. Did you say, 'Am I my lawyer's keeper'?"

"No. But I thought of saying it. The last time he called. He sounded kind of desperate."

"Of course he did. Okay, nothing we need to deal with until tomorrow, right?"

"That's right. Oh, and the Cadillac is back in the parking lot across the street."

"Really? Well now, they assume I'll be back."

"Apparently. Still the same cute guy. Would be okay if I asked him out?"

"What you do on your time is your business, kid."

"Thanks, boss."

"Listen, he may follow you home, so be careful."

"You mean, don't invite him in, right?"

"Right. See you tomorrow." He hung up, smiling. He'd almost said *I love you* because she was just so entertaining to talk to, but he didn't know how she'd take it. Phrases like that went to a holding area in his mind and waited, usually forever. Besides, he couldn't even remember if he'd said it to his dying father today, so it wouldn't be right to say it to his secretary. The sun went down on his left and a little bit behind him as he drove home.

It was only just seven p.m. when he approached town. Coming to the exit, he couldn't decide if he should go to the right and home or to the left to the club, where a restorative drink would put all the miles far behind. But he was tired and being tired was dangerous. He might give in to having more than one drink, and being tired and a little boozed up was very dangerous. He might say something before he could properly vet it in his head. So as he eased off the throttle and took the exit ramp, feeling the tired muscles in his foot and ankle give off their grateful shooting pains, he decided to just go home. He could drink all he wanted there.

He was surprised, to say the least, when he arrived at his place to find two cop cars, one with the lights still going, blocking his usual parking place in Shorty's driveway. The lights were on upstairs and he thought he saw Paula in one of the windows. He drove around the block, came back, and parked in the parish hall lot. He noted the Cadillac was there, but no one was in it. No one seemed to notice him as he walked up to his door with his little clothes bag and his briefcase. He was wishing he'd gone to the club and risked getting drunk. A cop was coming out with a man in handcuffs. It was Ray Kubiak.

"Hey, Ray," he said. "Tough night?"

"Fuck you," Kubiak scowled at him.

"Shut up," the cop said to Kubiak. He turned to Clarence. "Who are you, sir? This is a crime scene."

"My name is Clarence Keaton. I live in this crime scene."

"Do you have some identification, sir? Actually, could you hold on for a moment? Let me get this guy in the car." Clarence indicated that would be fine,

and put his bags down on the porch. The cop walked Ray to the cruiser and put him in the back seat. Then he came back. Shorty and Paula came down the stairs at the same moment.

"So you're Mr. Keaton?" the cop asked. Clarence showed him his driver's license, and he nodded. "Well, sir, there was a break-in here a little earlier."

"Hey, boss," said Paula, with a big satisfied smile on her face.

"Clarence!" It was Shorty. "What the hell is going on here? One night a peeping tom and now a break-in! What if I was having a dinner party or something?"

Clarence smiled at Paula and refrained from mentioning that Shorty hadn't had a dinner party since Eisenhower was in office. Two more cops came down the stairs with another fellow. Clarence recognized him. He'd actually defended him a couple of times. The name was…the name was…Corky something. Yeah. He worked mostly as a skip tracer for….a bail bondsman named Joe Bothwell. *Holy shit.* One of the cops escorting Corky down the stairs nodded to Clarence.

"Looks like we got here just in time, Mr. Keaton. They'd only just started searching your place." Your secretary called in and we happened to be close."

"That's great," said Clarence, "I appreciate it."

"Yeah," said the cop, smiling. "So maybe the next time you get me on the stand, you could give me a break." Clarence realized it was Officer Dillon, who'd arrested Otto Joyce for drunken driving.

"I do owe you one, Officer Dillon. Thanks."

"No problem, sir." He was clearly the senior officer on the scene, directing the other cop to take Corky and Kubiak in for booking. Then he motioned to Clarence to come look at the door.

"They really wrecked your lock, sir, and your door."

"Yes, I see that." It looked like they'd used two crowbars, and maybe a sledgehammer, too.

"I can put a temporary lock on it tonight, sir, after you've checked it out upstairs, but I would advise you to find another place to stay until you can get it fixed."

"Thanks, Officer Dillon. Give me a few moments upstairs, and I'll find a hotel."

"Do you have any idea what they might have been looking for, sir?"

"I'm afraid I don't." Officer Dillon made a note of that.

"And you were out of town all day, sir? Where?"

"I was out of town, yes. I just got back five minutes ago."

"Where out of town, sir?"

"I was in Marquette, Officer Dillon. I appreciate your getting here and taking care of my apartment. If you don't mind, I'll be down in a moment." He indicated that Paula should follow him and he grabbed his two bags and headed up.

The place looked just as he suspected. Slightly trashed. Some drawers had been emptied out and the bed was stripped and flipped, but nothing else had been touched. He turned to Paula, and was surprised that Shorty had come up as well.

"What happened?"

"I left the office and decided to drop some stuff off with Shorty for you to read," Paula said. "Tomorrow's schedule in court and the notes I made on all the calls today. I saw that there were two cars in the lot over there when I left and so I doubled back and saw them screwing with your door. So I went up the block and called the cops from a payphone at the gas station. They must have been cruising close because they were here in about two minutes."

"What do you suppose they were looking for, Clarence?" asked Shorty, looking through some of the stuff that had been in a drawer.

"I don't know, Shorty," he said. "I have a couple of cases at the moment that seem to be concerning people." I'm going to get some clothes and go to a hotel for the night. Thanks for being here and looking out for the place for me." She realized he was sort of asking her to leave, and she nodded.

"No problem. It was really your secretary. You want me to call about getting the door fixed tomorrow?"

"No, Shorty, I'll call and I'll pay. It'll be fixed in twenty-four hours. I promise." He knew that would satisfy her enough to make her leave, and he was right. She nodded to Paula and went back down to her place. He thanked God she had her own entrance, so he didn't have to pay to fix two doors. Once she was gone, he turned to Paula.

"Nice work, Slim. I owe you."

"We can talk about that later," she smiled. "But you shouldn't go to a hotel. Why don't you stay at my place?"

"Nice of you to offer, but probably not a good idea. I don't want whoever's following me to know where you live."

"Christ, boss. I'm in the phone book. You had a long day. How's your Dad?"

"He's dying. But we still had some fun. I took him out for a smoke, and we got in trouble. He told Crocker to go fuck himself."

"Keatons all seem to have that chip on their shoulder don't they?" she said.

"Something we never lose. It's good for the world that there aren't many of us."

"So come on over and stay in my spare bedroom tonight. I'll make you dinner."

"Okay," he replied. "What's for dinner?"

"What do you like?"

"I like fish." He went to his refrigerator and pulled the bag of fish Eddie had left him out of the freezer. "Here, can you make these?" She looked in the bag and shook her head.

"I can only make the fish," she said, reaching in the bag and pulling something out. "I can't make these." In her hand was a set of car keys. The Studebaker keys.

"Holy shit," he said.

"Is this what they were looking for?" she asked.

"Probably. Eddie left the bag of fish on the door of the Mercury and they keys got in there somehow, I guess. All right, I'll get some clothes together for tomorrow and see you at your place in about an hour. Okay?"

"An hour? I'm ten minutes away by car."

"I have to make one stop first. I'll see you around eight, okay?"

"Okay, boss." She turned to leave.

"Paula?" he said. She turned back and looked at him.

"Nice job today. Very satisfactory." It was his highest compliment and she knew it. She smiled a little, mostly to herself.

"My pleasure, boss." She left, and he started to collect what he'd need. Then he called Luther the lock man at home. He'd acted for him a couple of times and saw him occasionally at the club bar. He explained the problem and Luther said he knew a guy who could do the door in one day. They agreed to meet up at eight the next morning to measure and get it together. Clarence thanked him and then grabbed a suit and a couple of bowties for court and went down to the car. He checked the parking lot for anyone following and then remembered they were both in jail.

He headed over to the little strip of businesses behind the courthouse on Garfield Avenue. Tucked in between a cleaning store and hole-in-the-wall Chinese place was Bothwell's Bail Bonds. Joe Bothwell was an ex-cop and he did some investigative work on the side. He and Clarence knew each other peripherally, but had never locked horns or done business. If Clarence hadn't defended that idiot Corky he wouldn't have known it was Bothwell calling the shots. He sat in the car for a moment, collecting himself. He was tired and more than a little stressed, but he was also angry. An honest man shouldn't have thugs following him, he thought. Although, was he really an honest man? What if this wasn't about the Studebaker or the burglaries? He breathed in and out slowly and deeply several times, then opened the car door and headed into the confrontation. He looked inside the door of Bothwell's and there he was at his desk in the back, on the phone. He appeared to be yelling into the receiver as well. Clarence entered quietly and heard the last of the tirade.

"…well maybe if you hadn't fucked THAT up, too, you moron, you wouldn't be in fucking jail, would you? I don't know why I even…" He saw Clarence and abruptly stopped, staring. Then he said into the phone, "Stay cool. I'll be there as soon as I can," and hung up. He turned to Clarence, but didn't say anything. He just looked him straight in the eye.

"Do I owe you money, Joe?"

"Not that I'm aware of, Counselor." Joe smiled.

"Then why would two of your skip-tracer dickheads be following me around? Any ideas about that?"

"No idea."

"Corky and Ray. Corky in the Chevy and Ray in the Cadillac. They've been following me for a couple of days. And they work for you. I have the car license plates and I bet they're both registered to you, since neither of those assholes look like they can afford cars that nice." He reached into his pocket and pulled out a piece of paper, attempting to intimidate Joe into a verbal mistake, but Joe wasn't having any of that, either.

"Don't believe I know anyone by those names." He leaned back in his chair as though he was being entertained.

"And both of them broke into my house tonight, and they're now at the jail. That was Corky you were yelling at on the phone." He said it flatly, as though he didn't even need a confirmation. There was a flicker in Bothwell's eyes that told him he was dead on. There was also a freezing moment when he realized he wasn't welcome in this building any longer. It was rumored that Bothwell kept a shotgun under the desk, though Clarence doubted he would use it in this instance. "When I leave, you're going down there to bail them out, aren't you, Joe? I wonder if the cops already know you told them to search my place. I believe that's called conspiracy to commit robbery, or some such thing."

Joe stood up, slowly, and it was impressive. He was six-four and built like a hippo.

"Anytime you want to turn around and get the fuck out of here would be fine with me, Counselor. I have things to do."

"No problem, Joe. No problem at all. I just came as a courtesy, to let you know the two morons who work for *you* were caught breaking into my house tonight and you might want to go and bail them out. Just a heads-up. You'd better get to the jail before one of them talks and you lose your license to do any kind of business in this whole fucking *state*."

"Are you threatening me, Mr. Keaton?"

"Threatening? Are you serious? I'm doing you a favor. And whoever hired you might want to think about his political career. You can pass that along, too. Have a nice evening. Drive carefully."

He turned and walked out without looking back, leaving the big man staring at the back of him. He got in his car quickly and drove almost a mile before his heart rate started to slow. Threatening people wasn't really his style, but he knew this was a schoolyard situation. If you let the first one go, they never stop. And he really couldn't have people following him. His life wasn't that interesting, but it wasn't an open goddamn book, either.

He got to Paula's place a little after eight, parking out in front. He wondered if his Mercury would be safe since it was a black neighborhood, then was ashamed for thinking such a thing. *Besides*, he thought, *if they do steal it, I still have the Starlight.* He took his briefcase, his club bag and a garment bag inside, hoping no neighbors were watching. It was 1975, after all, but it also looked like he was moving in. He didn't know if Paula dated any white guys, but he doubted it. She opened the door before he got there and he smelled the fish cooking, a very pleasing odor. After a long day that began with almost certainly seeing his father for the last time, plus the drive, plus the break-in, and then the bracing of that goddamn bail-bondsman, he was about ready to pass out. There was an ashtray on the dining table, next to a glass of scotch. He dropped his stuff by the door and placed himself in the dining chair, lighting a Camel and taking a sip of the scotch. All three gave satisfaction.

THURSDAY

He woke up at six, knowing he wasn't in his own place, but unsure of his exact location. The motel in Marquette? An Elder hotel? No, the room was totally unfamiliar and then he remembered he was at Paula's. He'd been dreaming of his father and mother. And seeing his father so young and spry had been pleasing. It was as though his subconscious was trying to wipe out the events of the previous day, or at least remind him that it wasn't the whole story.

He had his own bathroom so he showered quickly and shaved. The soap in hotels and motels was always too small, and the soap in his secretary's house was too perfume-y. He smelled like a fruity Hawaiian beach ball when he was done. Dressed, he stole out of his room, hoping Paula was already up, but she wasn't. He found the coffee and started a pot, then sat down at her kitchen table to smoke one, possibly two, and go over the notes for the day's work.

On paper the day looked ridiculous and impossible. Two prelims, the Highfield kid's sexual assault and Elliot's burglary case, plus Jimmy Akens, the Odawa kid charged with possession. It seemed like a silly entrapment case, the kid being only seventeen, but one couldn't forget that this was Michigan, the state that gave John Sinclair ten years in the penitentiary for two, count 'em, *two* joints. And neither one a fatty. He saw that once he got out of court, if he did, he had two rescheduled appointments back at the office, plus his new door. It was going to be a long day for a working man.

He was pouring coffee for himself when Paula came in and got a cup for herself out of the cupboard. She walked over to him and held out the cup, but he hesitated, because she had come right from her bed to the kitchen, obviously. She was completely naked. He started to pour into her cup when she realized and giggled a little. He finished pouring and she took a sip.

"Sorry, boss. I forgot you were here."

"Until you saw me," he replied, going back to the notes.

"Well, now you've seen me, too," she said. She waited perhaps two extra seconds for him to say something more, but when he didn't, and didn't even look at her again, she walked back into her bedroom. He heard the shower go on, and assumed the next time she appeared, she'd be properly dressed.

She came out at seven fifteen, dressed as he saw her five days a week.

"I take it we're going in early today?" she asked. Clarence nodded.

"I am. I have to get a couple of things and then meet Luther's door guy at my place at eight. I want to talk to Elliot at the jail before his prelim, too."

"Ok, I'll get the mail and placate the clients until you get back."

"That sounds fine. And if I live through the day, we'll talk later this afternoon."

"About what?"

"The weather, sports, men and women, the usual Thursday shit."

"Got it."

"Thanks for the fish fry and the scotch and the bed, Paula."

"Anytime, boss. See you later. Oh, wait!" He stopped and turned.

"What?" She handed him the keys to the Starlight, which he'd left on her dining table. He shook his head, to make sure it was still attached, gave her a rueful smile of thanks, and left. He was inside the Merc and gone in less than thirty seconds. She watched him go, wondering if she would ever really understand what he was about.

He took the scenic route and got to the office in nine minutes, keeping a sharp eye on any cars around him. None seemed to be following. Once inside the office he got a few papers he might need, opening the briefcase to toss them in, and realized it was still full of the stuff he'd found in the Studebaker. *Aw, hell. There's just too goddamn much to think about lately.* He couldn't leave it at the office, since it was likely to be trash-searched next. Continuing to carry all of it around wasn't appetizing either. He wasn't going to put it back in the Studebaker, not in broad daylight, anyway. He realized he probably should have left it in his apartment. It had already been sort-of-searched, and it would have been safe there. But no, he would have awakened every hour wondering if he should go back and check it. He had to get all of this shit into his safety deposit box at the bank *today*, even if he was late for appointments after court. He repacked the briefcase with the files, swearing to himself, then down the back stairs again, out the back door, and over to his house, seven minutes at morning peak traffic.

He got to his place and waited an irritating four minutes for the door guy. He looked and measured and said he could do it with two new locks by four o'clock. Luther showed up and agreed to the timeline. They settled on four hundred for everything, about a thirty percent markup because it was a rush job, which seemed almost fair to Clarence. He said they should bring the keys to the office between four and four-thirty and he'd give them cash. He made a note on his pad. *Get cash at bank.* He put the odds that he'd remember it when the time came at eight to one.

From his house to the Courthouse/Jail complex was usually short but he hit every red light. He parked in the Court Officer's lot and walked to the jail. Elliot was waiting in one of the conference rooms. Paula had phoned ahead. Damn she was good. Like an OR nurse, a legal secretary had to have a sense of what her boss needed, rather than have him tell her all the time. Clarence sat down, offering Elliot a smoke. Then he got right down to it.

"Are there going to be any surprises in the evidence today?"

"What sort of surprises, Mr. Keaton?" Calm as a dead man.

"Will they have fingerprints or any other possible witnesses, besides the mayor's kid? Will they know about the papers in the envelope and the safety deposit box keys, and the diamonds, and the Beretta, things of that nature?"

Elliot would have made a hell of a poker player. Nothing registered in his facial muscles as he scratched his chin and responded to each query in turn.

"No fingerprints, certainly. I'm not a fool. I suppose there could be other witnesses, but I doubt it. I never left any of the other places hot or in a hurry." He paused, and the thing passed over his face again. The twinge. Clarence realized it was '*Should I tell the whole truth here*'? It was the kind of thing an honest man would register when he felt he *had* to lie about something. Clarence remembered the Bob Dylan line; *To live outside the law, you must be honest.* Or was that Ambrose Bierce?

"Mr. Keaton, I guess I should have assumed you would search the car. But anything you found there would be your property, not mine." He said it with an eyebrow shrug and a little sigh. That's the way it goes.

"James, that's horseshit."

"Excuse me? Which part?"

"There's a goddamned bag of *diamonds* in my briefcase right now. And you really think it's easy come, easy go? Could you *not* lie to me for one minute?"

"All right. I could try that." His tone indicated it wouldn't be comfortable for him.

"There was also a gun in the car."

"Not mine." No twinge, no pause, just a flat denial.

"You don't even own one?"

"The easiest way to never be caught with a gun is to never own one. I work alone. I've never needed a gun. Where did you find it?"

"It was under the driver's seat, in a kind of pocket."

"Aha, well it wasn't mine. The previous owner must have put it there."

"The little old lady who never drove it? A nine-shots-in-the-clip Beretta? Seriously?"

Again the smile. As though he was thinking, "Okay, I tried being truthful. What now?" He had a sense of humor, this professional thief. Clarence decided to pursue case strategy for a while.

"Do you want me to try and make a deal on this if the evidence looks bad? I might be able to reduce it to one or two burglaries. You plead to those, get seven to ten, possibly out in five?"

"I doubt you could get that deal, but on balance, yes, I would take it."

"Why do you doubt I could get it?"

"I escaped once. I'm a career criminal. And I know some odd things about people in this town."

"Things that could help us?"

"Maybe. Some people are doing some squeezing here. And other people are being squeezed."

"Wow, that's a load off my mind. Who are we talking about in these terms? And who owns the safety deposit box keys?"

"I would imagine whoever it is really wants them back."

"So much so that they might actually hire people to follow me?"

"Quite possible."

"Defending you has given my life a good deal of new stress, Mr. Elliot."

"I apologize for that." He took Clarence's legal pad and turned it around, grabbed a pen, lifted up to a new page near the back, and wrote something. Then he turned it back and took a drag off his smoke. Clarence didn't look. He didn't want to appear anxious.

"Thank you. I was afraid telling me would break Burglar-Victim privilege." Elliot laughed out loud at that. His first unmeasured response since they'd met. Clarence was struck by how prison shapes a man into a survival machine. How he lets very little affect him because anything involuntary can get him killed. It was a feeling he understood, in an odd way. Not that he would ever say *I know how it feels* to someone who'd done real hard prison time. But he empathized.

"Are you in danger, James? Are people here going to try and kill you for what you know, or what you took?"

"It's possible," Elliot shrugged. "But killing someone in a city or county jail is difficult. A big prison is where that's easy. I think I'm probably safe until they decide where to send me. Could you make sure I don't go back to Southern Michigan?"

"I can try on that, but no guarantees. How the hell did you escape from there, anyway? I don't even remember reading about it."

They kept it out of the papers. It was the first successful escape in fifty years. And I didn't really plan it or anything. It sort of just happened."

"Those things don't just happen."

"Sure they do. The trick is recognizing the opportunity and being willing to take the leap. There was a plumbing problem in D Block, a bunch of backed-up toilets. So, four plumbers and some pipe-fitters came on a Thursday. They set up in the small exercise yard behind D Block, which was usually deserted anyway. I had a job pushing a cart through that yard in the afternoons. Taking the debris from the metal shop to the garbage bins on the other side of D Block. I walked by that afternoon and I saw the plumbers and the pipe-fitters and a whole shitload of pipe and other plumbing stuff. I kept going and did my work. The next day, a Friday, I was a little late getting out of the metal shop, so it was really close to the guard's shift change. And I walked by the spot again and there was no one there, because it wasn't just Friday. It was Good Friday. They had the day off. But all the pipe lengths, which were ready to be coupled and fitted, were still piled up there. So I deposited the metal shop crap, rolled the cart back, stopped and coupled four lengths of pipe together. Then I leaned them up against the wall, shimmied up, pulled the pipe up and over, shimmied down, and that was it. It being Good Friday meant the guards weren't the regular guys. They were temps who worked holidays and vacations. And the two who were supposed to be in the tower on that wall were a couple of minutes late arriving, so they never saw me. It only took about six minutes." Elliot sat back, just a little flushed with achievement. Clarence guessed he hadn't told the tale to many people.

"An impressive feat," he said.

"It's all timing. Life is all timing. Something is impregnable but there's always going to be a day, or even an hour, when it's not. You just have to gear yourself to be ready when the hour comes."

"How long were you out that time?"

"About a year. I should have left Michigan. But I had an old friend who was out then as well, and we hooked up for some, uh, fun."

"I hope it was fun. What you get for the escape?"

"A double sawbuck. I had four years to do of a six year bit when I jumped the wall, and I did fourteen years after they caught me. It was foolish, but man, it was a thrill."

"Maybe I can thrill you this afternoon with a good deal."

"Thanks, Mr. Keaton."

Clarence exited the room and ran smack into Detective Ross, who was, as usual, a little pissed off.

"I left a message for you to call me, Keaton. The chief has been on my ass about this case. Why didn't you call me back?"

"I was out of town visiting my dying father, Mike. How was your day?" Clarence resumed walking and Mike fell in step with him.

"What?"

"And when I got back, someone had broken into my place and searched it. The same two guys who've been following me for two days."

"Someone searched your place?" Mike seemed concerned at first, but then he smiled. "I hope they found something that gets your ass disbarred."

"All they found were the naked pictures of your wife, Mike."

"Listen, you bastard…" Mike grabbed him by the shoulder and was about to slam him into the wall but there were a bunch of other cops around as they approached the main foyer of the jail. So Mike stopped and patted Clarence on the back. Clarence kept walking, turning as he got to the door.

"I apologize, Mike. It was your *ex*-wife."

"This isn't over!" Mike called as he went out the door and headed to the courthouse. Once there, in a small conference room off Courtroom number three, he found A.D.A. Gallo. Antoinette was against him twice today and she was in her best outfit for the occasion. Royal blue power jacket, off-white blouse that looked fantastic, a dark pencil skirt and nice blue pumps. Clarence felt a little less than professional in his suit, a Benny Pappas special blue single-breasted, since it was one of his oldest. A real workhorse. Toni smiled as he sat down next to her. She liked him because he never talked down to her, he considered her stiff competition at all times, and she was pretty sure he'd never lied to her.

"You've got some trouble today, Clarence," she said, in lieu of greeting.

"I know that, Toni. Although the big trouble seems to be where I'm going to eat lunch."

"Joke all you want," she said. "We have Elliot sewn up."

"Is that a fact? So we shouldn't even bother with a defense, then? Interesting."

Toni laughed at that, and he thought he detected a tiny little hitch in the laugh, a moment that betrayed a small lack of confidence. He decided to probe a little.

"Is there an offer on the table, Toni?"

"For Elliot, the best we could do would be fifteen years, unless he were willing to make restitution of the stolen property."

"And, just for the sake of argument, if he were willing to do that; what would the offer be then?"

"Well…" she began, not having expected this tack, "I don't think we could go lower than ten years. He's a career criminal and he's had a jailbreak."

"Could you guarantee me he won't be incarcerated at Southern Michigan again, Toni? He really wants to try and escape from a new place."

She laughed again. Ms. Gallo had been getting a lot of heat on this case, and without showing it, she was quite anxious to get it over with.

"I think," she said slowly, "that with restitution and a guilty plea to all the burglaries, I could get you that. Ten years and he'd go somewhere other than Southern Michigan. Though with a former escapee, the only other place would be Jackson." Jackson prison was the largest walled prison in the country and a real shithole, but the client asked for it, so that was fine with Clarence.

"Of course, Toni. I'll take that to the client and get back to you before the prelim today. Okay?

"Okay." Inwardly she was relieved. Get this one out of the way. "Now, about the Highfield case…"

"Another offer, Toni?" Clarence smiled. Dealing blackjack with a professional like Toni Gallo got his mental juices flowing.

"I can't offer anything on that one, Clarence, you know I can't. He tried to rape a fifteen year old, for Christ's sake."

"Attempted rape is harder to prove than actual rape, Toni. Here's what's going to happen: She's going to get up there, and you're going to lead her through the story, how she went to the party, and lied about her age, and met the man, and lied about her age *again*, the whole sad tale, and the jury will probably be sympathetic. But then I'll cross examine her, and we might discuss underage drinking, and lying about your age, and why she got into the man's car, and what she really wanted when she got in the car..."

"None of those things have anything to do with it."

"Of course they don't, morally. But by law I can bring them up, and the jury'll see a girl getting drunk, lying about her age, then deciding at the last minute it's not what she really wants. And my client didn't actually go through with it after she said no. He drove her home. We go to the jury on this and he walks. And you know it."

Clarence was bluffing, of course. There was no way to be sure of that outcome, but he was very good at convincing people that he was sure. Toni chewed the end of her pen for a moment or two, and then packed her briefcase.

"Let me get back to you on that one. Give me an hour or so."

"Of course, Toni. See you later." She left and he smiled at her until she wasn't in sight anymore, then packed his own briefcase. You had to like Toni. Honest, gung-ho, detail-driven and sharp as a new nail. If she ever decided to cross the line, he would love to have her as a partner. He tried out the name combo: Keaton & Gallo. No, that was wrong. Gallo & Keaton was better. His name always worked better last.

He looked at his watch. It was almost ten. Oh *shit*. He raced to the arraignment courtroom on the second floor, getting there in less than two minutes, his tobacco-stained lungs heaving. Eddie Two Crows saw him and directed him over to where that day's accused awaited their turn in the barrel. Jimmy was third in line, so there was time, though not much. Clarence crouched down, intending to confer quietly with Jimmy, but by the time he really got his breath back, they were called. Clarence stood and guided Jimmy to the spot before his honor, Judge Ronald Morton.

"Clarence Keaton for the defense, your honor," he said. An oddly comforting phrase. The courtroom was one of the only places on earth he felt really comfortable, anyway. Morton looked up.

"Yes, Mr. Keaton. Of course." He glanced at the prosecutor's table and saw no one. "Where is our prosecutor today?"

A low level Assistant D.A., Belkopf, a rookie, advanced to the table.

"Your honor," he began, "A.D.A. Archer is trying to find the detective who made the arrest."

"What's the charge?" Morton asked, turning to his bailiff.

"Possession of marijuana, your honor," the bailiff replied. Morton looked at Jimmy.

"How old is this boy?" he asked.

"Sixteen," said Jimmy. "I'm sixteen." Clarence, who had been about to say *seventeen*, nodded, and opened his mouth to say something when Judge Morton interjected.

"Did you say a detective arrested this boy, Mr. Belkopf?"

"Yes, your honor."

"Can someone tell me why a *Detective* in the Elder police force is driving around the Odawa reservation arresting teenagers for pot possession? This is the fifth damn case in the last ten days or so. Is there a shortage of genuine crime?"

Belkopf attempted to stall for a little more time, which was a mistake.

"Your honor," he began, "possession is a crime..."

"Indeed, Mr. Belkopf, and apparently we're experiencing an unprecedented wave right now. But your policemen, excuse me, your *detectives*, never seem to bring in anyone who actually sells drugs, just the teenagers who use them."

Jimmy started to say something, but Clarence knew they had a real chance here, and put his hand on the boy's arm, indicating, he was hopeful, that silence was best. The boy closed his mouth and lowered his head.

"I'm going to give A.D.A. Archer, let's see, one more second to get here," said Morton, pausing for the briefest of moments. "Let's get a plea, Mr. Keaton."

"Not guilty, your honor," said Clarence.

"Fine. I'm entering a plea of not guilty AND a finding of not guilty. And there better not be any more of these goddamn cases today. Next!"

Clarence led Jimmy out and Eddie joined them.

"Thanks, Clarence," said Eddie, turning to Jimmy and giving him the elbow. "Thank the man."

"Thanks, Mr. Keaton," said Jimmy, just a tiny bit teenage-grudgingly.

"No problem, Jimmy," said Clarence. "I do it for a living. Do you know anything about the other kids getting jacked by the cops for pot, by the way?"

"Yes, sir, they were all friends of mine. And they were all arrested around the marsh." The western edge of Tobico Marsh was the eastern edge of the Odawa/Chippewa reservation.

"Were they all in boats like you were, Jimmy?"

"Yeah. I think so." Eddie shot the kid a look. "Sir."

"Okay, thanks. You got lucky this time. Remember that. A pot conviction can follow you forever, so be careful, all right?"

"He knows," said Eddie, mock-cuffing the kid upside the head. "He knows now. Thanks again, man. Come for dinner soon, okay? Kiwi says you should."

"I will. See you Eddie."

Off he went to another conference room on another floor where Justin Highfield and his son Jamie were waiting. It was almost ten thirty and the preliminary was a half hour away. When Clarence walked in, Justin was somewhere between nervous for his son and really pissed off that this had come so far already. Normally his money could grease the wheels of any situation, but this minister and his damn daughter weren't playing ball. He was brusque with his longtime attorney.

"Glad you could join us, Mr. Keaton."

Clarence sat down and got out his notes. He looked at each man in turn. The physical resemblance was striking, but there it ended. Justin worked harder than three men, but Jamie, born to privilege, was a cutter of corners, and a little horse's ass to boot.

"My apologies, Justin," Clarence said, "I have three cases going on here today. Now, Jamie...we've pled not guilty, but what if Miss Gallo were to offer us a deal that included no jail time and short probation? Would that --?"

"No, sir!" his father thundered. "Jamie didn't do this, and we're not taking any goddamn deal!"

"Wait one moment, Justin, and think this through. He pleads guilty to a misdemeanor. Coercion, maybe. A misdemeanor is not a felony, there's no jail time, and we can most likely get it sealed because of the girl's age. It wouldn't follow Jamie."

"I thought we wanted to go to trial," said Jamie, clearly a little confused, or maybe just bored. For a twenty-five year old, he wasn't thinking clearly of the possible consequences of his actions. He was doodling bullshit on Clarence's legal pad. The temptation to reach out and slap his face really hard was almost irresistible.

"We don't want to go to trial," said his father. "We want this whole stupid thing to go away."

"Going to trial is always risky," said Clarence. "I think we'll win if we do, but we might not, and if we lose, then Jamie is a felon and that never goes away. And he goes to jail. Probably not for very long, but still, it's not what we want. If they offer a deal now, and I think they will, we can avoid the risks. I just want you to know all the options."

"Give us a few minutes to talk about this, Clarence," said Justin.

"Of course, I have to talk to A.D.A. Gallo anyway. I'll be back in fifteen minutes." He left the room.

In the courtroom hallway, always a madhouse , Clarence saw Gallo talking with Archer in a corner. He signaled to them both to come over, and when they did, he opened a side door that led to an alley where the lawyers smoked during breaks. Gallo didn't smoke, but she didn't mind, so they went out and lit up.

"Missed you in Morton's court this morning, Arch."

"I know. I got caught up," said Archer. "I heard the old bastard was in a shit mood, though I don't know when he isn't."

Toni Gallo looked a little sad and defeated, and Clarence thought he knew why.

"What's the dispo going to be on Highfield, Toni?" he asked. She shook her head as if to say, *I don't even know why I do this goddamn job.*

"They're dropping the charges."

"They are?" Clarence had expected a favorable deal, but this was too much. "Why?"

"The minister suddenly doesn't want his precious little virgin to be put through the wringer. I told them what you were going to do. Hell, I even did an impression of you doing it." She lowered her voice to a gravel-road timber and made them both laugh. "And after about a minute of it he stopped me and said no way. So we're dropping it."

Clarence was able to control the gleeful surge in his chest and keep his mouth shut. No sense in showing your cards if you weren't called, after all. And there would be other hands. He took a drag off his Camel.

"Thanks, Toni. What about Elliot?"

"That one you don't get," she smiled saying it. "Timmerman says fifteen minimum and only if he cops to everything and gives everything back."

"I'll pass it along. And I'll see you at the prelim."

"Count on it," she said, and headed back inside. Archer lit another smoke, and Clarence decided he would as well.

"Arch..."

"Yeah?"

"Why are Elder police detectives arresting a bunch of Indian kids for pot possession on Tobico Marsh?"

"You know, I've been wondering about that, too, and it beats the shit out of me." They smoked in silence for a couple of minutes, then flicked the smokes away and went back in. Clarence headed straight for the conference room to inform the Highfield boys of the good news. Jamie took it calmly and left quickly, but Justin was satisfied in a perfectly vindicated way. He thanked Clarence and pulled out his chequebook.

"What's the tab for this debacle, Counselor?" Clarence didn't like figuring fees on the fly, and he usually low-rated himself, but he had calculated it would have been at least fifteen thousand if they'd gone to trial. And since they hadn't, he asked for seven thousand. Justin wrote the cheque out in seconds and they parted with the lawyer paid and the client pleased. Nothing could be better. Plus, another victory in a business where word-of-mouth was the best advertising. He looked at his watch and saw it was only twelve-thirty. He hadn't planned on lunch at the club, but he had plenty of time and thought *Why not?*

Simon Roche was holding court at a table and Clarence was immediately spotted and called over so Simon could tell whatever the story was again. He sat down with the noon regulars, piss-tanks all, some already half in the bag. He decided it was not the day to break his pledge of not drinking during working hours and ordered a coke. Strict rules were a good thing. And he never wanted to believe he actually had *the disease*, as he called it. He wasn't even able to call it what it was, alcoholism. The word was too stark, blatant, familial. So it was the disease that dared not speak its name.

"Hey, Simon, how'd the parley end up the other day?" Simon, his mouth full of cheeseburger, gave him a thumbs down.

"Not great," Simon shook his head, "Joe talked me into the fourth horse, Moby Richard, and he farted his way into ninth. We were this close."

"Wish I could have been there." The talk of sports and betting and male generalities was soothing. He didn't have to talk much, and he had seven grand in his pocket. After a bit, he remembered that he should call Paula, so he went to the payphone by the men's room.

"Keaton Law Office, may I help you?"

"Hey. Anyone there?"

"Nope. All quiet on the festering front. How'd it go this morning?"

"One good, one not so good. But we got a big check."

"Lucky us."

"Yeah. What time are the appointments?"

"One at four and one at four forty-five."

"Okay, thanks. I'll go to the bank and see you soon."

"How much was the check for?" she asked.

"Seven grand," he said, noting that it didn't seem as large as it had when he got it. "Expenses plus this month!"

"Woo hoo," she said. He knew she was going to ask for a raise later today, and he didn't know how the hell he was going to say no. *The moment you make expenses they fucking go up*, he thought.

"By the way, boss, two more things," she said, "Your tailor called from Lansing, and the massage parlor upped its offer to four hundred and twenty five a month."

"You're shitting me."

"Nope. The lady said it was as high as they'd go, though."

"I don't wonder. What did the Bar Association say?"

"How did you know I asked them?"

"Because we're not turning that down, unless the B.A. says we have to. So what'd they say?"

"Well I can only paraphrase it," she said. He could see the smile on her face. "They said why would we give a shit who rents the first floor of the building your office is in?"

"They're as predictable as a blind weatherman. All right, schedule the Madam for last today. Make it five thirty. I should be back by three-thirty."

"It shall be done." And she hung up, knowing he was done. He hung up the receiver of the payphone, reflecting on how lucky he was to have her on his side. Then he remembered her naked body that morning. That had been so weird. And he couldn't tell if she'd meant to do it or it was just waking up a little foggy and not recalling he was there. He decided it had to be the latter.

He said goodbye to Simon and his disciples, all drunkenly planning the exactas and trifectas and parlays that would set them up for life, and he walked back to the courthouse for the Elliot preliminary. On the way he remembered Paula telling him Benny had called. He wasn't going to call him from a payphone, but he made a mental note to call him at some point later from the office. After everyone had left, perhaps. But he was drifting, digressing from the job at hand. The Elliot case. *Get in the game*, he thought. *Get on it*. He really wanted to secure a deal. This going to trial would be really time consuming and probably sensational, which would only be good for him if he won, and even then it could piss off all the burglary victims enough so they'd never hire him. It had 'disaster' stamped on it and he knew it.

He still believed a deal was possible. Elliot hadn't said a word, which was always helpful. There were no fingerprints. Children were bad witnesses for the prosecution, generally. Not only could you discredit them, you could often convince them that what they thought they saw was a mirage. He was pretty sure he could goad Toni Gallo into the ten-year range. Maybe give Elliot a little hope that he might see the sky again before he was seventy. That thought was depressing, not that Clarence had any shortage of things that punctured the spirit. His father, his career, his fear that he might be just like his mother, the death of his wife 18 years earlier, the destruction of his early ambitions. Even on the happiest days, the days when you win a case and get a nice cheque on the spot, something on the list would intrude and remind him that there'd be a price. Always.

Walking down the corridor to Courtroom five, he saw Toni Gallo. She walked past him as though she were going somewhere else.

"Hey, Toni," he said, stopping her. "Don't we have a prelim in two minutes?" She shook her head.

"Timmerman's doing it," she said.

"Timmerman? A burglary case?" Toni nodded and kept walking.

Jacob Timmerman, pronounced Yah-cob, as he told everyone he met, was the District Attorney of Tobico County, and other than really high profile cases, like corporate malfeasance, mob bosses, or serial killers, all of which were relatively rare, he never entered the courtroom anymore. He was content to make statements to the Elder Ledger, or the Detroit News when the chance came, and anytime the local TV news wanted him, he was available. He was waiting for the next election when he would run for the state legislature, and after that, eventually, for governor, provided there were no affairs or payoffs in his closet. And Clarence doubted he had those kinds of skeletons. He looked like someone who saw sex as a necessary form of alternative exercise, and he had always seemed to be scrupulously honest. Clarence admired that. Knowing Timmerman was doing the case meant one really depressing thing. There would be no deal. *Shit la-marde.*

It also meant a short afternoon. The courtroom was empty, save for court officers and lawyers, and Elliot, as always acting as though he was waiting for a bakery to open. Timmerman nodded to Clarence as he sat down, and then quickly asked the judge for a continuance, since the evidence was still being processed. That was bullshit, and the Judge knew it, but he held the case over anyway, until the following Monday morning. Being the D.A. had its privileges. The courtroom cleared in less than three minutes. Clarence walked out and decided to risk a chat with Jacob, a man notorious for never having any time to talk.

"Jacob, could I have a word?"

"Clarence, I wish I had time. How are you?" Timmerman, who didn't actually give a rat's ass how Clarence was, turned to go. Clarence's only hope was to make a statement that would stop him mid-stride.

"Regarding the restitution of the stolen property, Jacob…" he said. And Jacob stopped, like a professionally struck golf ball stopping on a soft green. He turned with his most sincere smile.

"Would you walk with me, Clarence?"

"Of course." Walking with Timmerman was a speed test, since he always went fast and with great purpose.

"Your client is prepared to return everything he stole?"

"That is a distinct possibility, Jacob, but we would have to know what you're offering in return."

"In return? How about I don't pursue a life sentence?"

"A life sentence for burglary? You're not serious. I'm willing to take five years right now for a large restitution and a guilty plea."

"Five years?" Jacob laughed. "Now you're not serious. That's ridiculous. He's a professional thief and an escape artist. The best I could start with would be twenty years and full restitution."

"That's a shame," said Clarence. "I guess I'll see you at trial. Have a nice weekend, Jacob." He walked away, and as he hoped, this time Timmerman stopped him.

"Clarence, be reasonable. I can't offer better than fifteen years."

"No problem, Jacob. When you can, get in touch."

"Clarence…" Timmerman started, but all he got was the back of the wrinkled Pappas suit as Clarence walked off. He waited one or two seconds, and then turned and went his way. He couldn't see that Clarence was smiling. He started on a hard twenty years and dropped it to fifteen in less than a minute. That boded well. He walked outside to the lawyer's smoking area and lit a Camel. He was alone, since every other case was still going on inside.

Jacob being personally involved meant there was some political pressure being brought to bear on this. And that suggested that the jewels weren't the bone of contention. It was the documents. Though why Elliot would steal documents was something Clarence couldn't figure out. Of course, it could have been he would just scoop the entire contents of a safe into a bag and look at them later, but the man was a researcher, a meticulous person. Thieves of this caliber tended to know exactly what they were going after. It had to be the documents. The ones he hadn't bothered to read yet. That and the safety deposit box keys. *Oh, shit, the bank!* His watch said it was 2:30, so he tossed the smoke and jog-walked to his car.

That's when the day started getting really weird. His trunk was open. Mercury's had very large trunks and his was up. He looked around and there was no one in sight. He wondered how long it had been open. Of course it could have been bumped and opened by accident. He took a look inside, but it didn't look too rummaged. The bag of burglar's tools was still there. *I should really get rid of those, or hide them somewhere other than my car*, he thought. Then the smell hit him. Urine. It was unmistakable. Someone had searched the trunk, found nothing, and then pissed in it. The tool bag was sodden. Jesus Christ. He was dealing with classy criminals here. He shut the trunk, grateful when it latched and stayed down, and drove to the bank. There was no sign they'd gotten in the car, though it was obvious from looking in the windows that there wasn't anything inside it.

He got to First National Bank, where he did business, and asked to see the manager, Desmond Vines. It was the first time in two years that he didn't owe him money. The giant settlement he'd received two weeks earlier had put them on equal footing. So Desmond, a proper gent, transplanted from England thirty years before, who still had the impeccable manners and the posh accent, received him warmly. If they weren't in a business relationship, one that occasionally frightened the shit out of Clarence, since he hated owing money almost as much as he hated talking about himself, they might have been good friends. But that was impossible. So they had a guarded, transactional acquaintance.

"Come in, my dear fellow," Desmond crooned. "What's on your mind?"

"I need to get into my safety-deposit box, Des."

"Of course. I'll have Lena assist you there, all right?" He picked up the phone and summoned her. "Anything else, old sod? Need an overdraft, or a loan against the office mortgage?" He smiled as he said it, his large, poorly cared-for teeth making him seem both kindly and evil at the same time.

"No, nothing else, thanks. Probably will be soon, though. Next month looks horrible."

"Yes, of course, well we're here when you need us, old boy. Just pop in whenever." Lena came in and Clarence nodded his thanks to Des as they left.

The box was brought to the private area and Clarence opened it. Inside was his will, his insurance policies, his passport, Rosalie's wedding and engagement rings, some letters they'd written to each other, and about four thousand in desperation getaway cash. Inside this he put the two bags of diamonds. He decided to keep the envelope with the documents with him for the time being, since he still needed to go through it. He was putting the keys to the other safety deposit box inside when he remembered that Elliot had mentioned they were probably for a box at this bank and – *Oh Christ, he wrote the name down on my legal pad!* He pulled out the pad, looked around to make sure he wasn't being observed, then felt like a fool. *You're in a privacy booth inside a fucking bank vault, you idiot. Who's watching?* He lifted the pages to where Elliot had written the name, looked, and thought, *of course*. He put the keys in his pocket, closed the box, and called Lena to take it back.

He got back to the office at 3:30, with plenty of time for some coffee and a couple of good smokes, but of course Paula had other plans. She appeared before he even got his jacket off.

"The Chemical company guy is due at 4:15, McLeish at 4:45, and the massage parlor lady at 5:30.

"McLeish? Doctor Alden McLeish?

"Yes, that's the name. He's a shrink."

"This is shaping up to be a banner month."

"There were no checks in the afternoon mail, and that's the good news," she said.

"Oh-oh. What's the bad?"

"The Mayor's here again."

"No shit. What a surprise."

"He's in the bathroom right now." They both heard a door close.

"Come in, your honor!" Clarence called.

"I hope he washed his hands," Paula whispered as she left the room. George Barnet came in with considerably less bluster than the last time. He seemed a little scared.

Clarence indicated the client chair, shutting the office door and retreating to his own chair behind the desk. He took a smoke out of his pack and lit it.

"You don't mind if I smoke, do you, George?"

"Actually, it does bother me a little…"

"Then let me apologize in advance." He blew out a plume of bluish smoke, relishing how good it made him feel. "What can I do for you today?"

"Mr. Keaton, if you remember our conversation of the other day…"

"I remember it very well, Mr. Mayor."

"I still need what was stolen from me to be returned, Mr. Keaton. I apologize for threatening you. I was extremely upset and I said things I shouldn't have. I apologize and I hope you understand."

"I'm not sure you can afford me, Mr. Mayor," Clarence replied.

"I can assure you that any fee you might designate for the return of the stolen articles would be fine with…"

"No, I mean, with you paying Bothwell to have me followed as well. His guys broke into my apartment last night and searched the trunk of my car this afternoon. Both crimes. Crimes you paid them to commit, sir."

Barnet clearly hadn't been expecting that little bombshell. He looked around for a moment, almost as if to see if there was going to be any help in this matter from the walls. He started to speak, but nothing came out. Then he started to cry. It wasn't unusual, having someone cry in his office, but Clarence hadn't been expecting it. Normally it was women who cried in the office as they explained what giant bastards their husbands were. He reached into his right-hand drawer and came out with a clean handkerchief and got up and gave it to Barnet.

"All right, George. It's all right. I'm sure it isn't as bad as all that. Why don't you tell me about it?"

"I…I can't…" was all Barnet could manage as he blew his nose and wiped his face.

"Somebody has something on you, don't they, George?" Barnet nodded, and as he did a thought occurred to Clarence. A pretty good thought.

"George," he asked, "Did you get the bill we sent you?" Barnet nodded and reached inside his jacket pocket and showed the bill.

"Do you have your checkbook on you?" The Mayor shook his head. "How about two hundred bucks cash?" He nodded that time. Clarence got up.

"Give it to me," he said, and Barnet obligingly took out his wallet and handed Clarence four fifties. Clarence patted him on the back and buzzed Paula.

"Bring in one of our standard contracts, would you, Paula?" A moment later she walked in and placed the contract on his desk. He asked her to wait, and gave George a pen. Paula indicated where he should sign the document and he did. Clarence handed her the two hundred cash and then the seven thousand dollar cheque Highfield had given him. She raised an eyebrow at the amount.

"Weren't you at the bank today already? Why didn't you deposit it yourself?" He curled his lip but said nothing. She realized she'd breached protocol by suggesting he was stupid in front of a client, and withdrew with the contract. She would fill out the relevant sections and kiss her raise goodbye. He shut the door behind her and turned to the Mayor of Elder.

"You're my client now, George. Anything you say to me will be privileged. I can't reveal it to anyone, even the cops, or I'll lose my license to practice law. So why don't you fill me in as to what this is about?"

Barnet started to talk, then stopped and blew his nose again. Two deep breaths calmed him enough to begin again.

"What I'm going to tell you is something nobody knows. I need you to understand that."

"Somebody knows, George, clearly. What you're afraid of is something somebody knows about you, right? You're being – what – blackmailed?" Barnet nodded.

"Yes."

"Okay. Blackmail is illegal, as I'm sure you're aware. So this person or persons can be prosecuted for it."

"NO!" Barnet shouted. "No. If I go after them they publish what they know about me and that's the end."

"The end of what?"

"Of everything! My job, my standing in this town, any political career or job beyond that. And it would kill my wife, it would *kill* her. And my boys..." he trailed off, staring at the stained handkerchief in his hands.

"Can you tell me what it is, George? I might be able to help if I knew." Clarence was relatively sure it was standard had-an-affair stuff. Barnet sighed deeply and spoke to the handkerchief.

"I have a predilection, Mr. Keaton. A fetish. It doesn't mean anything, you understand. It's just something I like to do that I never told my wife."

"Perhaps you should tell her."

"No, I don't think so. She sees me a certain way. If I told her, or anyone, that would be all they could see when they looked at me, if you understand what I mean."

Clarence nodded. He understood exactly. The Mayor continued.

"So...when I get the...what? Urge, I guess. When I get the urge, I have to..."

"You have to hire a professional," Clarence stated, without judgement.

"Yes."

"That's not unusual."

"A few months ago, I couldn't find the person I had been using, so I went to Grand Rapids to a new...a new..."

"Vendor?"

"Yes. Someone who was very reputable, apparently. Then, a month after that I received some photos in the mail. Two shots of me and... the other person, with my face clearly visible."

"Do you know who it is, George?"

"Who who is?

"The blackmailer," Clarence replied. He knew staying calm and reasoned was the way to go here. Barnet looked as though he was going to start bawling again any second, and Clarence really didn't want that to happen, since it made him uncomfortable, and there wasn't a great deal of time left before the next client was due.

"George," he said, "Please don't worry about this. I'm not here to judge you."

"I know, Mr. Keaton. But if my wife found out, it would destroy her." He was regaining some of his composure.

"Yes, you said that. We'll try and make sure she won't find out. Are you paying the blackmailer?"

No. Well, they haven't actually asked for money. Every few months I get more photos in the mail and they ask me to push something at council."

"I see. So they're trading silence on your affa – your predilection, sorry. They're trading silence on that for favorable council rulings. So it's most likely someone in town. Any ideas there?

"They said if I tried to find out who they were, they'd publish the photos."

"Well now George, that has to be one of the emptier threats I've ever heard. If they publish the photos, they'd no longer have control over you. It's in their interest to keep you as Mayor, as long as you're helping them." A look of realization came over George that showed this hadn't occurred to him. Clarence continued, "And among the things that were stolen was something related to this, correct?" George nodded.

"My safety-deposit box keys."

"And that's where you've been keeping the photos?" Again George nodded, and Clarence was a little flustered for a moment, since he couldn't imagine anything dumber than keeping the photos *anywhere*. Someone else had copies, fine, but if you send me copies, they are burned as soon as they arrive.

"If I may ask, George, what purpose does it serve to keep them?"

"I didn't know what else to do," George said.

Man, ain't that the truth.

"And you can't get into the box without the keys. Can't you go to the bank and say you lost them and get a new set made?"

"That just means more people know I have a problem."

Clarence couldn't get over how the fear of exposure had destroyed the Mayor's capacity for rational thought. It was time to play his magical trump card.

"Are you sure they were stolen, George?"

"What? Are you serious?"

"I mean it. You may have just mislaid them. It happened to me this week. Check your pockets."

Barnet looked at him like he might be insane, but his need was such that he couldn't stop himself from obeying, and lo, when his hand came out of the right hand jacket pocket, the keys he'd been looking for were in it. He looked right at them for several seconds before he actually believed that they were real. Then he looked at Clarence.

"I – how the – Jesus, were they in my pocket the whole time?"

"Let's assume they were, George. That totally works for me. Now, here's what I want you to do. Tomorrow when the bank opens you are there with a manila envelope and you take those photos out of that goddamn box and you do one of two things. You burn them, or you bring them here and I'll burn them. Those are the choices and either way, they're ashes by tomorrow afternoon. And I want you to think hard about the things you've been pushing for council and who, exactly, that would help, because whomever it helps the most is the one doing this to you. And, when they contact you again, the first person you call is me. Got that?"

"Yes, Mr. Keaton." He got up to leave.

"And try not to worry about this too much. You're paying me to worry about it now, okay?"

"All right." He didn't sound convinced, though. He went to the office door and then turned back with his hand on the knob. "How in the hell did you get those keys into my pocket? Clarence just shrugged.

"What keys, Mr. Mayor?" Barnet nodded, opened the door and left without saying anything else. Paula came in immediately after.

"Should I send him another bill?"

"No, let's wait on that. Having him as our ally is probably worth more."

"Are we sneaking into conflicts of interest here, boss?" she asked.

"I don't know. Are we? I thought that was part of your job."

"You're defending Elliot, accused of burgling half the wealthy people in town, and now you're representing the Mayor, who was a victim of that burglar."

"He also hired cute boy Ray to follow me. I'm not exactly defending the Mayor. I'm just representing him in case he has any legal trouble. And I think the thing he was worried about that may or may not have been stolen from him was amazingly, found today, so he would no longer be involved in the case, per se."

"Wow, that's some tightrope you're walking, boss.

"Life is on the wire. The rest is waiting. Did Luther come by for his door money?"

"He did. I paid him." She turned to leave, then stopped. "Who said that?"

"Life is on the wire? Karl Wallenda. Tightrope walker."

"Sometimes they fall," Paula said.

"Not so far. Who's next?" Paula went to the door and called out.

"Come in, Mr. Manafort."

A man in his thirties came in, introducing himself as Colin Manafort. He was dressed in work clothes and informed Clarence that he worked for a chemical refinery company, using a power hose to clean the tanks at the facility. He'd worked there for seven years and had been recently diagnosed with a brain tumor and given roughly a year to live. He wanted to sue the company, and though Clarence knew the chances were extremely slim in a case like this, he asked for all Mr. Manafort's employment records and health history. He doubted they could prove a causal link in time, but it was certainly worth an hour or two of checking. Maybe there were more people and he could get a class action going. Manafort wanted to get some money and leave it to his wife and eight year old daughter. He left as reasonably happy as someone with a year to live could be. Paula came in again.

"Should I do a contract on this guy, too?" Clarence shook his head.

"Start a file. He's going to bring in his medical and employment records tomorrow, and maybe we'll do a contract after we've looked at them. Who's next?"

"Doctor MacLeish."

"Alden, right. I though Tony Fleck represented him."

"Maybe he's changing lawyers."

"Send him in."

It wasn't a changing-lawyers thing. Doctor Alden MacLeish, a regular at the golf club bar, now had his offices in a building, in fact in the very office that Clarence had once occupied before he'd bought this house. Alden came in and handed him an envelope.

"We received this in the mail the other day. I kept forgetting to give it to you at the club, so I made an appointment in order to remember it." He smiled. Alden was a psychiatrist, and though the town had a hundred attorneys, it only had four shrinks, and he was one of them. Clarence thanked him and he left. A glance at the letter told him it was addressed by hand and most likely personal. He put it aside for the moment. Paula came in again.

"Is he ours now?" she asked.

"No," Clarence laughed a little. "No, he was just dropping off some mislaid mail. How long till the Madam is due?" Paula checked her watch.

"Wow, thirty-five minutes. Want to catch a movie?"

"I was thinking of something else."

"Do tell."

"I was thinking of paying you a hundred and fifty more per month. How would that strike you?"

"Well, now..." she said, "Two hundred would strike me a little better, as long as you're asking for my honest opinion."

"Yeah, well, I suppose everybody'd be happy with a two hundred dollar raise, wouldn't they? Would two hundred make you happy enough to not call me out in front of a client again? Could we make that deal?"

"I'm sorry about that, boss. I forgot there was a civilian in the room. Apologies."

"Okay, go home. I'll wait for this woman. You get two hundred more starting next month. Okay?"

"Absolutely. Thanks." He expected her to leave quickly but she lingered, as though there was more to discuss.

"Are you waiting for me to say 'you're welcome?'"

"Well, maybe kind of," she said.

"Maybe kind of? What the hell type of English is that? You sound like one of those idiots on television who say 'basically', or 'in terms of' as a preface to every stupid sentence." She smiled.

"Goodnight, boss."

"Goodnight," he said. "Pax vobiscum." She headed down the hall and he had the first really free moment he'd enjoyed all day. He waited until he heard the door close downstairs before he picked up the phone and called Lansing.

"Hey, stranger," said Benny, who answered on the first ring. "Those shirts are going to be ready tomorrow, if you wanted to swing by and pick them up."

"Thanks, Benny," A wave of relief came over Clarence as he realized the day was almost over – a red-letter day – and he had a big check and maybe he could take most of the weekend off, and here was his only real friend inviting him to come. A few seconds of happiness were followed by the realization that his father was dying alone 350 miles away, and the happiness dissipated like smoke at a breezy picnic.

"You there?" said Benny, and Clarence snapped back from his reverie.

"Sorry, Benny. A lot going on today. I could come up tomorrow. But I wouldn't be able to get there until around six-thirty."

"Great! I'll stay open late."

"Ok, I'll see you then."

"Bye, Clare. Drive safe."

Clarence hung up the phone and reached for his cigarettes, lit one and relaxed fully for a long moment, at the end of which, the door opened downstairs, and he heard someone coming up, no doubt the massage lady. He looked at the notes Paula had left for her name. Kimberly Bolton. He stubbed out the smoke after barely three drags and went to the door, seeing her in the hallway.

"Please come in, Miss Bolton. I'm Clarence Keaton."

A reasonably attractive woman in her late thirties walked into the office, shook Clarence's proffered hand, and took a seat in the client chair. In the five and a half foot range, black hair that wasn't so glossy that it looked dyed. She wore a flowing long red skirt almost gypsy-style below a tailored blouse with a pair of shoes he couldn't see underneath. She smiled as she sat down and the effect was substantial, though it didn't quite obscure the hard miles she'd traveled to arrive here.

"It is Miss Bolton?" Clarence asked.

"At the moment, yes, thank you," she said.

"I understand that you wish to rent the downstairs of this house for the operation of a massage emporium." Massage *parlor* felt as though it had too many negative connotations, so Clarence fell back on a more innocuous word.

"I do indeed, Mr. Keaton."

"And you are prepared to pay…" he consulted the notes as though he were cross-examining her, "…four hundred and twenty-five dollars a month to have me as your landlord."

"That is also the case," she replied. She was all business, which he liked. It bespoke commitment.

"I am prepared to take your offer, save a few logistical and legal matters I wish to iron out, in order that we have no misunderstandings, all right?"

"Of course," she said, flashing that thousand-watt smile.

"First: how long will it take for you to renovate the first floor to your specifications, and how loud will that renovation necessarily be?"

"I think it will take no more than a week, Mr. Keaton. We need to redo the reception area by the door, put in a door with our name and logo on it, and a sign that indicates your offices up here." Clarence was impressed that she understood and would pay for a sign for his offices.

"That sounds reasonable," he said.

"I'm fairly sure it won't be terribly loud. Or that we can accommodate you so that the loud parts don't occur during your normal office hours."

"Excellent. How many employees would you have on a daily basis?"

"There will be between five and six each day. Will they be able to use your parking lot, Mr. Keaton?"

"This could be a problem, Miss Bolton. We have my car, my secretary's car, and plenty of room for clients. If we were to put your five or six cars plus the customer cars in there each day, it could get very crowded."

"I anticipated that, Mr. Keaton, so I made a deal with the parking lot a block away, on the other side of the post office. I will pay them a monthly fee and we'll validate our customers and employees. Could two spaces be reserved for myself and my assistant?"

"Yes, of course. That'll be fine." Clarence was impressed. This woman paid attention to detail. He had hoped the parking problem would scuttle the deal, but she'd flanked him. *Okay*, he thought, *I have other scuttles.* "Now, as to the nature of your establishment…"

"The nature, Mr. Keaton? I'm not sure I understand your meaning."

Now it was Clarence's turn to show his once-dazzling smile.

"I'm sure you do understand, Miss Bolton. The massage business has a certain reputation, as you are no doubt well aware. It is often used as a front for other businesses, and forgive my bluntness, but those businesses are sex and sometimes drugs. I couldn't be involved or associated with those businesses in any way, even as a landlord."

"I understand your position, sir," she now showed an ability to turn to ice. "And I'm insulted by the insinuation."

"If you decide to be insulted, that's fine, but I wasn't insinuating anything. I was stating it as plainly as I could. If we're going to enter into a business relationship, we need to be honest with each other. I'm sure you appreciate that."

"We do massage, Mr. Keaton. Therapeutic massage. That is all. Every one of my girls is a trained massage therapist, as am I."

"All masseuses, then? Clarence asked. "No masseurs?"

Miss Bolton sensed a small advantage she could explore.

"Would that be your preference, Mr. Keaton? Males giving massages to males?"

Clarence paused, putting his hands together in a steeple at mouth level.

"Miss Bolton, my concern is not because I will be using your establishment. My concern is the police coming to *my* establishment and the subsequent difficulties that would pose for my business and my reputation, which are intertwined. If there was anything in that area I would have to worry about; anything at all, I would have to say no to you."

"Could you be more specific with regard to your worries, Mr. Keaton?" She gave her smile an extra Watt or two.

"I would prefer it if no one who worked for you had a criminal record."

"I think I can assure you, Mr. Keaton..." she began.

"I would prefer it that you had no criminal record as well. And you don't, in this country, under that name. I hope you understand that I'm not trying to insult you, I'm expressing concerns about how your business operating below my business will appear, especially if you have any legal troubles."

Miss Bolton reached into her purse, took out her driver's license, and wordlessly handed it across the desk. Clarence read it. Kimberly Joan Bolton, born June 14th, 1937. It looked perfectly legitimate. She handed another card to him, proclaiming her to be a licensed massage therapist. Clarence suddenly felt very tired and glanced at the clock, which showed it had been a really long day, of which there could be no doubt. He handed the two licenses back to Miss Bolton.

"All right," he said, "I'll give you a six month lease on the first floor of this house starting October first, which is sex days from – *six* days from now, if that's enough time. I'll have a contract drawn up and ready for your signature by tomorrow afternoon, and your workmen can start on Saturday. Will that be satisfactory?" She nodded.

"That will be just fine, Mr. Keaton. I will have a first and last month's check ready upon signature of the contract." She stood up, straight as a nun, and offered her hand, which he shook. She was looking at him very closely, he noted, and then she smiled, said goodnight, and headed for the stairs. When he heard the door close, he zipped down the steps, double locked it and turned out the downstairs lights.

Back in his office, he lit a smoke and was contemplating pouring himself a big glass of The Balvenie when the phone rang. *Shit fuck piss,* he thought. It was almost six p.m. Who in the hell would be --? It was Louise Merwin.

"Clarence," she said. "Sorry I forgot to get back to you about the guy following you."

"That's ok, Louise. I got it figured." *Or I thought I did,* he told himself. "You okay?"

"More or less," she said, her tone putting the lie to the statement. "I called the lock guy and he did it in less than 24 hours. He gave me half off. What the hell did you do for him?"

"Well, I can't comment on things I do for clients, Louise, you know that."

"I bought the gun, too." Clarence said nothing for a bit, and she continued, "You still there?"

"Sure," he said. "I was just trying to remember the last client who took my advice and followed it exactly."

"Who was that?"

"Nobody. It was you. Has Greg been obeying the restraining order?"

"Are you kidding? He calls at least once a day and tells me what a cunt I am. If he's drunk he says he'll come over and kill me."

"Where are you, Louise?"

"I'm in my kitchen with my new shotgun. I may bring a mattress in and sleep here."

"You can still have him arrested, Louise. He's breaking the law."

"He came over last night and screamed at me for an hour when he couldn't get in. A neighbor down the street finally convinced him to fuck off."

"Why didn't the neighbor call the damn cops?"

"Because I asked him not to. It's not the first time he's helped. Anyway, I only called to thank you."

"You need anything?"

"A boyfriend. A safe place in the world. Nah, I'm okay for now."

Sure you are, Clarence thought, *spending the night watching the door with a shotgun in your arms.*

"Call me if there's anything I can do," he said, somewhat at a loss for exactly what he should say.

"I will. Bye Clarence."

"Bye, Louise." He hung up and looked at the Scotch again. It beckoned him. He was powerless. He poured three fingers and lit a fresh cigarette. The first sip was smoky and delightful. He finished the glass and decided he would have another. He poured and then repaired to the sofa with the manila envelope and began going through the documents Elliot had stolen. He put the glass of scotch on the coffee table and stubbed out the smoke after a few moments of reading.

When Paula came in Friday morning and he was still there, the bottle empty, the ashtray full, and the contents of the envelope scattered around him in a protective circle.

FRIDAY

H e cried out when she woke him. Paula was surprised by it but said nothing. He noticed the look she gave him.

"What?" he said. "Am I in the hospital?"

"No, boss. You're in the office." His eyes began to focus and he realized his head was pounding.

"Shit," he said. "I drank too much last night." Paula held up the empty bottle of single malt for him to see.

"Based on the forensic evidence, I would have to agree," she said. "And what's all this stuff?" She gestured to the strewn documents as Clarence pulled himself into a sitting position, which required a supreme act of will and two loud groans.

"They were in the car Elliot gave me in lieu of the rest of my fee." Paula was down on one knee collecting them, glancing here and there.

"Did he steal some of these?" she asked, giving a particular one the eye.

"I can neither confirm nor deny that he probably stole every god-damn one of them. Why?"

"Because this is a land surveyor's report for the northwestern section of Tobico Marsh."

"What?" Clarence was still struggling to clear his head of the pain. His father used to say that hangovers were your body feeling guilty. "The northwestern section of the marsh is reservation land."

"Well, maybe someone bought it."

"How do you know it's a land surveyor's report, anyway?" She handed it to him and he took a look, still trying to focus his jangling eyes.

"My last boyfriend. No, wait, my second to last boyfriend, if you don't count the guy I saw three times who blew me off for that slutty bartender so maybe my third to last…"

"Paula?"

"Sorry. He was a land surveyor. And one night he thought I might like to learn a little bit about it and make a report with him. He thought it was sexy."

"Doesn't sound that sexy."

"It wasn't. He was just trying to get me to do it outdoors. He had a thing about that. But I looked at a few reports before he tackled me. How do you suppose people acquire those kinds of fetishes?"

"I have no idea. Something in childhood, maybe."

"Sounds like you have an idea."

"I can't confirm or deny that, either."

"Didn't you see this last night?" Paula asked.

"Last night is a bit of a blur," Clarence said, inwardly rebuking himself for lying. It wasn't a blur, it was a blackout. He had no recollection of looking at any documents. He remembered locking the door after Miss Bolton left, coming back up and thinking it would great to have a glass of scotch. After that he had no memory. He looked at the empty bottle, trying to remember if it had been half full, or almost full, and he couldn't even find that image. The blazing headache made him suspect it had been almost full. *Wonderful.*

"I could use some water, and a coffee, Paula, if you would…"

"Of course," she said, busying herself with those tasks. Clarence wrestled himself to a standing position and went down the hall to the bathroom, affecting a steady gait though every step jarred the pains he had everywhere. After the first concern was completed, he attempted to brush his pickled teeth. He was glad you had to clench them while brushing or it would have been even more painful. He returned to his office feeling slightly better than horrible, lit a smoke and sat in his chair. There was a glass of water waiting, and Paula soon brought a coffee, and then the full envelope, other than the two documents she was holding in her hand.

"I don't think he stole this one," she said, handing it to Clarence. "It's got his name on it." It was a medical report. Having done a number of malpractice cases, Clarence knew how to read one. As he scanned it, a phrase caught his eye, *acinar cell carcinoma*. He looked to see if it was in the 'Testing For' box or the 'Noticed/Found' box. It was the latter. No wonder Elliot wasn't worried about getting a deal for the burglaries. He had pancreatic cancer. Being a lifelong smoker, Clarence knew a lot of about different forms of cancer and their technical names. His anxiety about his own health was just high enough to be ulcerous, but not enough to make him quit smoking or drinking. Life was what it was. You were born, you worried, you died. Irish 101.

The second document was the land surveyor's report, regarding the top sliver section of the Rez. It was off the marsh a little but no one lived there. The dwellings and buildings were concentrated to the south, where the land was drier and easier to build on. The survey seemed to be on this parcel only, roughly one and a half square miles. The surveyor's name was on it, but not the company he was working for. Clarence didn't recognize the name, so it wasn't a local outfit.

"Paula, what have we got today?"

"We have no court and one client coming in at ten. Alison McMahon."

"The librarian?"

"That's her."

"Is she charged with something?"

"She's thinking about divorcing her husband."

"Aha. Well that could be fun. And Librarians are sticklers about fees."

"True, but what should we do until then?" It was just eight a.m. Clarence pulled a notepad from the pile on his desk, found the page he wanted, and handed it to her.

"Here, type this up and add it to Nate Erdmann's will. Then call around and see if you can find out where this surveyor is located. Use the old boyfriend if you have to."

"He'd know," she said. "They all know each other."

"Then call Central Michigan Correctional and schedule a visit with Tony Ferrera. This afternoon, if possible."

"Wow," she said, "I'm earning my huge raise today." She turned to leave and he stopped her.

"Do I have anything on the slate for tomorrow morning?"

"I'll look," she replied, heading to her desk. Moments later she came back. "There's nothing in the book for tomorrow."

"Okay," he said. "If someone calls and wants to see me tomorrow, tell them I can't and reschedule for next week."

"You going back to Marquette?"

"Yeah," he said, "maybe."

"Hey, boss?"

"Yes, longtime employee?"

"Who's Rosalie?"

The question startled Clarence, but he hoped that didn't show.

"Why?" he asked.

"When I came in you were calling her in your sleep. And you yelled her name as you woke up out of whatever it was you were dreaming about."

"She was someone I knew a long time ago. She comes when I'm sleeping now." *Or when I'm blackout drunk*, he thought. Paula nodded.

"The one that got away?"

"In a manner of speaking."

"You should call her. You could use some fun." She headed back to her desk. *Fun*, Clarence thought to himself, *yeah, that's what I need.* He was trying to remember if Paula had ever asked him a question that personal in all the years she'd worked for him. He couldn't recall one. He decided to go home and clean up, so he grabbed his keys and smokes, told Paula he'd be back before ten, and left. Then he came back up the stairs.

"What'd you forget?" she asked.

"If the Mayor comes in just leave whatever he gives you on my desk."

"Will do."

"And get the mail."

"On it."

Clarence walked around to the parking lot quickly, not appearing to notice if there was anyone watching. There was only one car parked nearby that he could see and he memorized its make and color just in case. *Blue Pontiac.* He hopped into the Merc and was home in six minutes, zipping upstairs, showering and putting on a fresh suit. He then drank several ice-cold glasses of water in succession, a hangover cure he'd seen his mother use. He was about to leave when he had another thought and went downstairs instead and double locked his new door from the inside. Back up in the apartment, he packed his little bag with to changes of clothes and some basic toiletries. Then he checked the window and what a surprise. The same Blue Pontiac was parked out there waiting for him. Maybe Joe Bothwell hadn't got the message from the Mayor to stop following him - one possibility. Maybe the

Mayor was playing him - another possibility. Or maybe this was something else entirely. He smoked a cigarette, noting that he still had close to an hour before Mrs. McMahon's appointment. He looked around the place for the keys to the Studebaker for a couple of minutes, just long enough to panic that he'd lost them again, then found them in the suit jacket he'd discarded. Then he turned on a couple of strategic lights that would make it appear he was still home when it got dark, and took the little packed bag and went out the window and down the fire escape. He walked to the office, taking a slightly roundabout route to get him into his parking lot unseen from the front of the building, and took the Studebaker out of the shed and parked it close to his back door, leaving the bag inside. He entered the office via the back door and got there in time to greet Mrs. McMahon.

She was somewhat distraught, of course, and they had a discussion about her philandering husband of fourteen years, a science professor at Central Michigan University Saginaw, who was apparently fucking two of his female students.

"Why do men *do* such things?" she asked, and Clarence was sorry he could give no reasonable answer. When she left, having paid a small retainer he gave to Paula, he got ready to leave. Paula informed him that Tony Ferrera was not receiving visitors at the prison today, as he was in the hole for some infraction. He would be out tomorrow, and visiting hours on the weekend were noon to five. *Okay*, Clarence thought, *I'll go Sunday on the way back.* He repeated what he'd said about the Mayor, and asked her to watch for a blue Pontiac. Then he left, down the back stairs, into the Starlight and gone, heading toward the reservation.

Roughly twenty minutes later, he pulled into the packed-dirt driveway at Eddie's house on the southwestern edge of the Odawa reservation. The house wasn't large, but it was sturdy, built around 1900 of good Douglas fir and yellow cedar logs, now whipped into a mild grey by the constant wind off Lake Huron, which was less than four miles east, over the marsh. Clarence was hoping Eddie would be home, rather than out tending to his semi-legal trapline, or hunting something out of season, two things he'd defended him for in the past. Kiwi came out the door as Clarence walked up and she hugged him. He had never known a woman like her. Kiwindok was her full name, meaning Woman of the Wind. Her mostly black hair had some white streaks in it and she stood a solid five feet nine inches tall. When her arms were around him, Clarence knew what true strength was. It flowed through her. He'd performed acts of friendship for she and Eddie, and the repayment Eddie gave was fish and game, but for Kiwi it was love. It was the passing on of strength. It was prayer and prayerfulness. And all were given as you would give a passing stranger a glass of water, without a thought of anything but the joy of giving. This was the woman his mother should have been. He didn't envy Eddie his wife, but he knew, with Kiwi, his potential and his dreams wouldn't have been idiotic to her. She wouldn't have used his weaknesses, his secrets as her weapons. She would have given him what he needed to be happy in life. It was as potent a fantasy as he'd ever had. She filled him with *if-only* thoughts. She broke the hug and smiled at him.

"Clarence, the spirit sent you to me again."

"The spirit?"

"Eddie isn't here, and I need someone to help me dig up the summer garden and turn the soil before it gets too cold. And you show up. The spirit sends help if you don't ask."

Though digging a garden hadn't been in his plans, he could never refuse anything Kiwi asked. She was one of the two or three people on earth with whom he felt safe. Sometimes he thought she might be the only one. And so, for part of that unseasonably warm autumn Friday afternoon, in borrowed work clothes, he used a spade and a pick to help prepare her garden for its winter rest. The two of them got it done in under three hours, and were enjoying an iced tea and some cookies in the kitchen when Eddie came home, carrying four dead minks and two porcupines. Kiwi rejoiced and set about removing the quills, washing and saving them for her embroidery, then preparing the bellies for their dinner. Eddie hung the four minks on hooks above his workbench and Clarence brought him a glass of tea.

"Aside from being in love with my wife, what brings you here, Clarence?" he asked, his sly smile making the accusation almost innocuous.

"How's Jimmy doing?"

"He's good, more or less. He smokes too much pot, and he runs around with a couple of morons, but he's got some heart, and he learns quick, so who knows?"

"Do you know why the cops have been arresting kids on the marsh?"

"No. Do you?"

"They're afraid they'll find something."

"Find what?"

"That I don't know, but someone had that part of the Rez surveyed recently." He handed the report to Eddie, who gave it a quick once over and handed it back.

"It's illegal to survey Indian land without permission of the tribe."

"I know. Probably why they didn't ask first. Maybe they know something they don't want you to know."

"You're talking in circles, Clarence. Like a lawyer."

"Keep your eyes and ears open is all I'm saying. Something's going on, and whoever's doing it has the cops in their pocket."

"Sounds like they're about to steal something from us. I, for one, am shocked," said Eddie. Kiwi laughed. "I've got to skin these minks. You want some of the meat?"

"No thanks, I'm heading out for the weekend."

"I owe you for helping Jimmy."

"No, you don't," Clarence replied. "I'll see you around next week. Tell Jimmy to be careful." He got up and walked to the door. Kiwi blew him a kiss and they walked out to wave as he got into the Studebaker and drove off.

Once on the main highway, he got it into fourth gear and reveled in the car's performance. It drove like a panther. Powerful, yet stealthy, her engine humming softly, never giving away how hard she might be working. The gears were beautifully tuned and every shift was pleasurable. The Merc had an automatic transmission, as did the Ford he'd had before it, so it's been a while since he'd driven as he'd learned, and the pleasure was palpable. He remembered his father being surprised during his first driving lesson at how well he grasped the concepts. But he'd been watching the old man drive for more than ten years. And Clarence was always a watcher. He had trouble acting in the moment of opportunity sometimes, since his own instincts frightened him, but he never forgot the things he saw.

His father had gone down to the licensing office in Marquette one day in 1947, and told them, "My son is an excellent driver, and you should give him a license." And they did. He had never taken a driving test, written or otherwise. He grinned thinking about it, and glanced in the rearview as he passed a state police car lying in wait behind deliberately high grass on the median turnout. He looked down and he was only doing seventy-one, so he wasn't worried. His exit off 1-75 was M-13 just below Elder. He took the county road, which was rarely crowded, even on Friday afternoons, past Saginaw to I-69 into Lansing. He wasn't going to Marquette. There'd be time for that next week. He was going to see Benny.

Pappas Tailoring was tucked behind a Chinese restaurant on Ottawa street. Clarence pulled in a little after six and parked in the alley by Benny's back door. He got out and had a smoke since he was a little early. The alley was alive with weird shadows as the sun going down threw images onto the brick edifices surrounding it. Clarence tossed the smoke and knocked on the door. The door opened to the round, thick eyebrows of his friend, a smile of welcome on his face.

"Hey! Glad you made it, I was getting worried."

"Worried? You said six-thirty. I'm early!"

"Come on in, I'm just finishing up for the day."

They went through the back room, suits and other garments in various state of completion hanging everywhere. There was a long cutting table with material sitting at the ready, but Benny headed straight to the front door to lock it and turn the OPEN sign around to CLOSED. He pulled down the blinds and set the aluminum barrier-curtain, then returned to the shirt rack, where Clarence was admiring some freshly made ones. Benny put his hand on Clarence's shoulder and said, "See anything you like?" And then they were embracing, their lips meeting, their arms and hands grasping each other as though something was attempting to rip them apart. There was an audible rush of air when their bodies came together, as though all the air they'd been holding in – it had been more than a month since they'd seen each other -- was now being let out in a frenzied relaxation of rigidly held standards as they kissed and groped with definite intentions.

There were a few people in Lansing who knew Benny was gay, since, being the capital, it was a slightly more cosmopolitan town than Elder, and Benny's profession wasn't necessarily one where the knowledge would cost him business. No one in Elder knew it about Clarence, because he had no intimate friends and never spoke about himself personally to anyone. He occasionally wondered if Paula might know, and if he could trust her with it. Her walking into the room naked the previous morning could have been a test rather than just something she did every morning. But he'd trained himself never to react visibly to anything, which was the proper policy for a lawyer. People were going to tell you shocking things since they knew you could never reveal them, and it was easier for them if what they said didn't spark a *Holy shit, really??* look on your face. In that odd way, being closeted helped. A lifetime of hiding one's true feelings made it second nature.

Despite his desires, Clarence had never even attempted to find out what might be available for him in Elder. That was simply too dangerous. As soon as one person knew everyone would know, and he'd be out of business. He never bought magazines, even by mail. Too risky. That policy had been confirmed as correct when his place was semi-searched earlier in the week. Blackmail would also end his career. He'd been hiding so long he didn't even think of it as hiding anymore. It was who he was. Or who he wasn't. He only loosened up a little bit in Lansing with the blinds down and the barriers up, with Benny. Benny never came to Elder, either.

Twelve years before, a client had come in wearing an exquisitely tailored suit, and Clarence had asked where he purchased it. *Fellow in Lansing, name of Benny Pappas*, the client said. A few days later Clarence had driven to Lansing to do an appeal and he stopped in to see this tailor. Some recent big-fee cases had him feeling flush and he liked Benny instantly and decided to order three new suits. Being measured for that first suit gave Clarence a bit of a hard time, since it'd been a long time since a man, or anyone else had touched him in an intimate way. Benny, who had a spider's radar for such things, clued in immediately, and when the measuring was done, he asked Clarence to try something on in his change room. While Clarence was doing that, Benny closed and locked the shop, just like today. His forcefulness in that first meeting was something Clarence was still grateful for, since he could never have been so forward himself. They'd been lovers ever since that day. Not exclusive, not '*I love you*', even though they did love each other, just a free '*when you can come over*' kind of thing. They were both more or less in the closet, Clarence more, Benny less; they had few intimates and led solitary lives, stealing weekends here and there. Benny talked sometimes of them going on vacation somewhere together. Somewhere it wouldn't matter that they were gay. But it was just talk. He was an only child as well, and had been taking care of his aging parents up until the previous year. But they sometimes discussed it the way children talk about how they'll grow up to be doctors or firemen. Benny had brought it up recently after returning from a trip to San Francisco.

Their standard weekend was Clarence driving to Benny's house on Saturday afternoon and spending the night, then leaving after breakfast Sunday morning. Benny lived in a nice bungalow well off the road in a quiet neighborhood with a private backyard, so it was perfect. After a few more kisses and clutches, they left to head over there. And other than Benny going out Sunday morning to get a New York Times, they didn't leave his place for thirty-six hours. Clarence's difficult week had given him a lot of tension to dissipate, and Benny was only too happy to oblige. Lying in bed Saturday night, Clarence having a post-coital cigarette before sleep, Benny had asked him when he could come back.

"Maybe next Saturday, or maybe not. There's a lot going on with these cases and my Dad."

"Right," said Benny, curled up against him. "Does your Dad know you're gay?"

"Christ, no! How the hell would he know?"

"He might know. Dads watch their kids a lot. They know things. How old were you when you knew?"

Clarence looked at his lover and fought his instinct to deflect or say nothing. He tried not to think about those things, and he was lucky that a lawyer's life required so much thinking about other people's problems, which lessened the time he could wallow in his own.

"I guess in school," he said.

"High school? That's when I figured it out."

"Grade school," said Clarence. "I was twelve."

Benny waited, knowing if he said nothing, Clarence might continue, and he did.

"Fell for a teacher, Mr. Prentice. Couple of big kids beat me up in the schoolyard. I cut my legs on some rocks when I fell. He took me to the nurse's office and washed the cuts."

"Where was the nurse?"

"Don't know. Out sick, I guess. He cleaned the cuts and bandaged them and he had to take off my pants to do it. And I got a boner."

"Did you and hunky Mr. Prentice get it on?"

"Not really. It was 1942 for God's sake. There was a war on." They both laughed, remembering the gravity of that familiar phrase.

"I wonder why he wasn't fighting himself," Benny mused.

"I never thought of that. Maybe he was too old. Though I don't think he was. He noticed my boner and felt it through the cloth. Told me not to worry about it. Put his other hand on my shoulder and then stroked me a couple of times and I came. It took about six seconds."

"You have more stamina now," Benny laughed.

"It was the most intimate moment of my life until I met you."

"Did he kiss you? Did you swoon" Benny was making fun of him.

"No, I melted. I cried. And I fantasized about having a man take off my pants ever since."

"It's fate that you met a tailor then, isn't it?"

"I always wondered if that experience was the decider. Can it really be as simple as that? I think I was born this way, but what if the nurse had been there that day. Would I be straight?"

"Was she nice looking, the nurse?"

"Sure. Miss Coyne. Tits out to here." They both laughed again.

"You're bi, you two-timing bitch," Benny joked.

They lay there in silence for a bit, both men remembering different formative experiences, before Benny had another question.

"What was Prentice's first name?"

"No idea. Mister. His first name was Mister. He was a science teacher, and I had already had a class with him by then, so we didn't see each other much after that. Maybe he avoided me. Then a year or so later I went to high school and never saw him again."

"So you never talked about it with him after?"

"No. Man, that was thirty-three years ago, and nobody ever talks about it even *now*."

"We do," said Benny.

"Yeah, but we're perverts."

They both laughed and Clarence put out his cigarette and closed his eyes. Sleep took him back to the nurse's office and the he saw the face of the teacher he revealed himself to when he didn't know how dangerous such revelations were.

SUNDAY

S unday morning came and by eleven, a fully recharged Clarence was ready to leave. He wanted to order a new suit, but Benny said he was swamped for the next month, so he said it could wait. They said goodbye, kissing and embracing inside the house, as was their habit, then Clarence went to the car and was gone. He had driven close to an hour when he saw the exit for the Central Michigan Correctional facility and remembered he wanted to see Tony Ferrera, so he exited. In the crowded parking lot, he squeezed the Starlight between a Toyota Land Cruiser and a Lincoln Continental, hoping it would be mostly hidden, although he was reasonably certain no one would try to steal a car in the parking lot of a penitentiary.

He generally avoided visiting clients in prison, and with good reason. One rarely got a private space to talk, and even if you did, there were always people listening in. Completely illegal, of course, but they did it. And you couldn't threaten or intimidate people who worked in prisons the way you could with cops and D.A.'s. They didn't give a shit who you were or that you could sue them, so once you were inside, you had to be careful and never pull the "lawyer rank". It was a lesson every young lawyer had to learn the hard way.

After jumping through the myriad hoops presented, he found himself sitting in a plastic chair at a small table in a gymnasium-sized room waiting for Ferrera to come out. Tony was curious when they brought him in, and then surprised when he saw Clarence. He sat down with a stare that could chip ice, taking the cigarette Clarence offered, his eyes never leaving the face of his advocate. He blew out the first drag and said nothing.

"Hello, Tony..." Clarence began.

"Yeah. Hello."

"How is everything?"

"What the fuck are you doing here?"

"I was wondering if you needed anything."

"Man, are you full of shit. I paid you off. Why are you here?"

"You recommended me to someone, Tony. I just wanted to show my gratitude."

"Recommended you as a lawyer? You're nuts."

"I must admit, I thought it was a little odd, too. But the guy said you steered him to me."

"What guy? Gimme another smoke." Clarence obliged, leaning and saying the name as he lit the smoke.

"James Elliot."

Tony blew out the smoke, his face utterly expressionless.

"Don't know him," he said.

"He knew you."

"Yeah, well, everybody fuckin' knows me. I'm famous."

Clarence was stumped for a moment. If Ferrera really didn't know Elliot, why use him as a reference? He couldn't find an answer, so he asked the only question he had left in his head.

"Has anyone else been asking about me, Tony?" Ferrera regarded him with a cynical air for a moment, and then sighed.

"My wife might need some legal help."

"I could assist her. Certainly. What kind of help?"

"She'll tell you."

"And I would provide this legal help free of charge, is that it?"

Tony nodded, reaching out and taking the pack of Camels, only three missing, and putting it in his shirt pocket, staring defiantly at Clarence the whole time. To mitigate the irritation, Clarence recited a Hail Mary in his head. It helped him to be patient and calm, both necessary, especially here. Finally Tony spoke again.

"Guy from the U.P. was in here when I came. I was bitching about how fuckin' stupid you were to lose my case, and he seemed real interested."

Clarence refrained from mentioning that Tony had been positively identified by no fewer than eight people who either worked at the bank he robbed, or were visiting when he robbed it, and Tony had talked to the cops for two full hours before Clarence got there and told him to shut his mouth. *Yeah, man, it was totally my fault you were convicted.*

"You remember his name?" Clarence asked, even though he didn't need to. He knew who it was. It could only be one person.

"Yeah," said Tony. "Walsh. Frank Walsh."

"I appreciate the info, Tony. Tell your wife to call and set up an appointment. I'll help her any way I can. Anything else you need?"

"Sure, a hundred in my commissary account wouldn't hurt. And a blowjob." He stood up and turned to leave. Clarence nodded to his back as he walked away, very quietly saying, to himself, "I can handle one of those." On his way out, he stopped and gave the hundred dollars to the commissary officer.

"What's the name?" the guy asked, opening his book to log the amount.

"Tony Ferrera." The officer shook his head.

"What?" Clarence asked.

"The guy's a fucking asshole." Clarence nodded. Good to know one's first impression is shared by others, he thought. He walked out to the Studebaker and sat in the driver's seat for a minute, looking for his spare pack of Camels in his bag. Finding it, he lit up and contemplated his new problem. Frank Walsh.

Rosalie's older brother, christened Francis, had always been bad news. A con man with the morals of a rattlesnake, he was unable to tell the truth about anything. Other than that, a hell of a guy. Made at speech at their wedding all those years ago – twenty now – and had everyone pounding the table with laughter. After he and Rosalie had been married about a year, Frank got in a little scrape in Detroit and got four years. So he'd been in jail when she died. Rosalie had been the good daughter, Frank the prodigal son. A month after the accident, he'd sent Clarence a letter, full of invective and threats. It was one of the smaller reasons he'd left Marquette ten months after his wife's death. *And now his name pops out of nowhere from Tony Ferrera, of all people.* As he drove, Clarence realized that he should have left Michigan entirely. Put half a continent or more between him and his past, and the people who still remembered him in it. That thought consumed him for the rest of the drive home.

Approaching Elder, he realized he couldn't park the Studebaker at Shorty's, and they might be watching the office, too. He drove by the office and looked around a bit. There didn't seem to be anyone in particular with eyes on his front door, so he circled the block and went into his lot, quickly jumping out and opening the back gate and securing the car inside the hidden shed. He then walked out through the property behind his and then walked home. It was a nice day, and he enjoyed the stroll. He got to his backyard via the driveway on the street behind it and went up the fire escape to his room. He wasn't going to take any more chances until he figured this thing out.

Once inside, he showered and changed into movie-going clothes, then went downstairs, trying not to look across the street to see if anyone was watching. He knocked on Shorty's door and she was surprised to see him.

"I thought you'd forgotten," she said.

"Never. What's our movie?"

"There's only one playing," she said. "Bite The Bullet."

"Let's go," he said.

They got into the Merc and as he backed out he saw the Blue Pontiac in the parish hall lot. And it followed them to the theater. The movie was a western, about the participants in a long distance horse race. Gene Hackman, James Coburn, Candice Bergen and assorted others. Clarence laughed out loud once. Gene Hackman hired a prostitute the night before the race and they went up to his room. She was taking her dress off, revealing two large breasts and some fancy embroidered bloomers, and Gene was unvested and removing his gun belt, as she laid back on the pillows of the bed, looking at him, and said *How do you like it, Mister?* To which Gene, advancing toward her in long johns, replied *Without conversation.*

Shorty liked westerns so she was pleased. They had an early dinner at Chang's Chinese Palace and repaired to their apartments in Shorty's house afterward, well fed and entertained. Clarence hadn't noticed anyone following them after the movie, which might be a good sign. Getting back to his room, he badly wanted a drink, but it was Sunday, his day of not drinking that proved he didn't have *the disease.* He tried a couple of rationales on himself and rejected them both. Instead he had a ginger ale and three cigarettes and went to sleep. *Without conversation.*

MONDAY

Monday mornings were bad enough, he supposed, even if you were going to a job you loved, but waking without a hangover always reminded him of the wisdom of the No-drinking-On-Sunday rule. He wasn't happy to have to get up, shower, shave, dress and go to work, but at least he felt all right. He took the short route to the office and didn't see anyone tail him there. Once inside, he found workers already on the job, setting up the first floor to look more like a massage parlor than it ever had. The foreman said they'd worked the whole weekend, so not coming in on Saturday was a smart choice. The place looked professional, and they were putting in a partition so the way up to his office would be obvious, and people coming to see him wouldn't see anything other than a reception desk. He made a mental note to ask Miss Bolton if they could share the cost of a receptionist. *You need a lawyer, mister? Or someone with big tits to rub your back? Your choice.*

Coffee was made and a cigarette lit and enjoyed and then he dove into the paperwork for the week. The new discovery date for Elliot was tomorrow, so he tackled the envelope again, and discovered a small folder that held a parole notice. When he took it out, there was a photograph behind it. An old black and white, bent in one spot and grainy as hell. It was of two boys, no more than eleven or twelve years old, standing by a lake – Teal Lake, he realized. Southwest of Marquette. He'd fished there as a youngster – holding up their catch and smiling as though happiness would follow them all their lives. The back of the photo had three words scrawled, *Me and Jim, 1937*. He looked at the photo again. On the right, clearly, was James Elliot. The boy on the left he knew but couldn't place. But there was something in the face, a smirk that was very familiar. He closed his eyes and concentrated on it, and another face appeared. He looked again. There was no doubt. It was his brother-in-law, Frank Walsh.

He'd deluded himself for years that Frank wouldn't be interested in finding him, and even if he was he'd never look in Elder, which the majority of Michiganders considered a backwater. He'd deluded himself about a lot of things.

But here it was. He sat back in his chair and rolled his neck one way six times, and then the other way for another six. The implications were many and not one of them boded well for him. First off, Elliot choosing him as his attorney wasn't an accident. Or was it? He probably didn't think he'd get caught; criminals, in Clarence's long experience, never thought that. But no, he came to Clarence before he'd been arrested, knowing he would be. How did he know that? And then he offered the car, knowing it would make someone Clarence's age salivate. And then he left a shitload of incriminating stuff in the damn car. He heard his mother's voice, a constant when he was in crisis. *How can you be so goddamned stupid?* And she was right this time. Played by a client at his age. Unforgivable. The whole thing was a setup; it had to be. And he needed to find Frank, to know exactly where that asshole was. He picked up the phone and called Louise at her house. She answered right away.

"Listen you motherfucker! Stop calling me or I'll have you arrested!"

"Louise? It's Clarence."

"Oh, my God, I'm sorry Clarence. Greg's been calling me; four times last night. Screaming at me, saying he's going to come over and kill me."

"I can go to court today and have him charged. Swear out a warrant for his arrest. Say the word."

"No, he came over Saturday night and pounded on the door for a half hour, but he couldn't get in, the lucky son of a bitch."

"Lucky?"

"I was waiting for him. I almost shot him through the door."

"There are better ways of dealing with this, Louise. Less stressful ones."

"I wish I could think of one."

"Can you call me the next time he says he's coming over?"

"What good would that do?"

Clarence had to admit she had a point there. He had no idea what good it would do, except that maybe he could talk her out of killing the prick, or get over to her house in time to head him off.

"Louise, I hate to ask, but I need a small favor."

"What?" Her tone suggested it had better be a simple favor, easily done.

"I need the record and current whereabouts on a felon from upstate."

"You have a stalker too, Clarence?"

"Something like that. His name is Frank Walsh. Francis Walsh, actually. Born around 1925, I would imagine, in Ishpeming. Anything you can find out about him."

"I'll have to call the state criminal archives in Lansing," she sighed. "Okay, I have a friend down there. Call me this afternoon at my work number, unless you want me to call you a motherfucker again."

"Nothing I haven't heard before. Thanks Louise."

"Will you defend me if I kill this bastard?"

"What? Greg?"

"Of course Greg. Who else am I going to kill?"

"Of course, Louise. And I'll get you off, too. I'll use the 'He Needed Killin' defense."

"Thanks, Clarence. I'll call you later." She hung up .

Clarence lit a smoke and looked at the photograph again. But it didn't tell him anything. There were too many questions. He knew they were playing him, but they could also be setting him up for something. He was glad the car was hidden and no one, not even Paula knew where it was. There might still be something in it that could incriminate him. He went through the scenario to see if he could spot a mistake he'd made. He accepted the car as his fee. He'd had the car registered in his name and insured. That made it his, legally, without question. Was that what Elliot or Frank wanted? He'd searched the car and found a bunch of things. But they were Elliot's things, not Frank's. Unless...and it hit him. *The car.* The Starlight, with a gun in a special holster under the driver's seat. That's what it was. It was Frank's car. That had to be it. Everything else was safe in the box at the bank, unless the cops got a warrant to search it. He doubted that would happen. He couldn't shake the idea that Elliot was generally an honest person, or as honest as a criminal could be. When he'd lied it'd been obvious that's what he was doing, and that suggested someone who only lied when it was absolutely necessary. That was Clarence's criteria for an honest man. He decided he needed to get out of the office and think. His watch suggested the post office would be open, so he put on his suit jacket and grabbed his keys and left.

He was locking the office door when Mayor George Barnet came up the steps. He was carrying a manila envelope. After a short greeting Clarence suggested they walk to the post office together. Going down the steps Clarence risked a quick glance at the Library parking lot and saw no blue Pontiac, or anyone even sitting in a car. *Excellent.*

"How is everything, Mr. Mayor?" he asked.

"You know goddamn well how things are. I'm being blackmailed."

"Yes, of course. I've been meaning to ask you about that. Who's doing it?"

"Are you crazy, Keaton? I'm not telling you on a public street."

"Of course not, and most prudent of you," said Clarence, realizing his nonchalance in the face of the Mayor's desperation wouldn't make him feel and easier, but it might very well serve another purpose later, should the tale of Clarence's sexuality ever start to travel around town. "What's in the envelope, George? The things I told you to bring over the other day or burn yourself?"

"Yes," Barnet replied, "and not so goddamn loud." He unclenched his teeth to smile at a citizen and wave at another. While he was waving, he passed the envelope to Clarence without looking, sticking it under his arm.

"So it's just the photos?"

"And the last note they sent me. And a list of everything that was stolen from my house by that asshole you're defending. How do you live with yourself?"

"I drink a lot and only look in the mirror when I shave, George, same as you."

"Sorry. I'm a little fucked-up about this. I shouldn't be lashing out at you."

"Ok, shake my hand." They were almost at the post office.

"What?"

"Stop, shake my hand and keep walking. Maybe a smile and a wave. People are watching."

"Right," said Barnet, and then executed all three moves to perfection. Clarence was duly impressed. This guy really knew about public perception. He went into the post office, collected his mail, and then found a chair off to the side and tore open the manila envelope. He'd been hoping it would only be the photos, but the blackmail note and the list of stolen items would be very useful so he had to extract them, hoping it could be done without seeing anything else. It was a vain hope. He got out the letter, but had to look inside to find the list, and then had to look to make sure only the photos were left. That last glance gave him an image he'd been hoping to avoid, and he wondered if he'd ever be able to look at the Mayor again without seeing the dog collar and the diaper. Probably not.

He walked past the mailboxes again and turned down a long empty corridor, walked to the end of it, and knocked on a door that had neither name nor department written on it. A weathered older woman opened it and peered out.

"Clarence, hey," she said, opening the door wide enough for him to slide in and then closing it. Her small office, if it could be called that, held a desk, two chairs, a large paper shredder, and lots of bags of shredded paper.

"Ellie," Clarence said, "could I shred something into your pile?"

"Of course," she replied. "I was going for a smoke anyway. Come and have one with me when you're done. I'll be on the verandah."

"I will," he said. "Thanks." Ellie left. Clarence decided to do the whole envelope in one shot, rather than have to do each photo separately. It went into the slot fairly easily and came out looking like black and white and yellow candy strips. He watched closely and decided none of it could be reconstructed, and then selected four pieces of his own mail, all junk, and shredded those on top of it. Satisfied, he went out and heard the door click behind him.

The 'verandah' Ellie had mentioned was around the back of the building, where she'd set up three folding chairs under the awning of a large umbrella. It wouldn't be long before winter came and she'd have to retreat to a basement room in the building for her five or six daily smoke breaks, but it was still nice enough, and Clarence sat on one of the chairs, noting he had plenty of time for one or two before court.

Ellie was one of his first clients after arriving and setting up shop. She'd hired him to guide her parents' estate through probate in 1958. She didn't trust the lawyer her parents had retained, with good reason, it turned out. She'd picked Clarence because he'd held the door for her a couple of times at the post office and always said hello. His parents had told him time and again that good manners and courtesy cost nothing and would bring dividends, and in this case they had been right. Ellie was a tart-tongued post office spinster type even then, and very little had changed, except that she'd retired two years ago. Four months after that retirement, she went back to her boss and asked if there wasn't *something* she could do for them, since she was going insane with boredom. The job of shredder had come open and despite its lonely mindlessness, she loved it, so they brought her back at a reduced salary with no benefits, since she already had plenty of those in her retirement package. And everyone was happy. Clarence was still her attorney and having a client who did nothing but shred paper all day had turned out to be very useful. Ellie was also a world class gossip.

"Anything in the wind, Ellie?" he asked, blowing the delicious smoke out on the morning breeze.

"Word is Bayne Oil is coming in. They're going to build a pumping station and a refinery and hire at least two hundred people."

"That's news. You know where?" He was trying to sound only vaguely interested, because Ellie picked up on everything.

"Don't know where. But they're doing a presentation at the council meeting on Wednesday night."

"Should be riveting. I know where I'll be."

Ellie laughed, and flicked her burned-to-the-end smoke through the back fence and into the parking lot.

"Gotta go destroy the evidence. See you Clarence."

"See you, Ellie." He was lost in the reverie that good tobacco brought for a couple of drags until he realized he should get his ass in gear too.

Back at the office, he handed the mail to Paula.

"You were late," he said.

"I'm aware of it," she replied.

"What do you mean, coming in here at this time of day?" It was a line from *A Christmas Carol*. He loved saying it. She was supposed to say, *I am behind my time, sir,* as Cratchit did in the movie, but he could see she was struggling to remember the line.

"I wasn't…I am…I can't remember the damn line, boss," she said. "And this is the silliest role-playing game ever."

"Commitment, Slim," he said, "Be committed to the part you're playing."

"You remember every movie, every line. How do you do that?"

"My mind is trained to remember," Clarence said with confidence, even though it was a lie. He did have a good memory, but he knew movies by heart because he felt safest when alone watching other people grapple with their fictitious problems. He was a devoted late movie watcher and it didn't matter if the movie was one he'd seen twenty times. All the better, in fact. He handed her the mail.

"Any checks?" she asked.

"I didn't look," he said. Her face registered real shock.

"Are you all right, boss?"

"I'm fine. When does the brothel officially open downstairs?"

"Wednesday, I think."

"Right, and what time am I due for the Elliot preliminary?" Paula consulted her calendar, which Clarence trusted more than his own.

"Ten-thirty."

"Okay, I'll be looking at notes. No calls, unless it's a client I know, or a new client, or someone wanting to be a client, or Hallberg, or the Madam from downstairs."

"That's virtually everyone who might call," she said.

"No personal friend calls."

"Got it," she said, thinking, *you don't have any.*

He went back to his office, made a coffee and had a smoke while looking over the preliminary notes. He still thought he could strike a deal even though Timmerman was going to be a hard-ass about it. He remembered the medical report and got it out of his briefcase. Elliot had maybe a year to live. *Maybe I should go all out and try to pull a 'lack-of-proper-evidence' play to get him kicked,* he thought. Nobody should spend the last few months of their life in a penitentiary. Paula came in as he was looking at his watch. It was 9:20.

"There's a guy downstairs…" she began.

"A lot of them," he replied.

"He's trying to open the back gate," she said.

"What? In the parking lot? Shit." He stood up so fast he banged both knees on the desk's edge. "SHIT!" Paula motioned him to the bathroom and he limped over, cursing himself softly. They both looked out and someone was now picking the lock on the gate, in broad daylight. Jesus, what balls these fuckers had. He opened the gate and went in. Clarence rushed back to his desk to get a small pair of opera glasses that had been his mother's. He came back and got a better look. The man wasn't picking the locks on the garage/shed, but he was looking intently in the window.

"What the hell is he looking for?" asked Paula.

"The car," Clarence said. "the Studebaker. I've been keeping it in there."

The man came out and carefully closed and relocked the gate. Then he walked quickly across the lot and Clarence and Paula went to the other side of the house to watch him as he crossed the street and got into an Oldsmobile Cutlass and drove away. Clarence trained the opera glasses on the plate and recited it so Paula could write it down, for all the good it would do them.

"Now what?" Clarence said out loud, not realizing he had.

"So they know it's there," said Paula, "but I have a question."

"Yes?"

"Who is they? Who's interested in this car?"

"Yeah, that's the question. See if you can get your guy at DMV to run that plate."

"Why not your guy? I hate to ask my guy. It makes him think I want to get back together."

"I used my guy already this week. Two in one week is bad luck."

"Right," she said. They were back at her desk now and she made a note of it. "What do we do about the Studebaker?"

"Yeah, and whatever we do it had better be fast. I have to be in court in an hour."

"I have a two-car garage," she said.

"Yeah, you do. That might work, as a temporary fix. I'm pissed that they know about the shed, though. It means I can't hide it there anymore. All right, here's what we'll do. I'll drive it over to your place and you follow me. We put it in your garage and then you take me back here and I go to court."

"That's stupid."

She said it flatly, as though stating a mathematical fact. It pissed him off, but only for a second.

"Tell me why."

"We don't have enough time, and we don't know if you're still being followed in which case we would show them both my house and the next place you're hiding the car." He frowned at her, trying to literally hurt her feelings with the look. He knew she was right.

"So tell me what we should do," he said.

"You go to court in the Mercury. I watch and see if someone follows you. then I go out and get the car and take it over and put it in my garage, and take a cab back." Clarence nodded as she spoke. It was solid. The point was that whoever came looking for it tonight would find it gone.

"Okay," he said. "We'll do it that way. You have the spare key to the gate?"

"In my desk."

"Here are the keys to open the shed..." he looped them onto the ring of Studebaker keys. "Lock the shed again after you get the car out and lock the gate again, too. And do it as fast as you can."

"Right. Of course. You don't have to tell me that."

"And here's a sawbuck for the cab," he said, handing her a ten from his wallet. "Please be careful. I like my secretary and my new car very much. I'll be back later."

"I've got this, boss. Really, you don't have to worry."

"Don't speed or anything with the car. You're not insured on it, and cops might pull you over just for driving something that fancy"

"I've got it *covered*," she insisted. "Go get Elliot off."

"Right." He went into the office and grabbed his briefcase, looked around, pocketed his smokes and lighter, and left. As he pulled out of the lot, he noticed a car pulling out of the Library lot behind him to follow, but he couldn't make out what kind it was. It was dark blue. *Good luck, Slim*, he thought.

He was waiting outside Courtroom A for Timmerman and his crack team of yes-men and women, and going through his notes he found the blackmail letter to the Mayor. *Dear Mr. Mayor,* it read, *A zoning ordinance will come before the council on Wednesday night. You will instruct your majority to vote YES on this ordinance, without debate. When this is done, you will have satisfied your debt to us. Failure to pass the ordinance will result in your disgrace and removal from office. Do as we say and you could remain Mayor of this shithole town for many years to come. Have a nice day.* At the bottom, the writer had drawn a smiley face. Of course the sop of "you will have satisfied your debt" was horseshit. They had the photos, and the next time they needed something, they'd use them again and tell him *that* satisfied the debt. Blackmail was a soap opera. It never ended. The Mayor could only stop it by announcing it was happening and why. And that was unlikely. Clarence realized he was going to have to go to that council meeting.

He rolled his neck back and forth for six again, trying to ease the knots. He was stressed and tense. This case was too close, Frank was too close, every goddamn thing was too close. Death was passing him to go take his father and looking back to say, *Next time I'm coming for you.* Maybe he should hand this off to another lawyer and take a short holiday. He was having a good month, after all. *Someone good enough to get Elliot off. Someone who isn't in the closet.*

He remembered a case many years before in which he defended two men in their twenties charged with robbing and beating an older man inside his home. The two men were quite obviously guilty of the crime, but it came to light in discovery that they'd met the older man in a bar and agreed to go home with him. Clarence had interviewed the man, and realized that he was gay. He got him on the stand and led him to admit that he'd invited the two young men to come to his house in order to have sex with them. The jury, appalled, acquitted the men in under an hour. The older man lost his job, moved away, and was heard of no more in Elder. Of all the things Clarence had done as a lawyer, that one remained on his conscience. The quote from Ecclesiastes came up from the cauldron of Catholic learning one could never fully digest or forget, *Be not righteous overmuch; neither make yourself over wise; why shouldst thou destroy thyself?* He decided it was okay. He was vigorously defending his client, doing his job. Then he laughed, imagining himself saying that at the gates of heaven. Then he laughed harder at the idea that he was even going to heaven. People were looking at him and he composed himself, realizing he was too happy for a courtroom hallway on a Monday morning. His watch informed him that he had time for a smoke so he headed to the back alley.

Coming out, he spotted Mike Ross lighting up and went over to him. Mike was mildly surprised to see him, but pulled out his lighter and lit the Camel dangling from Clarence's lips.

"I need to ask you something," Mike said. "What's going on with Louise?"

"How would I know, Mike? She's your partner."

"You're her lawyer, asshole."

"Well I'm not allowed to discuss anything about her with you then, am I?"

"You know her ex is an asshole. He's doing something that's fucking her up. I know that"

"If you're sure, then you should do something about it, Mike."

"Very diplomatic, very lawyerly. You have no trouble destroying a good cop on the stand, when he was only doing his job, but when it comes to keeping your own client safe, you can't do a fucking thing."

"I wish I could tell you something, Mike. I was planning on enjoying this smoke and now I'm not."

"Good. Your day should be as bad as mine."

"If it's any consolation, it probably will be."

"That's what you think, asshole. Your burglar's gonna get a deal."

"A deal? And how would you know that?" Clarence didn't want to sound too eager, knowing that if Mike was angry, he'd stop talking.

"The witness is a kid. They have nothing other than him. And his parents don't want the little shit traumatized. And none of the rich pricks he stole from want to stand up and have it counted. Maybe they were hiding stuff from the tax people. Same old story. We do the legwork and you waltz in and get it kicked."

So which is it, Mike? Is it a deal or will the whole thing get kicked? Clarence took the last drag on his smoke without asking the question.

"Thanks, Mike," he said. "You take care, now."

He walked back to Courtroom A and saw Elliot was seated at the defense table already, with Toni Gallo back at the prosecutor's table.

Toni instead of Timmerman meant it was a defeat of some kind for the D.A.'s office, and when Toni didn't even acknowledge him or call him over to discuss the deal, he realized that Mike had good information. It was a free and clear kick. Amazing. He sat down next to Elliot with a curt nod. He wanted him to be surprised and really grateful. Maybe grateful enough to tell him a few things.

The Judge came in, everyone stood; the Judge sat down, everyone sat. The Judge asked if the prosecution was ready and Toni Gallo stood to say that they were asking for the charges to be dismissed. Clarence tried to see the look on his client's face without making it obvious by turning his head. Elliot was certainly surprised but not to the extent that most people would be. Clarence figured that the long stretches of prison time had made him just generally unwilling to show emotion about anything. The Judge was more surprised than the defendant, giving his sternest look to Ms. Gallo and asking what the problem was "Lack of evidence, your honor," she said, sounding just a little rehearsed on it, "and our witness has refused to testify."

"A subpoena wouldn't help compel the testimony, Ms. Gallo?"

"The witness is a minor, your honor, under thirteen years of age."

"I see. Very well, Mister…" his eyes scanned down the report page in front of him, "…Elliot." Clarence motioned for Elliot to stand but he was already up.

"Mr. Elliot, the charges against you have been dismissed. You are free to go. Bailiff, take Mr. Elliot back to the jail to retrieve his personal effects. This court is adjourned." The Judge stood, everyone stood; the Judge left.

Elliot turned and looked at Clarence, betraying nothing, merely a hint of a smile on his face. He was about to say something when the bailiff touched his arm and he left with a small nod. Clarence watched him go, then walked over to Toni Gallo who was repacking her briefcase.

"Sorry, Toni," he said.

"Bullshit you're sorry," she replied with a smile. "Another victory for the good guy who reps the bad guys."

"He's not that bad a guy. He never hurt anyone."

"Get you next time, Clarence."

He nodded and she left. There would be a next time, a lot of them, and she would get him most of the time. His winning streak of the last ten days was a fluke, a bending of the continuum. It would straighten out soon enough. He packed his own case and headed to the smoking alley for a quick one.

The release door at the jail was on the west side of the building, not facing the road or visible from the windows of any other building. Roughly forty minutes later, it opened and James Elliot came strolling out, a free man. He walked around the corner of the building, thinking about how he was going to get where he was going, and saw his lawyer waiting for him.

"Mr. Keaton," he said. "You weren't lying about how good a lawyer you are."

"No, I wasn't," Clarence replied. "But you were lying about why you chose me."

"Was I? I don't remember lying to you about that."

"Well, memory loss among career criminals is a chronic condition, isn't it? Where'd you grow up, Jim?"

"Me? I grew up in, uh, Niles." There it was again, the hesitation-hint. The 'Me?' moment which gave someone a chance to think of something other than what sprang to mind, which was the truth. The great liars trained themselves to have the lie spring to mind. Elliot was a good liar; excellent even, but not a great one. Not born with the ability. He was self-taught. The ones born into lying were impossible to trap or decipher. You just had to assume they were lying all the time.

"Niles, eh? I don't think so. You sound more like a guy from the U.P. Ishpeming would be my guess."

"That's an odd guess."

Clarence held out the photo of the two boys at Teal Lake with their fish. Elliot took it and nodded.

"You know, I was actually wondering where this was."

"And I am the King of Rumania," said Clarence. He'd almost said *Marie* of Rumania, which was the actual Dorothy Parker quote, but he had one of those last second *this-could-be-misinterpreted* moments as the word formed in his mouth, and he reset it to say *King* instead, which had the effect of strangling the line and weakening its punch.

"Why did you come to my office that day?" Clarence asked.

"I was about to be arrested and I needed a lawyer."

"Tony Ferrera said he'd never heard of you. So who was it who recommended me again?"

Elliot looked him right in the eyes, steady as a rock. Later, Clarence realized that it was the first and only time he'd ever done that.

"Well, I'd heard about you from Frank Walsh. But I wouldn't call what he said a recommendation, exactly."

"No, I would guess not."

"I was in town for some weeks, Mr. Keaton, and I asked around about the best criminal lawyers. You were one of the names mentioned, and since Frank hated you so much, I figured you were probably a straight shooter. He isn't."

"What exactly did Frank say about me?"

"He thinks you killed his sister."

Clarence nodded. It wasn't a surprise. He knew protesting his innocence or saying it was a car accident would only make him look guilty. So, as he'd advised countless people over the years, he said nothing. Elliot waited a moment or two to allow him the chance to speak, then realized he wasn't going to. A look that might have been admiration passed across his face.

"Mr. Keaton, I wonder if it might be possible for me to retrieve something from you. I know I said it was yours, but I would like it back all the same."

"I assume you mean the bag of diamonds."

"Yes."

"Come on, they're at my bank." They walked to the Merc and got in. Pulling out of the parking lot, Clarence, trying to be as casual as he could, asked another question.

"Jim, does Frank Walsh know I live here in Elder?"

"I'm afraid he does now." He sighed. "Frank and I were in prison together for four years, and there wasn't a single day he didn't mention you. Not one. He was going to get out, and find you, and etcetera, etcetera."

"Right," said Clarence. What else was there to say? He'd been thinking the same thing for almost twenty years, though he'd only mentioned it to whichever bottle of Scotch he was currently emptying. "Did you tell him where I was?"

"No. He wrote me and said a guy at Southern Michigan told him."

"Tony Ferrera."

"That's right. I know you didn't kill his sister, by the way."

"You do?"

"She died in a car accident. I looked it up. And you don't strike me as a man who arranges those kinds of things."

"I appreciate the vote of confidence."

They arrived at the bank, Elliot staying in the car as Clarence went in and got the diamonds from his box. He came out and handed them over. Elliot started to get out of the car, but Clarence stopped him.

"Jim, I need to ask one more question."

"Sure."

"Why'd you give me Frank's car?"

Elliot smiled, and actually laughed a little at that one.

"'Well," he said, "I figured you'd sell it."

"I'm afraid I've decided to keep it, Clarence said, and Elliot smiled again.

"Frank might think it's his car, but it isn't. He sold it to me for a thousand bucks just before he went in for his last bit."

"Forgive me, Jim, but this really sounds like a setup."

"The car was legally mine and now it's legally yours. He has no real claim."

"That may be true, but if he has proof that it's his he can kill me and take it back and walk, provided he has the right lawyer."

"Would another lawyer defend someone who murdered a lawyer?"

"Are you kidding me? They'd form a line."

"He does want to kill you. It's something he talks about a lot."

He looked at Elliot, sure now that he'd been played in what was now going to be a life and death game. But Elliot didn't look back and seemed calm, as always. Maybe that was because he was dying of cancer. Maybe that focused a person. Or maybe he'd always been like that. Then he remembered the gun.

"Was the gun part of the set-up?" he asked. "Was it going to be used to incriminate me?"

"Mr. Keaton. I didn't even know the gun was there. Where is it now?"

"You'll forgive me if I don't put much stock in what you tell me. The gun's been disposed of. And I think our professional relationship should end here."

"No problem," said Elliot, opening the door and swinging his legs out. "I appreciate what you did, Mr. Keaton, and I wish you good luck."

"Thanks. I might need it."

Elliot exited the car and Clarence pulled out into traffic, silently cursing his stupidity. He glanced in the rear view a moment or two later and couldn't see Elliot, a ghost to the end. He decided to drive back to the office and stake out the gate to see who might be coming. Then, as he turned right, it occurred to him that he could take the Studebaker and his four grand desperation cash and just leave. Head west. Find a place where a gay man could live openly without worrying it would cost him his living. Then he started laughing. He laughed all the way to his parking lot.

The activity downstairs seemed to be abating a little, and it was only Monday. The place looked fairly presentable already and the partition was up, with a sign that said LAW OFFICE UPSTAIRS with an arrow. *How about* that? He walked up the stairs and saw a woman in the waiting area. He recognized her but couldn't find her name in his jumbled brain-rolodex. He stuck his head into Paula's office.

"Name?" he whispered.

"Angie Ferrera," she whispered back. "Tony's wife."

"Right, thanks. Everything good with the relocation thing?" He didn't want to say *the car* and hoped she would understand. She did.

"No problems. We're the only ones who know. And they'd have to kill me before I told them." She smiled.

"How would you tell them after they killed you?"

"You know what I mean. How'd the prelim go?"

"He walked." Clarence turned and headed down the hall, leaving Paula a bit open-mouthed.

"Mrs. Ferrera, how nice to see you. Please come in."

Angie Ferrera was forty years old, and she didn't look anything like a woman who was married to an armed robber doing hard time. Her dark brown hair had a couple of little gray streaks in it and she dressed like someone who worked in an office; proper matching blouse and skirt combinations, sensible but nice looking all day shoes. Clarence couldn't recall what she did for a living. He ushered her into the comfortable client chair and shut the office door. He really wanted a cigarette but couldn't remember if she was a smoker, so he decided to wait.

"Tony said you could help me, Mr. Keaton," she began.

"Of course. How is Tony doing?"

"Fine, I guess. He has a new punk."

Clarence wasn't totally sure how to respond to that, rejecting the one that came to mind – *We could all use a new punk* – so he just nodded and attempted a smile, hoping it would be reassuring.

"Actually, I'm really glad he's there," she continued. "He's kind of psychotic sometimes. And you wouldn't believe the things he used to make me do in bed."

"Well you certainly don't have to tell me about that, Mrs. Ferrera," he said, trusting she would stay with the implied *it was horrible,* but she didn't. The attorney-client vow of silence only applied to the attorney. Once the office door closed, clients so often felt that unburdening themselves of all their secrets was the thing to do.

"He was an animal. He liked it rough, you know? And I don't like it rough, but did he care? No, sir. And regular positions? Regular screwing? Not for Tony. Had to put it in my—"

"Mrs. Ferrera? Was there something I could help you with legally?"

"Well, you know I went to a doctor after Tony went away and he told me all that punishment wasn't good for a person's anus."

"I would imagine not." Clarence wondered what look his face was projecting. "Are you wishing to sue your doctor?"

"No. Of course not. He's a nice man. And he's good in bed. Not like an animal."

Good to know. Clarence decided a cigarette was in order so he pulled one out and lit up without asking.

"Are you here to begin divorce proceedings?"

"What? No. I'm Catholic. I'm only allowed to get a divorce if he dies."

"Right, of course," Clarence said, deciding not to point out that wasn't true, since it would serve no purpose.

"I was recently hired by Bayne Petroleum, as a legal analyst," she said.

"You're a lawyer, Mrs. Ferrera?"

"No, I'm a paralegal. I got my certificate two years ago. I was in the first class ever trained in that job in Michigan."

"Well, congratulations." *More useless information.*

"Thank you."

Clarence was genuinely wondering why Bayne wouldn't have hired an actual lawyer. Not that it should have been him, but paralegals were such a new thing. A lawyer would be safer, though more expensive. That was undoubtedly the reason.

"I've been looking at some documents, Mr. Keaton, that suggest Bayne is attempting to circumvent Michigan law in several respects, and as an analyst, I want to make sure they don't fire me for telling them so, which is illegal, as you know. And I don't want to be found liable under the law if they get caught."

"Do you have the documents that prove this, Mrs. Ferrera?" he asked.

"No. I'm not allowed to copy them or take them home."

"But you're absolutely sure that the law is being broken?"

"I finished third in my class, Mr. Keaton. I'm sure."

"All right, don't tell anyone what we've just discussed. Go to work as usual and do your job. What I'm going to need is some idea of the laws being broken, written down. So, tonight, and for a night or two, you write down everything you think they're probably doing that's illegal. Don't do it while you're at work, do it at home. Come back and see me in a couple of days and we'll go over it and plot a strategy. All right?"

"Yes, thank you so much, Mr. Keaton. I'll be back with all the information." She got up, clearly relieved, they shook hands and he walked her to the door. As she went down the stairs he called to Paula. She came in with her notepad.

"What's the story on Mrs. Convict?"

"Shush," he said, but he was smiling. "Have there been any cars in the Library lot today watching us?"

"Nope. Not that I could see." But he knew they hadn't given up. They were coming back for the car, most likely tonight. *They must be really sure whatever they want is still in there,* he thought.

"By the way", Paula said, "Louise Merwin just called. She said you should call her back as soon as you got in. She's at her desk, although why she needed to tell me that, I don't know." Paula never missed anything. Clarence knew Louise wanted him to know it was about work, not the other thing. He called and she didn't waste any time.

"Frank Walsh got paroled from Southern Michigan four months ago. He was doing an eight year stretch for forgery and fraud. Did six years. He was in Grand Rapids for three months, regular parole visits, but he didn't show up a month ago and they don't know where he is now."

Of course. It had been too good a month to imagine anything else. "Thanks, Louise."

"Do you know this guy, Clarence? Have you defended him? His record is pretty long. The stretch in Jackson was his third."

"I only know him peripherally and I've never defended him." *We're related by marriage.* "Please let me know if his name comes up in any context, ok?"

"Ok. Is he looking for you?"

"I can neither confirm nor deny that."

"All right," said Louise. "Hope I don't have to call you tonight."

"Louise, say the word and Greg is in jail. I mean it."

"Yeah, but only overnight, and he'll come out angrier the next day." She was right.

"I owe you for this, Louise. Payable on demand."

"Thanks Clarence. Someday I'll come and collect." She hung up.

He lit a Camel. *How many will this make today?* he thought and then decided *who cares*. He felt tired and it was only Monday. A weekend with Benny usually fired him up. Too much going on. The sofa looked like a young male hooker someone else paid for beckoning to him. He stubbed out the smoke, walked over and laid down. He was asleep in seconds.

When he awoke, it felt like he'd slept a long time, but his watch proved this to be untrue. It had been barely forty-five minutes. But he felt good. He sat up and saw Paula coming down the hall towards him. *Please God no more clients today*, he thought. It was ever thus. Suffer through the times of no clients and no money coming in, or suffer through the times of plenty when there were just too many people unloading their problems on him.

"Boss?"

"We have anyone else today?" he asked.

"Nope. Open book until Wednesday."

"You have a date tonight?"

"No."

"Want to stake out the shed with me?"

"Stake it out? What do you mean?"

"The guy broke in today and saw the car. He's going to be back tonight to steal it, or search it, or something."

"How can you be sure of that?"

"I'm not. I'm betting on it. We leave and sneak back up here. Get a camera and photograph whoever comes to get the car."

"Why don't we just call the cops?"

"Because we need to know who these people are."

"What if they just send flunkies?" Paula's logic was so blade-perfect, it was irritating. It was why he always ran plans by her first, even though he hated how easily she could dismiss what he thought were excellent ideas.

"We can't call the cops. Until we know what they're looking for. And we need to know who and why."

"So who, and why, and what are tonight's questions?"

"Yes."

"How about we call the cops, have them stake it out, and then if they arrest anyone, you ask them who it was? Doesn't that seem simpler than doing it ourselves?"

Clarence had to admit it was the best plan, even though he didn't like it. He hated asking the cops for favors. He liked it better when they owed *him*. But there was no escaping the logic of what Paula proposed. He picked up the phone.

"Okay, we'll do it your way, Slim. You got a big date tonight or something?"

"I might," she said. "I was wondering if I could take off a little early, too."

"Sure. Hope you have a good time." She smiled at him and left. He thought about having a smoke and a drink of scotch, but then remembered he'd finished his bottle of The Balvenie. *Aw hell.* He smoked an Egyptian and then called Louise. She said it was no problem for a patrol car to stake it out, and if they wouldn't authorize it, she'd do it herself. He thanked her, not mentioning payment of a two-favors-in-one-day debt. It would come in good time.

The golf club bar was sparsely populated that Monday evening, but Simon was there. He was always there. Clarence sat with him and

had two beers, followed by a sandwich. They discussed the Detroit
Tigers, who were about to finish last, having lost nineteen games in a
row in August. Simon had made a bundle on that streak, betting them
to lose from the fifth game to the seventeenth. Then he decided he was
on the edge himself and stopped. They lost two more before they won
and he was still congratulating himself for having the courage to stop
what he called 'A winning streak on losing'. Gamblers were always
patting themselves on the back. Since baseball was ending, Simon was
now heavily betting football.

"The Lions are 2-0, you know," he said.

"Yes, I know," said Clarence. "They print the scores in the paper."

"It's a good omen."

"A good omen of what?" Clarence snorted. "They always start hot
and cool off just when you think they might win something. Dallas is
going to kill them next Sunday."

"You're wrong. This year, they're going to be good. You just have to
know how to bet them."

"I do. Don't bet on them, ever. And try not to bet against them.
That's how you bet them, by not betting."

Simon laughed.

"No, dummy. When they should win; when they're obviously so
much better than the other team it's a joke, you bet against them. They
always lose those games. But when they should get the shit kicked out
of them by a superior team, you bet on them. They either win or cover
in those games."

"That's the trick, is it?"

"Damn right."

"Well, you make a living at this. I don't."

Clarence decided to have a third beer, which turned into a fourth.
Simon called for some vodka shots and he had at least one. He was
halfway through his sixth beer when he heard a really loud laugh from
the other side of the room, and he realized that it was his, echoing off
the walls. One of the signs that he was getting over-the-line drunk was
his laugh got so loud you noticed, even if everyone else was laughing
too. The sound jarred him and he saw it was closing in on ten p.m.
He went to the pisser for a long one, ran his head under the tap, dried
off, combed his hair, came out and ordered a large black coffee, which
he knew meant he wouldn't sleep at all, but there wasn't a choice.
Forty-five minutes after the coffee was consumed, he took another piss
and judged that he was all right to drive home. He kicked himself for
letting it get so far along. On a Monday, no less. He said goodnight to
Simon and some of the other die-hard drinker-gamblers, and headed

for his car. He sat in the driver's seat for at least ten minutes, enjoying a smoke and trying to make absolutely sure he wasn't too drunk to drive home. Finally, at around eleven, he pulled out of the Golf Club parking lot and turned the car toward his street.

Being arrested for drunk driving wouldn't destroy his career as a lawyer, certainly. Not in this town. It might even garner some new business. But it was still too much of a risk. So he drove a careful, speed-limited route to his house and was relieved to turn right on his block and have his driveway to park in. He saw no one and was upstairs quickly and quietly. He took a blazing hot bath, figuring it might help him get to sleep faster, and it did. Before he nodded off, it occurred to him that it hadn't been a bad Monday at all.

TUESDAY

Tuesday started much earlier than it normally might have. The phone by his bed rang and shredded the dream he was having. He picked it up after the second jangle.

"Hello?" His voice sounded like tractor tires on gravel.

"Clarence?" It was Justin Highfield. Clarence sat up to orient himself and put his hand over the receiver to cough out the crap.

"Yes Justin? What can I do for you?"

"I need you to go down to the station and bail Jamie out. He was arrested. I'd go but I'm in Lansing tonight on business. I'll be back tomorrow."

"Do you know what he was arrested for, Justin?"

"I don't know for sure. He says it's bullshit, of course." *Of course.*

"All right, I'm on my way."

"Use Bothwell's Bail Bonds, Clarence," said Highfield, and then hung up. Clarence was out of bed and putting on clothes before that registered.

He wasn't in his best humor as he pulled out of the driveway and headed for the jail, so when he turned right at the second light, he barely noticed the three police cars barreling the other way, and he didn't check his rear view or he would have noticed that they turned left onto his street. He got to the cop shop and when he told the desk sergeant Jamie's name, the guy looked kind of funny at him.

"What was the charge?" Clarence asked.

"Breaking and entering."

"Did he make a statement?" Hoping against hope.

"Not according to this. He was bailed out about twenty minutes ago."

"What?" said Clarence? "You mean I came down for nothing? Who bailed him out?"

"Joe Bothwell."

Hearing the name a second time made it clear to Clarence, *finally*, that the setup he was fearing was coming from the oil company, not the burglar and his ex-brother-in-law. But he barely had time to put those pieces together in his mind when he heard his name screamed from the entrance, about thirty yards away.

"Keaton! Stay right there! Don't move!!"

He turned and saw Mike Ross, Louise, and several uniformed patrolmen and women, a veritable phalanx, coming toward him. Mike called again.

"Keep your hands where I can see them, Keaton." Clarence obligingly put both his hands out in front of him above his head. Moments later he was handcuffed and being led away to an interrogation room. The desk sergeant watched him go, asking "Want me to call Bothwell for *you*?" as he disappeared down the hall.

Mike Ross, bearing a two-canaries-grin, led Clarence into one of the rooms and sat him down. Louise followed them inside and shut the door.

"Counselor, I think you know I've been waiting for this day. You're under arrest."

"Of course, Mike," Clarence said, "Could you un-cuff me now and may I ask the charge?"

"Suspicion of murder. We found Elliot."

Clarence was stunned, but made a great effort not to show any emotion at all.

"Keaton. Where's your car?"

"It's in your parking lot, Detective. I'd give you the keys but my hands are cuffed." Mike unlocked the cuffs.

"I take it you want to search it, Mike? And you probably have a warrant to search it that you're now going to show me?"

Mike brought out the warrant and Clarence read it and gave up the keys. He realized they were going to find Elliot's burglar's tools in the bag in the trunk and that wasn't going to look good, so he tried a bluff to see what they thought they had.

"I hope I can get it back as soon as its searched, Mike, because I'll need it to drive over to the courthouse and file the false arrest lawsuit against you and the department tomorrow. Thanks."

"You're not under arrest, Keaton. You're under suspicion and being questioned."

"So I'm free to go, then?"

He knew already that since he wasn't booked, so they weren't sure yet, which was a good sign. A patrolman came in and gave him a cup of coffee. He demanded his phone call, and a phone was duly brought in. Once they'd left him alone, he called Paula.

"Hey, it's me."

"What's up boss? It's four in the morning. The car's fine."

"Shush. I've been arrested."

"Arrested? Were you driving drunk?"

"No. They think I may have killed someone."

"Who?"

"Elliot."

"What? That's insane."

"Yeah, of course. So you need to call Flacco and have him come down here and get me out."

"Flacco? It's that serious? Aren't they going to just find out you didn't do it?"

"Sure, but with Flacco, I can also sue them."

"Are you really sure? His retainer will wipe out all our gains this month."

She was right.

"Ok, wait on calling him. I'll try and call you again when you get to the office. Go back to bed."

"Oh, sure. Like I'm gonna sleep now."

"The cops might come over to your place, so...."

"So...?"

"Put something on." She laughed out loud and he said goodbye.

He hung up the phone and considered the options. The nagging thing was, of course, who killed Elliot and why? He doubted they could frame him for it. He was with people almost the entire time since he dropped the guy off outside the bank. So he probably wasn't killed to set up a frame. It would most likely be someone Elliot stole from. And that list would be miles long. He wondered if he could get any information out of the detectives when they came to question him. That was a very dangerous line to walk, because they were professionals and he would have to do some talking in order to get them to tell him things. Probably too risky. The cop came and took the phone away, forgetting to unplug it from the wall so it jerked him backwards when he got to the door. Clarence stifled a laugh. Two minutes after the patrolman left, Clarence lit a smoke in defiance of the new No Smoking sign, and Ross and Merwin walked in, their faces grave. Louise sat across from him and Mike stood against the wall. They were actually going to try good cop-bad cop on him. He wished he hadn't had so much to drink earlier, because although he felt fairly sober now, he knew he would get tired easily. He stubbed out the smoke and took a deep breath. Louise spoke first.

"It looks bad, Clarence," she said.

He looked at her questioningly.

"We found Elliot shot in the head." Clarence wondered exactly where they'd found him. He hoped his silence would draw that out "We have witnesses who saw you drive him away from the courthouse and others who saw him in your car parked outside the bank. Why'd you take him to the bank, Clarence?"

"And why'd you dump him by the marsh, in the open? That was stupid, Keaton." Mike couldn't help himself.

"Mike, please," Louise said. They were doing the script very well, although Mike had given him some information. It was puzzling why he would be dumped in an open spot by the marsh.

"Why don't you tell us what happened?" Louise said. She had a silky voice that was very seductive. He wanted to speak, but he knew every word he said would give them ammo, so he just shook his head, eyes down. That made him look guilty, of course, but – and he had spent twenty years trying to drill this into clients' brains – you can *look* guilty all day and never be convicted, but once you open your mouth you look and *sound* guilty and they write down all the sounds, they prove you guilty almost one hundred percent of the time. So he stayed quiet, though it took great willpower. He wasn't going to talk until he was sure what they had.

"Did you shoot him in your car and then dump him at the marsh, Clarence? Was he threatening you? Maybe it was self-defense. You have to tell us if we're going to help you."

Man, she's good. Clarence could see Mike taking deep breaths, actually warming up for the explosion that was coming. Louise would try to hold him back and sternly rebuke him, or send him out of the room after he'd scared the shit out of the suspect. Clarence wondered if he could say something that would speed up the process. He cleared his throat, which got both detectives a little excited.

"I would like to call my lawyer, Robert Flacco," he said.

"Come on, Clarence," Louise said, "a guy who wants a lawyer looks guilty."

"I would like to speak to Mr. Flacco before I say anything else to you about the lawsuit."

"What lawsuit?" They were momentarily confused, which was pleasing to Clarence.

"The lawsuit he and I are going to file against you and the department for false arrest, illegal search, and harassment."

"Fuck you, you lying bastard." Mike broke into bad cop a little early. Clarence could tell by the look Louise shot at him.

"That was hurtful, Detective. I'm going to have to add pain and suffering to the lawsuit."

"I'll show you pain and suffering, you fucking – ."

"Mike, back off! I mean it!" Louise said. Clarence couldn't believe they were still trying to play this on him. Plus they hadn't threatened him with any evidence, other than the witnesses seeing him with Elliot, so they hadn't found anything in the apartment or the car. Well, maybe just the apartment. The car would take longer, but all they could really prove was that Elliot had been in his car, which wouldn't convict him. *So it's not a frame,* he thought. There would be some real evidence in the apartment if it was.

"Why don't you just tell us what happened?" she said.

"Yeah, Keaton," said Mike, holding his temper. "Regale us."

"I should probably have my lawyer present for this," Clarence said. "Can I call my lawyer, Bob Flacco?"

"You've already had your phone call," Mike said. He was getting angry for real, so Clarence decided to try a trap. If it worked, Louise probably wouldn't be able to stop Mike from punching him, but it would end the interrogation.

"I would really like my phone call," he said again, and Mike took a bite.

"You had it! If you didn't call your lawyer, who the fuck did you call?"

"Your ex. Told her I couldn't make it till later."

From the wall, Mike launched himself across the table, his hands striking Clarence high on his chest, with full angry-cop weight behind them. The chair flipped back as both men crashed into the back wall. Clarence had deliberately tried to relax his whole body before he made the wife comment, knowing what would come, so the fall wasn't too painful for him. But Mike got in two punches to his head before Louise and a uniformed patrolman pulled him off. The second punch caught him flush on the left eye. It wasn't a knockout blow, but it was painful and enough to raise a solid shiner. Mission accomplished.

They took Mike out of the room to cool him off. Louise and a uniform helped Clarence up and put him back in the chair, where he lit a smoke as best he could. They brought him some ice, which he refused, since he wanted the eye to swell up and look horrible so he could use it against them. He shut his good eye against the pain, which was considerable, and asked for some aspirin. He wondered who he would get to photograph his face tomorrow, because that's what he was going to do. Louise sat down next to him.

"I'm sorry about that, Clarence."

"Yeah, well, you're probably going to be in the future."

"I know."

"You can book me now and face the consequences later or cut me loose and face the consequences later."

She sighed. The reason she'd hired him as her divorce lawyer was exactly this. He was tough and smart, and not afraid to take his lumps if necessary. He'd fucked the whole department tonight because he knew how to get Mike's goat. And it was also why she liked him. What had always escaped her was why he didn't like her the same way.

"You're free to go," she said. "Let us know if you're going to leave town."

"What about my car?"

"We're going to keep that for a little longer."

"Sure. Let me know if you decide to sell it." He picked up his cigarettes and stood up, too quickly. He was still a little woozy and he sat back down to clear his head. Then he got up and walked out of the room and down the hall toward the front entrance. As he got close to the door, he saw Bob Flacco coming up the steps.

"Clarence! What the hell is going on?" He saw the black eye. "Did someone beat you up?"

"No, Bob. I was questioned a little strenuously by Mike Ross."

"He HIT you??"

"He did."

"Well, I hope you're going to sue his dumb ass. Hell the whole department."

"Certainly a possibility, Bob. Did my secretary call you?"

"No, I'm here on another matter. New client."

"Well, then, good luck."

"You should have that eye looked at, Clarence. And call me if you want to sue them, ok?"

"I will. Thanks Bob."

Flacco walked inside and Clarence saw him talking to the desk sergeant. Then he walked to the payphone and called Paula.

"You okay?"

"Sure. Come get me, will you?"

"On my way. Ten minutes."

"Thanks."

He hung up and sat on the bench in the reception area so that every cop and civilian who walked by would see a man who'd been beaten up.

Paula took him to the emergency room where a doctor clucked over him for ten minutes and wrote a prescription for painkillers, which he filled, but would use sparingly, since he knew they mixed very poorly with alcohol. Then she dropped him at his apartment so he could change clothes and shower, while she went home and did the same. Then she picked him up again and they went to the office.

The new sign was up and it wasn't horrible. Not too big or ostentatious, simply adorned with gold edging, easily seen from either end of the street, and not blocking his sign. It said BOLTON MASSAGE THERAPY in dark red letters. *It might work out fine,* he thought as they drove in and parked. The rent being paid would make each month marginally easier and that was a good thing.

He got upstairs, started the coffee and went to work on his eye with the cover-up Paula had lent him. His touch was clumsy, but he got it looking slightly better. He laughed a little to himself while he did it. *A real homosexual would be good at this. Why can't you be a better stereotype like the other fags, Clarence?* Eventually, he decided it looked presentable. A run in with a drunken door, maybe. Not a bar brawl. The coffee tasted great and the first office smoke was a perfect companion, almost a meal by themselves.

He'd tried to quit cigarettes only once, about ten years earlier. The Surgeon general's report came out, labeling tobacco as a serial killer, and he'd taken notice. He went eight consecutive days without one, and the agony was not only palpable, but it increased every day. The only times he wasn't aching for a smoke were when eating or sleeping. He blew a case, a simple goddamn easy little case, because he was so wired up about it that he missed something he normally would have pounced on, and the client went away for three years when he should have been acquitted. On the eighth day, he had nine small meals at a diner near his office, and decided that was enough. The non-smoking experiment came to an end. Yes it would no doubt shorten his life, but he determined it was worth it and everyone else should just mind their own damn business. Benny sometimes tried to bring it up, but not too often. He knew it was about happiness. Clarence was generally unhappy, but when he'd quit, he was depressed all the time. Now he was back to being generally unhappy, which was so normal for him it occasionally felt just like happiness.

But enough with the morning blues, he thought. Things to do. He called Paula in, but she had gone to her car to retrieve something. Then the phone rang. It was Kiwi.

"Clarence, are your eyes all right?" she asked.

"I have one that's black and blue from a punch I got last night."

"That's all?"

"That's all."

"Good. I saw you in a dream and you were blind." She said it like you'd tell someone what time it was. It was unnerving.

"I'm all right, Kiwi. It's just a bruise."

"I'm glad. Come and see me."

"I will. I promise." He hung up, and lit a second smoke. Fourth of the day. Actually the eighth or ninth, but he rationalized. *I was up early.* He looked at his book, and just as Paula had promised, it was a free day. *Good.* She walked in with her notebook.

He doodled around the desk, looking for anything that might catch his interest. He wondered who'd killed Elliot. It could have been Frank Walsh, but he doubted that. They were friends. And he wouldn't kill someone he trusted just because he gave the car away. He also doubted that Frank would have the resources to have him followed or send people to surveil his parking lot and garage. He hoped Elliot's death was quick enough that he didn't have time to get frightened. And did the police recover the diamonds? Hard to say. The only real fence currently operating in town was Cosmo Montini, who ran a small hot goods business from the back of his vacuum cleaner store. Clarence had unsuccessfully defended his competition a couple of years back, and that guy was doing ten years in Jackson. Bob Flacco was Cosmo's attorney.

He got the envelope full of odd documents out of his briefcase and looked at them again. The surveyor's report was the most interesting thing. He was reading it a third time, the words starting to blur into each other, when Paula came in. She was surprised to see him.

"Jesus," she said. "I thought you said you knew how to use cover-up."

"Does it look that bad?"

"You look like someone who was frightened to death, but only on one side of his body."

They both laughed. She got her makeup kit out of her purse, a formidable valise with many compartments, went to the bathroom and got a damp washcloth, came back and went to work on him. She cleaned off what he'd attempted, making him wince in pain only once, then put a thick coat of cover-up at the center of the bruise, blending it out in a soft circle with the tips of her fingers. Then she did the same with a much lighter coat on his other eye. When he complained that his other eye wasn't bruised, she said they should match, it would look better. He felt helpless, but her face and hands in the tiny space that he could see clearly were oddly comforting, so he let it go. Then she got out a powder and a brush and applied a light dusting to each eye to set the cover-up. She stepped back to survey the work critically and decided one side needed just a little more, so she bent in again and fixed it. Then she kissed him.

It was one of those kisses that happen without either person thinking too much about them beforehand. Like a match strike, something flames up and then is quickly shaken out again. He did return the kiss very briefly, and it wasn't unpleasant. Her eyes met his and both of them were trying to think of the appropriate thing to say when they heard a voice in the doorway.

"Mr. Keaton?"

It was Kimberly Bolton, just dropping in. She stood there in his office doorway with a little smile as though she now knew something she shouldn't. Paula backed up quickly, but naturally, and nodded to each of them as she left. Clarence coughed and lit a post-makeup-kiss smoke and gestured to Ms. Bolton that she should take a chair, which she did.

"Miss Bolton. I trust all is in order downstairs?"

"Yes, Mr. Keaton, thank you. We will open tomorrow on schedule. We've had ads in the paper and on local TV for a few days. It's very exciting."

"It is," he replied, knowing neither of them thought it was that exciting. It was just something you were supposed to say. "I saw the sign today, and it looks very good."

"Thank you," she said. "I hope the proportions are correct."

"They are. Thank you."

"You know, you could advertise. It does wonders for a business."

"No, I'm afraid not."

"Lawyers are forbidden to advertise?"

"No, we're not. I just think it's unseemly. It's huckster-ish, which I don't think I want to be."

She nodded, opened her purse and took out a check, handing it across to him.

"First and last month's rent, Mr. Keaton."

"Thank you. Much appreciated."

"You should also know that I have engaged a weekly cleaning ser-vice. Dominion Maintenance. They'll do our towels and linens, etcet-era. The truck will be in the parking lot by the back door for a couple of hours each Monday morning, if that's all right?"

"Of course. Not a problem." He knew there were going to be prob-lems, but so far she had circumvented every one he could imagine.

"Excellent. Very nice to be doing business with you, Mr. Keaton." She rose to shake his hand, he thought, but instead handed him a pamphlet, which upon perusal, turned out to be a coupon for a five massage treatment at a large discount. He smiled.

"Thanks you so much, Miss Bolton. I'll treasure this."

She laughed.

"Good day, Mr. Keaton." She left and went down the stairs. Paula came back in.

"Listen, boss…" He stopped her with a raised hand.

"Slim, you know I like you, right?"

"I have always assumed it, yes," she replied.

"I hired you, and I give you raises…"

"If I bug the shit out of you."

"Yes, but we work together, and I *love* that, you know? I love that you understand what I need every day and I don't have to tell you what to do because you goddamn well know your job."

"Thanks, boss. What's the other shoe going to sound like?"

"The fact that we're attracted to each other is certainly nice, but if we were to act on it, it could and probably would ruin the great thing we have going on as boss and employee. I need you here helping me and I won't jeopardize that for some fleeting pleasure, okay?"

He looked at her as kindly as he knew how, praying she would take it in the spirit and understand. She smiled.

"So it's not because I'm black?"

"No, of course not." He was relieved, since that was at least a rea-sonable direction for her to think, and he didn't want her thinking in any other direction, but he still had to be honest. Her being black had nothing to do with it. If he was heterosexual, it might. She smiled again and nodded and went to the door. Then she stopped and turned back to him.

"Fleeting?" she said. "That was all. Fleeting?"

"All glory is fleeting, Slim. Miss Bolton came in before I could properly digest the extent of the glory, the pleasure. Let's put it that way."

"Boss, I appreciate working for you, too. And just so you know, if you ever need anything outside my normal stuff, you only have to ask me, okay?"

"Okay, thanks. I appreciate it." She went back to her desk and he sat down. He did like her. She was the best employee he'd ever had. They had something like a marriage now – a sexless one, yes, but a partnership nonetheless. Sometimes he wondered why the Lord or whoever made those decisions had decided he should be homosexual. It came with so much stress. He remembered a priest in high school who told him, seriously, that God would never put any burden upon a man that He felt the man couldn't handle. *Really, Father? Then He must think I'm the strongest man on earth.* It was stress compounded on stress the way a loan shark compounded the vig. You simply couldn't tell anyone you didn't completely trust, and you soon learned that meant everybody. So you lived inwardly one way and outwardly another, in two different realities, with no real friends, or damn few, because your desires were slightly different from the majority of people and that fact utterly horrified 98 percent of them.

He shook himself out of his self-pitying reverie and looked at the papers strewn across his desk again. *Who killed Elliot?* Paula buzzed him.

"Yes?"

"Louise Merwin is here."

"Send her right in."

Louise didn't look too bad for someone who'd been up most of the night. Better than he did, anyway, although she hadn't taken a good shot to the eye.

She walked in and sat in one of the chairs, pulling it up to his desk as though she didn't want them to be overheard.

"Louise, everything okay?"

"I could ask you the same thing. Sorry about last night. Mike got the bit in his teeth and wouldn't let the goddamn thing go, even though he knew it couldn't have been you."

"When will I get my car back?"

"Today, maybe. We have to check for blood traces."

"Blood traces? You said he was shot in the head. If it happened in my car there'd be more than traces. There'd be giant stains, sticky blood residue and brain matter everywhere. Who are you kidding?"

"Clarence, relax..." she said.

"Relax? My client was murdered. You have the balls to accuse me of doing it, plus I get punched in the face by Mike Ross, Elder's finest. Are you even looking for who really did this?"

"You deliberately provoked Mike into hitting you to stop the interrogation."

"Is that what I did?"

"And I have to say, it was a ballsy thing to do. I admired you for it."

"I want my car back."

"Are you going to sue the department?"

"Why do you care?"

"He's my partner. He has my back when I go through doors. And if you sue, I'm going to have to fill out so many fucking forms. It'll take days."

"Well, I might not sue, but then you'd really owe me."

"Even after I saved your car last night?"

"What car?"

"The Studebaker, in the shed. The patrol guys caught three asshole breaking in and arrested them."

"Shit, I totally forgot. Who were they?"

"Two petty guys from Lansing and, get this, Jamie Highfield."

"*What?*" Clarence caught himself. "Wow."

"You want to tell me what this is all about, Clarence?"

"Not right this second. Maybe later. Who do you think killed Elliot?"

"We don't know. But it was pretty clean."

"Professional?"

"Maybe. One shot through the temple."

"Scorches on the wound?" Clarence had studied a lot of wounds and knew they often yielded surprising evidentiary secrets.

"Yes…" she said it reluctantly.

"So whoever it was must have gotten quite close to him. Was he tied up?"

"Nope. No ligature marks."

"So it might not have been a pro."

"Possible," she said. "And I have another question."

"Shoot," he said.

"Why don't you want to fuck me?"

It hung in the stale air of her car as he waited for the right words to come to him. He got out his cigarettes and put one in his mouth as a stall. When he lit it, it occurred to him what he could say in reply.

"Louise, goddammit, we have a professional relationship. Plus I can't fuck anyone when I'm scared her ex might come bursting in and blow my head off at a crucial moment."

"I have a shotgun now. He comes in, I'll take him off at the neck."

"I hate loud noises during sex." They both laughed and the moment passed. There had been several between them. He wished her husband would go away and she'd find someone to fuck and get off his ass about it. She stood up.

"I'm going down to Albert's to get a coffee. You want to ride with me?"

Albert's Rolling Lunch, best coffee in town, probably, always visited the courthouse just before ten, so the cops and the lawyers could top up their caffeine tanks. Clarence nodded.

"Sounds good."

He told Paula to leave any messages at the golf club bar, and headed out.

They were in line to get their coffees in less than fifteen minutes, Clarence paying.

"Louise, if you find out anything about who did Elliot, could you please let me know?"

"What if we find out you did it?"

"I didn't. And, in that case, you would let me know in a different way. And I need my car back ASAP."

"All right, but there's a price for both those favors."

"What?"

"Don't sue us. Don't sue Mike."

Clarence thought it over for about three seconds and decided it was a fair trade.

"I won't sue you guys."

"Your word?"

"Yes."

"All right. I'll call you when we figure it out and try and get the car back to you as quick as I can. Later today or tomorrow."

"That's fine."

"Okay, I have to go to work now," Louise said, and gestured toward the lot. "And I see Mike coming, so you should probably get lost."

Clarence nodded and headed the other way, toward the smoker's alley. When he got there he realized he had no car and no ride back to the office. The club, however, was a short walk away and the bar was open. So he walked there and called Paula from the payphone in the back.

"Hey, I'm at the club. I'm going to have lunch."

"Lunch? It's only ten thirty."

"An early lunch. Call me here if anything happens."

"Got it."

Simon Roche was at his table, with a coffee and a Danish, going over the Racing Form and several other pieces of paper with bets, teams, odds, points, and parleys written all over them.

"You should get a secretary," said Clarence, sitting down across from him.

"I like to keep my overhead low." Simon circled a horse on the page, hesitated, then circled another. "If you had to bet one of two horses, would you go with, Bulwark or Steam Donkey?"

"What are the odds on Steam Donkey?"

"Eight to one, but how the hell can I bet on a horse with Donkey in his name? Who the fuck would give a horse a name like Steam Donkey? What is that?

"It's a winch. A steam powered winch they use in logging. Looks like a little train carrying a silo."

"How do you know these things, man? You've never been near a logging operation in your life."

"I was near a library once and it had books in it. And they let anybody read them. What are the odds on Bulwark?"

"Ten to one. He looked strong early in the season but lost his last three races."

"I think you have to bet Steam Donkey."

"Yeah, but that name is just hard to bet on. You put a hundred on him with me? I'd feel better about it then."

Clarence started to laugh.

"How the hell do you make a living doing this?" he asked.

"I told you, low overhead." And it was true. Simon had no car of his own, paid no rent, had neither girlfriend (at the moment) nor ex-wife, and no children. Clarence reached into his pocket and pulled out his wad, somewhat diminished from the original withdrawal, but still substantial enough. He counted out five twenties and handed them to Simon.

"Steam Donkey," he said. "On the nose."

"Great!" Simon got up. "I'll call my guy and get it down." The waitress came over with a message from Paula. *Crocker called from Marquette*, and the number. Oh, well, so a good day would be spoiled. He waited until Simon came back, got some change from the bartender, and called Mill Creek. Crocker seemed glad he'd called and there wasn't any somber, *your-father-died-I'm-afraid* tone, which was encouraging.

"Mr. Keaton," he said, "your father has rallied a bit in the last couple of days."

"I'm glad to hear it, Mr. Crocker. Thank you for informing me."

"And the doctor now thinks he may live another one to three weeks."

"I will be unable to get up to see him for at least a day or two, I'm afraid, Mr. Crocker."

"I understand, Mr. Keaton, of course. It's just that the month is about to turn and…" It was September 30th. *Of course, the check.* Crocker felt that he needed to get his monthly rent in case Jay Keaton defied all expectations and lived another three weeks. Clarence put on his *That's not unusual* face so his voice would not betray him.

"Of course, Mr. Crocker. I'll send a bank transfer from here today."

"Thank you so much, Mr. Keaton. We pray for your father, of course." And he hung up. *You could also pray for your own black soul, you bastard*, Clarence thought as he cradled the receiver. He called Paula and told her to send the money. Back to the table, the waitress had brought him coffee. Clarence drank a bit of it and then looked out the window towards the eighteenth green and saw Eddie Two Crows standing by the large bunker that the regulars called Death Trap. The strangeness of seeing Eddie at the Golf Club propelled Clarence to his feet and swiftly out the door. Simon got back to the table prepared to tell some stories about getting the bet down that would make them all rich and found it empty of his erstwhile lunch companion. Clarence fast-walked up the little hill to the parking lot and Eddie nodded to him and they repaired to Eddie's truck.

"Paula said you'd be here," said Eddie.

"Why didn't you come in?" Clarence asked.

"I'm not a member. And they built this club on an Odawa burial ground."

"They did?"

"Yeah, about eighty years ago. So we're not supposed to set foot on the earth here. The parking lot is as far as I can go. But I needed to see you."

"I could have come to the office."

"Paula said you didn't have a car."

"Well, that's true. The cops confiscated my car."

"What for?" They got into Eddie's truck.

"They think I might have killed someone."

Eddie started laughing as he started the engine.

"Is it that funny?" Clarence asked.

"Yep. It's that funny."

"Can you drive me back to the office?"

"No," Eddie replied. "We have to go to my house."

"Why?"

"Trouble. We'll talk there." They drove in silence, Eddie constantly checking the rear and side-view mirrors, convincing himself no one was bird-dogging them. Finally, as they got within a mile or so of the rez, Clarence asked him.

"What's the trouble?"

Eddie glanced at him as though he'd broken protocol.

"It's Jimmy."

"Jimmy the pothead?" Eddie laughed at that.

"Yeah."

"Another possession arrest?"

"No. He hasn't been arrested. He saw something."

"A murder."

"How the hell do you know that?"

"At the marsh. He was getting high there and a car drove up so he hid, right?"

"He figured they were cops."

"But they weren't."

"No, two guys. And…"

"And one killed the other with a single shot to the head. Did the guy see Jimmy?"

"Are you a spirit, Clarence? How do you know what happened?"

"The cops arrested me for the killing last night."

Eddie looked at him again and they both started laughing like hell.

They arrived at Eddie's house and went inside. Kiwi welcomed them with coffee and sandwiches. They sat at the kitchen table.

"Where's Jimmy?" Eddie asked his wife.

"In the other bedroom," she replied. Eddie went to get him and Kiwi turned to Clarence.

"Are you all right?"

"Sure," he said. "Everything's fine." She gave him a look that unmistakably said *Don't bullshit me*, and then Eddie came in with Jimmy and they all sat down. Clarence had taken a bite of his sandwich but then decided a smoke would calm him, so he lit up. He was tingling all over, knowing he was about to discover something important. Other than being in the courtroom, the only thing he really enjoyed about the job was this part, the finding out.

"Can I have a smoke, Mr. Keaton?" Jimmy asked.

"Sure, Jimmy," said Clarence, tossing the pack of Camels across the table. Jimmy fished one and lit it, the first drag's strength surprising him. He coughed.

"Okay, Jimmy, tell me what happened at the marsh."

"Okay…well, I was there yesterday smoking a jay…"

"What time was that?"

"About two thirty, I guess."

"School let out early?"

Jimmy gave him a sheepish look and nodded.

"Okay," said Clarence. "Just tell me what you saw."

"I heard a car coming. And then another. Two cars, I figured it was cops, so I went down a bit into the weeds and behind a little scrub tree. Two cars pull up and one of them…"

"What kind of cars? Can you describe them?"

"A green Chevy. And a blue Pontiac, I think. Five or six years old, each of them."

"You see the plates?"

"Both Michigan, I think."

"Not sure?"

"Pretty sure. Anyway, one guy driving the Chevy, and two guys in the other. The passenger gets out of the Pontiac , and the Chevy guy meets him. And they hug."

"Hug? They embraced?"

"Yeah. And then they talked a bit, but I couldn't really hear what they were saying."

"Right. What'd they look like, Jimmy? Describe them."

"One guy was shorter, about sixty, kind of skinny. The other guy wasn't as old and he was taller and had long sideburns and was balding on top."

Clarence nodded. The kid was a keen observer.

"What about the driver of the Pontiac? What'd he look like?"

"He never got out. Younger though, blondish kinda hair."

"Okay, what did the two guys who got out do?"

"So they talked and then it got a little weird, like they were arguing. The taller guy got really mad about something, and then the little guy put his hands up like, you know, I'm done, and got back in his car."

"Which car was his?"

"The Chevy. And when he started the car, the taller guy started calling to him, like "All right, all right," and walked over to the car with his hands up like it was okay, right? The other guy rolled down the window and as soon as he did, the tall guy whipped out a gun and shot him. Man, it was loud. Then he turned the car off, took the keys and opened the trunk and looked through it, for a while, then he started swearing and slammed it."

"He didn't see you?"

"No, pretty sure he didn't."

"What happened then?"

"He opened the door of the Chevy and pulled the dead guy out, left him on the ground there. Then he went back to the Pontiac and talked to the driver a bit, and he left. Then he got back into the Chevy and left."

"Shit," said Clarence. Then he pulled out his wallet, a large pigskin billfold he'd had since he was seventeen, reached in and extracted a small photo from one of the secret compartments. It was a photo of him and Rosalie at their wedding, with the best man and maid of honor flanking them. He showed it to Jimmy, who, after a moment, gasped.

"Shit, that's him. He's a lot older now, but that's the guy. You know him?"

"I used to," said Clarence, replacing the photo and feeling Kiwi behind him. He turned and she was offering him a drink, which he gratefully accepted.

"Okay, Jimmy, here's what we're going to do," he said. "You're going to tell no one about this. And when I say no one, I mean *no one at all.* Do you understand me?"

"Yes, sir."

"And that's not going to be easy, you know. Your friends and you will be hanging out, and they'll have stories about shit they saw or did, and you'll just be dying to tell them your cool story about the guy getting murdered, but you have to stop yourself from doing it. You have to, understand?"

"Yes, Mr. Keaton. I know."

"Do you know why?" Jimmy thought about it for a moment.

"Because if I tell anyone someone might come and kill me?"

"Exactly right, Jimmy. Dead on. As soon as you tell anyone besides us, it starts the process of someone coming to kill you, and maybe your friends or your family, too. Got it?"

"Got it."

"And please stop smoking dope around the marsh, will you?"

"Where, then?" Jimmy asked.

"Here," said Kiwi. Eddie and Jimmy looked at her as though they'd forgotten she was even in the room.

"Here?" said Eddie, more than a little surprised. She'd never let him smoke pot in the house.

"Yes, Jimmy," she said firmly, "You want to get high, you come here, okay?"

"All right, thanks."

"Now, Jimmy, there's something else," said Clarence.

"What?"

"The cops might come looking for you. They probably won't, but it's possible. If they do, you don't run. You go with them. They ask you questions, what do you say?"

148

"Oh, I know this," said Jimmy, almost smiling. "What you said last time." He was straining to recall it, the thoughts creasing his cheeks with effort.

"I have nothing to say, and I would like to see my lawyer, please."

"Right. I ain't gonna say anything and I want a lawyer. I got it."

"That means in the station, in the interrogation room, and most important, Jimmy, in the cop car, too. They're going to try and get you to talk to them, and in the car it'll seem like they just want to chat, shoot the shit, nothing going on. But no matter *what*, you say one or both of those things and that's it until I get there. No exceptions. Okay?"

"Okay, Mr. Keaton."

"Eddie, take him home," Kiwi said. Eddie got up and headed to the door.

"Come on, Jimmy." Kiwi started putting dishes in the sink and Clarence lit another smoke. *So Frank Walsh has no problem killing a friend,* he was thinking, *which means I'm in trouble.* He felt Kiwi behind him, her hand was on his shoulder. He turned his chair and faced her.

"Was that a photo of your wedding?" she asked.

"Yes, it was."

"How long ago was that?"

"20 years, give or take."

"Why would you get married, Clarence?"

"What?" The question was so simple and honest it flustered the hell out of him. "What do you mean, Kiwi?"

"You're homosexual, Clarence. Why would you get married?"

He stared at her, his mouth opening and trying to force words out, but failing. Finally his voice returned.

"How do you know that? How *would* you know that?"

"You're part of the earth, Clarence. I'm part of the earth. The earth knows who we are. It's obvious to anyone who looks right at you."

Again Clarence could find no language or single words that would explain his state of mind. He had feared this moment for most of his life, and all seventeen years in Elder the fear had been a mortal one. And yet, here it was, someone knew.

"I guess no one ever looks right at me," he said at last. She nodded.

"I've seen you in town and you hold yourself differently. Maybe that's why they don't see it."

"Does Eddie know?" the question came choking out of him like a small sob, which he checked, though not as fully as he'd hoped.

"Of course not," she said. "Eddie doesn't see those things." Clarence nodded, a little relieved without knowing why, and then he started to cry. An instant high tide of sobs and tears came sluicing out of him, over the sandbags he'd put in place and held for so long. He put his head on the table and the tears poured out, down his arm, snuffing out the cigarette in the ashtray with a hiss. Kiwi bent slightly and put her arms around him and held him while he sobbed, without saying or doing anything to suggest he stop. She rocked him a little as the relief-torrent began to subside, and when he was finished, she got him a towel and a bowl of cold water to wash his face with. He put his face in the bowl, actually enjoying the shock of the cold water. After he toweled off and turned back to her, she gasped.

"Where did you get that black eye?"

"Oh, last night. Some cop thought I was being an asshole."

"Were you?"

"Absolutely," he said, and they both laughed. "I should get going." He didn't tell her not to tell anyone he was gay. He knew instinctively she never would.

"Eddie wanted to ask you about something," she said.

"What?"

"He and some of the other Elders are going to the council meeting tomorrow night

"The Tribal Council?"

"No, the city council. Eddie wondered if you could come as well and sort of represent them."

"Is this about Bayne Oil?"

"I don't think so. Eddie said it's some developer who wants to build houses for white people along the marsh with a lake view. They offered us a price but the Council turned it down."

"The Tribal Council."

"Right. They're trying to get it declared Eminent domain or some such thing. Whatever that means."

"Eminent domain is a license to steal land from Indians, more or less."

"But this has been Indian land forever, since before the white people even considered coming over the ocean."

"So was the golf course," said Clarence. Kiwi nodded.

"Be careful, Clarence. There are strange ghosts around you."

"I know," he said. "But most of them have always been there."

He walked out of her house, fully prepared to head back to the office and get to work, realizing only moments after Kiwi shut the door behind him that he had no car and was stranded until Eddie returned. He watched the clouds roll over Lake Huron as the afternoon got a little dark. The view was beautiful and would be even more beautiful over by the marsh. No wonder kids liked to smoke pot there. He lit a smoke – what was this, the twentieth today? – and waited for Eddie to come and drive him back.

He got back a little after three, and Paula was full of news.

"Your car was returned a little while ago, and there's a guy here to see you."

"Name?" He looked at his watch, annoyed. He wanted to go to the club and relax. It had been a long day and he just wanted to think about nothing until he had to think about something again.

"Andrew Berger. I think it's a real estate thing."

"Okay. Send him in." *Shit.* A real estate deal meant real money, in that he got paid immediately for those jobs. One of the drawbacks of criminal and corporate work was the constant slow-walking of his payments. Having to call people and send them letters asking for the money you *earned* was such a pain in the ass, not to mention degrading. But real estate paid pretty well and fast, so they were always welcome.

Berger came in, a little shy since he'd waited to hire an attorney until it was almost too late on this particular deal, but they spent an hour going over it and got everything on the square by a little after five. Berger signed the standard contract, wrote a check for the small retainer, and went away happy. Paula came in one last time.

"I'm heading home early again, since I got up so early."

"Of course," he looked up. "Could you redo my eye thing?"

"Sure." She got out the necessaries and did a repaint. "You going to the club?"

"Thinking about it."

"Go easy tonight. Get a good sleep. We have people tomorrow."

"Right. Thanks for all the help today. I'd give you a raise if I hadn't already done that."

"Yeah, sure." But she smiled.

The bar was full of the early evening drinkers and Simon was holding court at his table. There was a seat open and Clarence took it. Simon beamed as he sat down and poured him a glass of draft from the pitcher on the table, then pressed something into his hand. A wad of cash.

"Eight hundred, cash money, counselor. Steam Donkey came through like a gladiator. Won by three! You had the touch today, kid." It was the exact amount of the transfer he'd sent to the home in Marquette. Maybe it was a lucky day, a serendipitous one. He knew a lot more about what was going on, but not enough yet. His client was dead and the guy who killed him was going to be turning up sooner or later. *Maybe he's laying low till the murder thing blows over.* But he knew that hopeful thought was bullshit. The cops were looking for Frank but he was probably smart enough not to be using his own name. A man with a prison record like his had to make allowances to get work. Lots of people he felt responsible for were in danger, which was comforting in a kinky way, since it took his mind off his own danger.

About an hour later, when a third glass of beer came around, he took a sip and got up, saying he had to go to the bathroom. But he walked past it and straight to the parking lot, checking all around the car and his rearview before starting home. Nothing attracted his interest. Simon and the Steam Donkey revelers wouldn't even notice he was gone for at least half an hour. He got in The Merc and drove it home, seeing nothing suspicious at all. But he wasn't satisfied, so he went up to his place, found some twine, three empty beer bottles and three full ones. He tied the clinking lot together and took them downstairs. No one was about and it was full dark when he unlocked the Merc, put the bottles on the driver's seat, and tied the other end of the twine tightly to the inside door handle. If somebody got that door open, the bottles would come tumbling out and it would be heard, which was the point. He went back upstairs, lit a last smoke, took four big drags, put it out and laid down on his bed. His last thought before he fell asleep was that even the easy days were getting hard lately.

WEDNESDAY

For a smoker, waking up in the morning was the best and worst of times. Five to eight hours since you'd had any nicotine so you would come to with your skin just crawling for it. Your lungs, lying somewhat dormant for those hours, would need to be cough-started like a recalcitrant car. And that had to be first, while you were still dying for a smoke. Maybe some water and a nice long spit, since chronic dry-mouth was another fact of life. But most smokers – the dedicated ones, like Clarence – had the hacking and mouth-splashing down to only a few seconds, leading to the blissful part of waking up: the first drag of the first smoke of the day. Wednesday's gave full satisfaction.

Shorty knocked on his door at seven and offered him coffee down-stairs, which was a surprise, but it turned out he'd forgotten to pay his rent, which he immediately did from the wad of cash Simon gave him. She was impressed.

"You defending stickup men again, Clarence?"

"No, Shorty, just a bit of luck with a horse."

What the hell happened to your eye?" she asked.

"I walked into a door," he said.

"A door shaped like a fist?"

"Similar, I guess." He smiled and took a large sip of coffee and got up to leave.

"Hold on," she said, "I'll get you a receipt." He was about to protest that it wasn't necessary but stopped himself in time. Shorty had been audited by the IRS a couple of years earlier, and they'd read her the riot act about keeping canceled cheques and giving receipts to whomever might be renting rooms in her house, which they called her 'establishment'. It enraged Clarence, but he didn't say or do anything, lest it might put *him* on their radar. He'd commuted to Lansing each night for the three days – *three goddamn days* – it took to audit a 72 year old widow. She brought him the receipt and he headed for the door.

"Hey," she said, "What's our movie gonna be on Sunday?"

"What's playing at the Odeon?"

"The Redford one. Three Days Of The Condor. It sounds like a documentary on bird ecology."

"I think I read it was a thriller," Clarence said. "I'll knock on your door at 3:30."

"Don't forget, like you forgot the rent."

"I didn't. I won't. Put that money in the bank. Don't leave it lying around."

"I look like an idiot to you?" She was in her housecoat and wearing a hairnet, so he wasn't totally sure how to respond. He went upstairs and put on his favorite suit, thinking *if I get killed today at least I'll look good*. At the car door by seven-forty, he had a moment of unease he couldn't place, and then he jerked the door open and the six beer bottles came clinking out, one full one breaking against the window knob and spraying his suit pants, socks and shoes with beer. He looked at it with the pure exasperation of being privately stupid, and thought *well, at least I know it works*.

He got to the office in the usual six or seven minutes and found his secretary already at her desk.

"You smell like beer," she said.

"Yeah, well, that can't be helped."

"You're that stressed?"

"No, I'm that stupid." And he told her the story of his clever trap that he ultimately fell into himself. She laughed a little, and shook her head in that rueful way women did when there was nothing they could do about how impossibly stupid their men were.

"I'm sure it will wear off soon. And you're open this afternoon."

"That's nice."

"Want to go to a movie?." He knew she was kidding.

"I was thinking more of having a long nap."

"I think that's an excellent idea."

Clarence nodded, appreciating her kindness. He was stressed. It was a good month and a bad week. Lots of money he wouldn't be able to spend if he got killed or wouldn't be enough if he was found out. He looked out the window as he sat in his perfect chair. What would he do if it came out – if *he* came out? Where would he go? Lansing? Live with Benny? As it occurred to him, he realized it might not be the worst thing. Paula interrupted his reverie, as she had a tendency to do. Another reason she was so valuable.

"Angie Ferrera is coming at nine. There's a motion on the Robb lawsuit at eleven and one on the Sanger case at eleven thirty. I have the paperwork ready. After that, only whatever walk-ins who think they'll get a massage."

"You know," said Clarence, "we might get a bump in business if Ms. Bolton's place brings in a lot of people. Our sign will be noticed and when they get in trouble, they might think 'Hey, what about that guy over the massage joint?' or words to that effect."

"Sounds dreamy," she said. They both heard someone coming up the stairs. It was Detective Merwin, who put her head in view.

"Come in, Louise – Detective." She noticed his eye, since the coverup had rubbed off on his pillow during the night. It was now turning a sort of purplish plum as it healed.

"Jesus, Clarence, Mike really clocked you one, didn't he?"

"All in a day's work. Thanks so much for getting me the car so quickly.

"My pleasure. And you're cleared on the Elliot murder."

"You can imagine my relief," he said, lighting a cigarette. "Are you okay, Louise?" She looked a little rough.

"Oh, Greg came over last night. Pounded on the door, screamed at me. The usual shit."

"What'd you do?"

"I wasn't there, the neighbors told me."

"Louise, I'll say it again. He belongs in jail."

"Lots of people do, but I'm not going to have every other cop on the force think I'm a weakling."

"A weakling who worked her ass off to make detective."

"Damn right," said Louise, twirling and shaking her ass at him.

"I stand corrected," said Clarence, knowing this flirting was just a bad idea, but she was cute, even if women weren't his thing.

Paula, pouring coffee, saw the exchange through the door and noted it. She thought it was a little weird that Clarence had never come on to her, even though she'd really tried to show him that door was open, and now she saw another woman flashing *her* sign at him. But it ended quickly and Detective Merwin thanked him and left the office. For the first time, a thought struck Paula about her boss. A thought so ludicrous she dismissed it immediately into the 'That Can't Be True' section of her brain. She got his coffee ready and he was already at his desk smoking when she brought it in.

"Is Mrs. Ferrera here yet?" he asked.

"Not yet. Expected very soon."

"Slim, I hate to say this, but your raise, as it turns out, brings on some new responsibilities."

"You want me to do your makeup before she gets here?"

"Yes. Until this thing heals, that's one of your new duties."

"What will you do on Saturday mornings?"

"I guess I'll have to hire a temp." She went back to her desk, got her purse, came back and sat on his desk and did his eye. He was careful to keep their bodies apart for it, and he tried to stay very still so she could do it properly. Just as she was finishing, they heard someone coming up the stairs. Paula packed the makeup kit away and was gone to greet the visitor, who turned out to be Angie Ferrera. While he waited, Clarence checked his book. October wasn't looking very good. September has been excellent. Expenses plus plus. He tried to remember the last time he had two really good months in a row. He stood as Mrs. Ferrera entered. She was carrying a file folder full of papers and had clearly been weeping some this morning.

"Please come in, Mrs. Ferrera," he said, guiding her to one of the two client chairs, a brown leather wingback with nail-head accents in French style. He'd purchased both of them in his first year as a lawyer. Another Ben Yawkey bromide had prompted it. *Son, spend a little money on two nice chairs for the clients and a nice one for yourself. They'll appreciate it and so will you.* He'd gone out and spent a large chunk of his savings on the two wingbacks, still fine chairs after almost twenty years, reupholstered only once, and for himself, a Dunbar Wormley. It cost $500 in 1956, a ridiculous sum, but he'd never regretted spending it. It had tufted ebony leather on a dark walnut base, and was as pleasurable to sit in today as it was the first time, if not better, since over 19 years the leather had tufted itself to the exact contours of his lower torso.

"May I offer you a cup of coffee?" he asked. She shook her head.

"No thank you, Mr. Keaton." Then she started to cry again. Clarence got the box of tissues and placed them on the arm of her chair. He let her cry, which was always his policy unless severely pressed for time. She found her emotional footing after a few moments and handed him the file folder. He opened it and saw a bunch of copied files, which horrified him.

"Are these files from Bayne Petroleum, Mrs. Dalton?"

"Yes," she nodded. "You told me to copy them and bring them to you."

"No, ma'am," he said flatly, closing the file and handing it back to her. "I most certainly did not tell you to do that. No."

"What?" She seemed confused. "You told me to…"

"I told you to *write down* every way you thought your employer might be breaking the law, and then bring me that list. I *did not* tell you to copy or remove private documents, under any circumstances!" He raised his voice just a little at the end, because he was angry, and also because he realized she might be wired up. She had stopped crying now, and was looking at him with an expression that might have been trepidation.

"I'm sorry, Mr. Keaton. I thought you wanted copies of the files."

He was torn, because something smelled weird about this, and yet it was also typical of how many clients acted. You gave them advice; they ignored it, did what they wanted, and then blamed you when it turned out you, the person they were *paying* for advice, were right. And you couldn't get really angry, since they were paying you, though why you'd pay anyone for advice you were going to ignore was beyond Clarence's intelligence to conceive. He wondered if doctors had the same problem. She was starting to cry again, but she had huffed and puffed a bit beforehand so he suspected she'd been warming up to achieve more tears, and that made his decision for him. He stood up.

"Mrs. Ferrera, I'm afraid I can't represent you anymore."

"But I only did what you told me, Mr. Keaton."

"No, Angie," using her first name was a rebuke, even though she wouldn't know that. "You did exactly what I told you not to do. So we're done."

"But you promised Tony you'd help me." She sounded like a child now.

"I will recommend another lawyer in town and pay the first retainer, if you'd like."

"But I want you!"

Now he knew for sure he was being set up. He led her to the door and out into the corridor.

"Forgive me, Mrs. Ferrera. Goodbye. Feel free to get a massage downstairs." He shut his door in her face. He heard Paula usher her out and he went to his window to watch her leave. From the side, so he wouldn't be seen watching, he saw a car across the street in the Library lot, off by itself. There was a man behind the wheel, but he couldn't make him out. But his erstwhile client helped him, because she went straight to that car and the man got out to greet her. And it was Frank Walsh. He watched them talk for a moment, then get in and drive away. He was congratulating himself when Paula came in and noticed something on the wingback chair.

"She left her file folder." *Oh, shit.* The stricken look on his face frightened her, but he recovered and knew what had to be done. He pointed to the folder.

"Okay, I need you to take that, go down the back stairs, drive to the post office and go in the back way. You know what room Ellie's in, right?"

"Of course."

"Okay, knock on that door, tell her I sent you, hand her that and say I owe her one." She went over and picked it up.

"What's in it?" she asked.

"I'll be goddamned if I know. But they're stolen and they can't stay here even another minute. Do you have a large purse or a bag you can carry them in?"

"You bet. It's big purse Wednesday."

Clarence laughed, in spite of how freaked out he was.

"Go. Now. Tell Ellie it's top priority."

"You got it." She walked out and then came back immediately. "You want it shredded, right?"

"What? Of COURSE!"

"Right. Just making absolutely sure." And she was gone.

Clarence sat in his chair like he was dead weight. *It's not even nine thirty for Christ's sake.* The phone rang and he was so tired he let it ring three times before he picked up. It was Justin Highfield.

"Clarence? Something rather urgent has come up and I need to see you."

"Of course Justin. I have two motions this morning. Can it wait until this afternoon?"

"I guess so. We'll be over at say, 2:30?"

We'll be over? Who was *we*?

"That'll be fine, Justin. See you then." He hoped his voice did not betray him. He hung up, lit a smoke, pulled out the notes for the motions and started going over them. Paula came back after a bit and stuck her head in.

"Ellie said you owe her."

"Of course. A debt to Ellie is a given. You didn't have problems or see anyone who looked odd?"

"Nope." She turned to go back to her desk.

"Wait. Highfield called. Put him in the book for 2:30 today."

"Got it."

"I'm heading out to do these motions," he said, stuffing the papers in his briefcase. A quick look around once he was outside showed no ominous people awaiting, so he got in the Merc and drove to the courthouse; one of his places, the courthouse, the men's bar at the club, the office, and his apartment; each a place where he knew all the ins and outs, all the nuances, the people, where he felt safe. He sometimes included Benny's place in Lansing as one of those, but not always. He could never get over the forbidden nature of those pleasures in that place. Sometimes, on long weekends with Benny, he would see what could be, the other side, visible for a few moments, but he always pulled back. He was a lawyer in a medium sized city disguised as a small town. He knew no other way to make his living. Starting over wasn't possible at 45, either. He prided himself on his reputation for honesty and above-board dealings, even though he wasn't completely sure it was deserved. He liked to think he only lied when it was absolutely necessary, but his judgement of when it might be necessary didn't always dovetail with his conscience. Kiwi knowing and telling him she knew had been revelatory. He wondered how many other people he knew who were that intuitive. Were women more attuned to such things? Paula had kissed him, Louise wanted to sleep with him, without any idea of how disappointing that would be, and Shorty didn't seem to care much about him as long as he paid the rent and took her to the movies on Sunday. So maybe it wasn't *that* obvious. And maybe he could cling to that for the rest of the day.

The usual throng of lawyers, stenographers, bailiffs, judges, reporters and the indicted mingled at the courthouse. Clarence headed for courtroom eight, a tiny justice theater for the Robb motion. Dennis Robb was a general surgeon who was being sued by the family of a man he'd operated on six times. The man had died on the table during the sixth operation. The family were convinced it was blatant malpractice, despite the fact that Dr. Robb had prolonged the man's life by several years with the first five – successful – operations. They had managed to convince a local attorney to file suit and were asking for half a million dollars in damages. Clarence was hoping to get it dismissed out of hand. Even though he knew he was right, and on the right side of this – for a change – he didn't think the motion would be granted. It asked that the grieving family pay his fee, which was standard, but didn't make you many friends. Judge Lang was presiding and he discussed the motion for ten minutes and then ruled against it. The suit would go forward. Dr. Robb would be displeased.

Clarence then had a smoke and went to courtroom four for the Sanger motion, which was requesting that a man recently convicted remain free on bail pending an appeal. An appeal Clarence was mildly confident he could win. The motion was granted, which surprised a lot of people including the defendant.

After which he sailed to the club for a mediocre dry lunch, calling Paula to make sure the time was clear until 2:30. Hanging up the phone and walking down the hallway towards the bar, he saw the Mayor standing at the other end, by the men's locker room door, gesturing to him. He walked over and went into the locker room with Barnet following. It wasn't completely deserted so they walked to the sauna change room, which was. Barnet checked the sauna and the shower room to make sure.

"What have you found out?" he asked.

Found out? I'm your lawyer, George, not your investigator. The photos have been destroyed. It's most likely that Bayne Oil is blackmailing you but other than that eminent domain ordinance tonight, there's no proof."

"How do you know they're going for an eminent domain ordinance?"

"Oh, well I don't, actually. I just assumed that's how they'd do it."

There was a noise from the locker room, and Barnet, skittish at the best of times, jumped up and checked. He returned to the change room and started taking off his clothes.

"Let's go in the sauna," he said. "It'll be safer there."

"Safer how?"

"Who the hell has a sauna in the middle of the day on a Wednesday?"

"George I don't want a goddamn sauna. What do you need me to do?" By now Barnet was almost naked.

"Come on," he said. Clarence remembered that heterosexuals had no idea that something might look gay. Even the dog-collar-and-diaper heteros, apparently. He reluctantly removed his clothes, hung them up and grabbed a towel. He disliked saunas, preferring steam rooms, where there was more anonymity, though he rarely went to gay steam rooms, either. He rarely went anywhere, in point of fact. Benny often bugged him about that. He sat down on the wooden bench, took as deep a breath as he could, and coughed for a solid thirty seconds. Another reason he hated saunas.

"What are my options tonight?" asked the Mayor.

"Your options are to vote the way they want you to and then wait for them to use the photos again the next time they want something, or vote against them and be exposed, plus lose the vote tonight anyway."

"How would I lose the vote if I vote against them?"

"George, you don't rig a vote by blackmailing one person. They've got more people on council who'll do what they want. People who do this sort of thing are prepared for all contingencies."

"So there's nothing I can do?"

"No. There are many things you could do. But I wouldn't."

"Because every other option means I'll be exposed…"

"I'm going to have to be honest with you here. The odds are you'll be exposed anyway, no matter what you do."

"What?" The look on the Mayor's face was one of extreme self-pity, bordering on tears. Clarence continued.

"The vote will go the way they want, and there might be a further vote or two in the next year or so, depending on what they'll need while they're setting up the drilling, zoning and the like, but when that's done they're established, they won't need you anymore. They'll be in a position to pay the money to elect their own Mayor. And then the photos will come out."

Barnet stared at Clarence, digesting it, then sighed deeply and nodded.

"Right. You're right. There's really no other plausible scenario. So, for whatever this is costing me…"

"A bundle, George. I charge an extra two hundred an hour for consultations in rooms over 98 degrees Fahrenheit."

"Of course," Barnet laughed, "Of course you do. I would, too. Okay, what actual choices do I have here? Any?"

"They're all unpleasant, but in my opinion, the best one is to tell your wife." Clarence could hardly believe he was saying it.

"Tell her about the sex…"

"You love her, she loves you, you fucked up that one time; you were drunk, you blacked out, something along those lines. Is she by nature a forgiving person?"

"She is….I guess…I'm not sure her forgiveness has ever been tested to this degree."

"Well it might be better for her to hear it from you, rather than to get a letter in the mail with those photos in it."

"I suppose you're right, Clarence," he said, after a moment or two.

"It doesn't give me any pleasure, George."

"I guess I should probably resign as well."

"The next election is over a year from now. You might hang on until then. Maybe you could hand it over to the deputy mayor. Plead illness or something."

"Manning? That jerk-off as Mayor? No fucking way. They've probably got his ass in their pocket, too."

"Think about it, George. I wouldn't go against them tonight. Let this one go and we'll see what the next move is. Now, if you don't mind, can we get the hell out of this goddamn sauna?"

"You go ahead, Clarence. I like a sauna."

Clarence treated himself to a quick shower before dressing again. His watch informed him there was still ample time for lunch so he had a halfway decent club sandwich and another chat with Simon about how to bet the Lions. The conclusion they came to was that it was safest to never bet on them or against them.

At twenty minutes after one, Clarence realized he could zip back to the office and get in a 45 minute nap before Highfield came in, and that sounded like a good idea, so he said goodbye to Simon and headed to the parking lot. He was a fair distance from the Merc when he saw someone standing by it. A tall man, brush-cut black hair with some gray in it, lean and wiry. As he got closer, the man turned, and it was Frank Walsh. He smiled his conman's smile.

"Hey, brother-in-law," he said.

Clarence had taken a good look on the walk up and there wasn't anybody around. He eyed Frank's hands and was relieved to find them empty. His heart was suddenly beating so fast, realizing the danger before his brain could fully compute it, he was sure it could be seen bursting out of his shirt. He tried to keep his face impassive, knowing he would fail.

"Hey, Francis," he replied, assuming Walsh would still despise his given name. "Something I can do for you?"

"Yeah, motherfucker, there is," said Frank, taking a step forward, bringing him closer but still not in punching range, "You can give me my fuckin' car."

"This is my car, Frank," said Clarence, indicating the Merc.

"You know what I mean, you fuckin' snake. The Starlight. *My* Starlight."

"I didn't know it was yours." Clarence kept his voice steady and widened his stance just a bit so he might have some leverage in case of a sudden frontal assault. A voice in his head reminded him that Frank was no doubt schooled in man-on-man prison fighting, and suggested running might be a good option. But a heavy smoker knows exactly how far they can run, and it's not very far.

"The guy who gave it to you was holding it for me, Keaton."

"I have a pink slip and it was signed over to me, so I doubt you could prove that." He remembered his father telling him to stand up to bullies, saying, *ninety-nine times out of a hundred they'll back down*. His father had neglected to mention the hundredth guy, who beat the living shit out of him. And here was Frank, number 101, who could easily kill him. But even while the voice was screaming *run*, Clarence was finding inner reserves of bravado.

"Here's how this is gonna go, Keaton. First, you hand over the keys and tell me where the car is. Second, you tell me how you fuckin' killed my sister!" As he said it, his hand went behind his hip and came back out with a medium sized blade in it.

"Rosalie died in a car accident, Frank. On 550 on the way to Big Bay." The parking lot wouldn't be deserted forever, and the slower this went, the better chance someone would come and spook Frank into bolting. Or at least, that was the clearest thought Clarence could find in his head. Everything else was the soundless screaming a passenger makes when the driver is going to hit something and there's no avoiding it.

"You killed her!" he shouted. Why was she driving to Big Bay that night anyway, you lying bastard?!"

"I don't know, Frank." *Not true.* "I do know that if you kill me with that knife, you won't get your car back. I can fuckin' guarantee that."

It was as if someone who was stronger and more confident than he was doing his talking for him. He was listening to himself being courageous and not really believing it at the same time.

"What if I just cut you up a little, you lying prick?"

"Hey, that's certainly an idea," he said backing off a couple of small steps. "Is there any other way we could deal with this?"

"I know you had a fight with her. You probably beat her up! She was all bruised up when they found her." *I remember*, Clarence thought.

"That happens in car accidents, Frank. I didn't touch her." *True.*

"She wasn't even 23 years old, you son of a bitch!" And he came at Clarence with an obviously practiced two-short-steps move, the knife flashing in front of him. The first step had alerted Clarence to what was coming, and he managed to execute what he would later call a backwards broad-jump, combined with a mini pole-vault lower body suck-in, trying to avoid the blade. Frank was so sure the first thrust would be decisively crippling that he lost his balance. He turned his head toward Clarence as he fought to regain it, and Clarence saw the lower jaw exposed and close even as his right hand was preparing to strike out. Not even realizing what he was doing, allowing instinct to take over completely, he pivoted slightly and hooked a solid right dead on the point of the exposed jaw. Not the best punch ever, but it was accurate and thrown by a man in control of his balance against a man who wasn't. Frank went splashing down to the gravel, the knife spinning out of his hand. Clarence didn't wait to see what would happen next. He went straight to his car and was out of the parking lot in less than five seconds. He considered running Frank over, but only for a one second fantasy-moment. He had driven two blocks away when he became aware that he could barely breathe and his heart was pumping as though it had been too long confined inside his chest and wanted out. He started to laugh and it caused a coughing fit, which miraculously slowed down his heart. He got to the office without knowing how or what route he took, and dashed upstairs as though wild dogs were behind him. When Paula saw him, her normal reserve was shattered.

"Holy shit, boss. What the fuck happened to you?"

"What?" he managed, between rasps. "What? I'm...fine."

"Yeah, you look good. Did you leave the house with that jacket and shirt?"

He looked down and noticed that his suit jacket was sliced below the buttonholes on the left hand side, as was his shirt front in the same spot. He was bleeding slightly, but the garments seemed to have taken most of the damage.

"Jesus," he said. "I'll have to go home and change before Highfield gets here. Were there any calls? Did you get the mail?" He was still so adrenalized that he couldn't hold onto a single thought for more than a second. Paula took his arm and sat him on the couch before he fainted.

"You sit," she said. "Give me your keys and I'll go get another suit from your place." He tried to get up in protest but she stopped him, held him, and eased him back down. It was the second intimate lawyer-secretary moment they'd had that week, and just like the first one, as it was ending, Kim Bolton walked in.

"Is everything all right, Mr. Keaton?" she asked. "You seemed quite rushed as you came in – oh my God! Were you attacked? Are you all right?"

"I'm fine, thank you, Miss Bolton." She gave him a look that said, I don't even have to verbally refute that idiotic statement, but he didn't see it. He was looking at Paula, and feeling just a bit restored. "Paula, bring the light blue serge, and a tie. They're in the big wardrobe next to my bed."

"Okay, boss." They both looked at their watches. It was five after two.

"Move it," he said, and she was gone. As he sat up and considered standing, Miss Bolton came over and began to undress him, which he found insane, but he couldn't come up with a verbal protest. She took off the suit jacket and removed the torn shirt, all very matter-of-fact, as though she were his mother, and then she studied the belly wound, which was still weeping small amounts of blood.

"Do you have a first aid kit up here, Mr. Keaton?"

"No, I'm afraid we don't. Never occurred to me we'd need one."

"Yes, until today. I'll be right back. Please stay still and don't try to get up."

She let and he heard her going down the stairs. He lay there wondering why he felt so good, despite still being a little short of breath, half-naked and bleeding. *I hope there aren't any walk-in clients in the next few minutes.* Then he realized why he was happy. It wasn't beating Frank Walsh through freak luck, it was what Frank clearly still didn't know. He thought Clarence had killed Rosalie, but that was fine, since it wasn't really true. But he didn't know anything else. Then it dawned on him that Frank still wanted to kill him, and that dissipated the last part of the high and the good feeling. He would have to call Louise and see if he could get Frank arrested. He sat up as his head began to clear and the thoughts inside it became a little more orderly, and Kim Bolton reappeared and began to address the cut that was still bleeding. She applied pressure with some gauze and then painted it with mercurochrome before placing a bandage on it. When she was done, he sat up again.

"Thank you, Miss Bolton," he said. And he meant it.

"Mr. Keaton, how intimate an experience will we have to have before you can call me Kim?"

"I'm not sure..." he began.

"May I call you Clarence? Such a charming, old-fashioned name, by the way."

"Thank you. It was my grandfather's name. Yes, I suppose you can call me Clarence, if you wish, Miss – I mean, Kim." He hated being casual with business associates. *Business is business and Christmas is bullshit.* She smiled.

"Clarence, if I may say, you seem a little bit overexcited by whatever happened to you, so may I suggest you lie back down on your stomach and let me try and relax you a little?"

He knew this was both an excellent idea for him personally in this moment and a horrible idea in every other respect. He wanted to say, *We're in a goddamn office during goddamn business hours,* but she was already kneading his shoulders and he didn't even get the first word out. He moaned a little and lay on his stomach while she gave him a ten minute mini-massage. Her hands were strong, like a man's, which he noted in his head as they heard steps on the staircase, and she stopped and he stood up, amazed that he was no longer dizzy. He reached for his cigarettes and almost had one out when he realized he didn't want it. He looked at Kim Bolton and started to say something true, but it got strangled from his throat to his mouth and came out as a coughing *thank you* as Paula came in with a suit. She saw he'd been bandaged and was impressed. She turned to Kim.

"Were you a nurse?" she asked.

"No," said Miss Bolton. "Just someone who's been around, picked up a few things. You know."

"Thank you, Kim," the words were out of his mouth before he realized he should have used the formal, and Paula noticed it. You bet she did.

"Glad I could help, Mr. Keaton," she said, a tiny smile flickering through her face. She walked out and they heard her on the stairs.

"You've got about fifteen minutes," Paula said as she laid out the clothes. She waited for one extra moment for a 'thank you' and when it didn't come, she left him alone to change. Clarence could tell by the way she left that she was piqued about something, but his failure didn't register. There were too many other things crowding his brain. He dressed quickly. As he put on the suit jacket, he felt a crinkling in the inside pocket. Reaching in, he found the blackmail letter and the list of stolen items the Mayor had given him. He put the on the desk as he poured a cup of coffee and lit a smoke. Not wanting one had lasted four minutes. He picked up the letter and gave it more than a cursory look, because there was something odd, something he hadn't noticed before. At the bottom was a smiley face, which was certainly a strange thing to put at the bottom of a blackmail letter. Whoever had drawn it was pretty stupid, and this case hadn't been rife with stupid people so far, other than Frank. He looked again. The eyes were slanted a bit and the mouth was more a sneer than a smile. Why was that odd? Then he realized he'd seen it before.

Paula buzzed to say Mr. Highfield and Mr. Hay were waiting. *Mr. Hay?*

"Send them in."

And in they came. Justin Highfield and Charles Hay. Two of the richest men in Elder. Clarence had never acted for Hay, and was impressed by the expensive tailored suit he wore and the expensive watch that wasn't flashy. He arranged the the two Wing chairs to face his desk and he shook their hands as they entered and walked them over. The formalities that wealthy clients observed in his office fit his own personal style very well. He went to his desk and at facing them.

"What can I do for you, gentlemen?"

"Clarence, you have acted for me in certain matters," Highfield began, taking the lead, "But not all matters. I have always found you to be honest."

"Thank you, Justin." Mr. Hay, a square-shouldered man with a Marine haircut of white fuzz on the top of his head, took up the next thread.

"Mr. Keaton, Justin and I have joined forces recently and purchased an oil company, Bayne Petroleum. We are currently attempting to get the city to allow us to buy a particular piece of land on the Odawa reservation."

"I see."

"We believe there is a very large oil deposit under that land. And since we're proscribed from drilling in Lake Huron by the assholes in Lansing and the goddamned EPA, we hope to access the deposit from the land we wish to buy. It isn't valuable otherwise, and no Indians live on that part of the reservation."

"The northeastern edge? Is that the parcel you're trying to get?? Clarence asked, as innocently as he knew how.

"Correct. The edge of Tobico Marsh," Hay replied. "The city council will be voting for our proposal at the meeting – pardon me, voting *on* our proposal at tonight's meeting."

"But we have a small worry, Clarence," said Highfield.

"And what would that be, Justin?"

"Well, Charlie's house was burgled by a certain Mr. Elliott, and some documents were stolen. And then Mr. Elliot turned up dead."

"Yes, a most inelegant way to turn up," Clarence said, unable to help himself. Hay almost laughed, but managed to curtail the impulse. Highfield continued.

"We believe the stolen documents might be in your possession, Clarence. Would we be correct in that assumption?"

"You would be. They're not here in the office, but I would be able to lay my hands on them if it became necessary."

"We would, of course, be willing to pay you a large sum for their safe return, Mr. Keaton," said Hay. Clarence noticed Justin wasn't happy that his partner had said that.

"That wouldn't be necessary, Mr. Hay," said Clarence. "The documents belong to Bayne Petroleum and I would be happy to return them, since Mr. Elliot is dead and the case closed."

"Thank you, Mr. Keaton." Hay was smiling now. "And then there would be the matter of the council meeting tonight. Do you plan to be there?"

"I'm sorry?"

"Will you be at tonight's meeting to represent your Indian friends?" He said it with a touch of disdain, a sort of 'look who *you* associate with' attitude.

Clarence's face betrayed nothing of his growing disgust, unless you looked very closely at the lower part of his neck, which was beginning to get red. To relax and give himself a moment, he picked up his pen and opened his legal pad to a fresh page. But his estimate of where there was a blank page was incorrect, and he saw some notes and doodles on the page. One of them, he noted quickly, was a smiley face drawn exactly as on the blackmail letter.

"An Odawa elder did ask me to represent them at tonight's meeting, Mr. Hay, but I declined, because I also represent Mr. Highfield, and that would be a conflict. They told me the original interest in the land was from a real estate company, to build condos at the edge of a marsh."

"That was the original idea, Clarence," Justin chimed in, "But the surveyor's report, which I believe you might have, suggested there was a large oil deposit." Hay nodded and continued.

"So we changed what was a zoning ordinance request to an Eminent Domain request. And we've offered the tribe another plot of land of similar size on the other side of the reservation, away from the water."

"I see," said Clarence.

"Surely it's no matter to them what side of their property they get drunk on, is it, Mr. Keaton?" Hay smiled as he said it. A classic, 'We're all white people here, right?' smile. Clarence's dislike of the man was now complete, and he noticed that even Highfield had found that last remark to be over the top, to his credit.

"So then," Clarence began, "since it was an honest mistake, you need only to get those documents back from me, which we can do right now. They're at my bank."

Both men showed visible relief, giving each other a quick look and nodding. Clarence smiled. "We can certainly deal with the matters of robbery and blackmailing the Mayor another time."

That stopped their relief. Hay coughed his surprise, but Justin kept his composure.

"And then the matter will be at rest," Clarence continued, with another smile.

"I hope you have some proof, making an accusation like that, Mr. Keaton," said Hay, attempting to huff himself into a state of righteous indignation.

"I have proof that the three men who broke into my apartment and my garage out back here were hired by you gentlemen, through an intermediary, Joe Bothwell." He didn't actually have *proof* of it, but he decided to act as though he had. Justin didn't change expression. Hay snorted.

"Bullshit. There's no way Bothwell would admit that."

Highfield turned to his business partner for a look, as though to prove to himself that maybe he hadn't just said something so comically stupid, that it might be a dream. And Clarence worked hard not to grin at either of them. The bluff worked. Then he shot his big gun.

"I also have proof that the blackmail letter was written by Justin's son Jamie, Mr. Hay." And he did. The sneery-face on his legal pad had been drawn by Jamie Highfield during the short sexual assault discovery the previous week. That was where he'd seen it before. If the kid had been smart enough to type the letter, he wouldn't have known. No one would have. But thank heaven for little dumbbells.

The look on Justin's face was now one of desperate calculation, first looking at Hay, then back to Clarence, and finally he forced himself to be calm and spoke.

"Is there something we can do to work this out, Clarence?"

"Wait a minute…" said Hay, and Justin shut him up completely with a look and one motion of his hand. Clarence had guessed, correctly, that Justin was the major partner in this deal. Hay was rich, but Justin was *wealthy*, and had more power, more at stake.

"I think an arrangement could be made that might be satisfactory, Justin."

"What would that be?"

"You draw up a partnership agreement over the oil profits."

"We already *have* one, for Christ's sake!" said Hay.

"Charlie, shut the fuck up. Go on, Clarence."

"And three percent of those profits go to the Odawa Tribe."

"For how long?"

"In perpetuity, Justin. For as long as the field is producing oil. And when the oil runs out, the land ownership reverts back to the tribe."

"That's ridiculous," Hay snorted.

"Really? Once the oil's gone the land will be worthless to you, and you're losing only one point five percent of your profits apiece. Surely you can scrape that up for people you're fucking out of several billion dollars? I'll draw up the contract here this afternoon…"

"No, thank you, Clarence," Justin replied. "The terms are acceptable, but we'll do the contract. We'll have the papers drawn up and sent over here to be signed."

"Before close of day tomorrow, Justin. And I will read that contract very carefully."

"Of course."

"Oh, and there's one more thing, Justin, Mr. Hay."

"What?" they both said it at the same time.

"Along with the new contract, you will return to me whatever it is you're blackmailing George Barnet with. All copies. And then the matter will be done and you'll have your oil field." He looked at them as they exchanged a couple of *what the fuck, there's nothing else we can do* glances. Then Justin nodded.

"We accept those terms. We get the documents, you don't appear at the meeting tonight, the tribe gets three percent and ownership when the field is played out, and you get – "

"Whatever you're holding over the Mayor's head." Clarence was careful not to reveal that he knew that that was.

"Of course," said Justin, letting a long breath out. "We'll have the contract out to you tomorrow."

"I expect it by noon, Justin. And it will be signed and back to you by Friday morning."

Justin stood up, indicating to Hay that they were leaving now.

"Where are we going for the documents, Clarence?"

"I'll meet you both at First National on Michigan Avenue in a few minutes. Gentlemen." He walked to the office door, opened it and saw them out and down the stairs. As they neared the bottom of the staircase, he heard Hay say to Justin, "Massages? Seriously?" Clarence stuck his head in Paula's office when he heard the downstairs door close.

"Call the notary and have him here tomorrow at two."

"Which notary? Albright the motormouth, or Melman?"

"Melman," said Clarence, after a moment's thought. "He's a stickler. That's what we'll need. Tell him to clear out the rest of his afternoon."

"Got it." She made a note.

"Anyone else today?" he asked.

"I called the cops. They said you had to come in and report it."

"What?"

"You were assaulted! You have to report a man trying to kill you with a knife."

"Slim, that's not your business."

"Really? And if whoever it is kills you the next time, there goes my raise."

"You could always work downstairs giving massages."

"You have to promise me that you'll go in and report this. *Today.*"

"Okay, I'll go in and report it."

"I need your word," she said.

"I promise I'll report the assault to the cops, okay? Now I'm leaving. Thanks for your help today. You earned your raise, again." She nodded and smiled. "Call Melman and then go home yourself. Or..." He pulled the discount coupon for Bolton Massage out of his pocket and tossed it to her. "Go get a goddamn massage."

He left by the back stairs, got in the Merc and headed to First National. Arriving, he found Desmond, the world's smarmiest banker, fawning over the two rich men who were waiting. When he realized they were clients of Mr. Keaton, his occasional deadbeat lawyer-customer, Clarence could see his respect went up a few rungs, which might be useful another time, when business was shitty again. Next week, perhaps. He went into the safe deposit room, retrieved the relevant documents and brought them out. Hay took them and went to a table to go through them to make sure, and Clarence had a moment with Justin.

"Thank you for this, Clarence," he said.

"Always a pleasure, Justin. Please send my regards to Jamie." Highfield bristled a bit at the mention of his boy's name, but recovered. Hay came over.

"They're all here." Justin nodded.

"Goodbye, Clarence."

"Nice doing business with you boys." Clarence replied. They left the bank without replying, or acknowledging Desmond, who had positioned himself at the door to shepherd them out. He acted as though they had acknowledged him, and strutted back to his office like a man who owned the street, which he probably did.

As Clarence walked to the Merc, he knew in his bones that this would be the last time he acted for Justin Highfield. He'd have Paula send him a large bill for this little transaction, but that would no doubt be the end of it. The disappointment on Justin's face, the fear for his son, plus the fact that Clarence had forced him to give money away spelled it out. That avenue would now be closed. And Hay would never hire him unless he got caught murdering his wife or fucking his dog.

He drove to city hall. It was almost four-thirty and he was hoping the Mayor would still be in his office. He walked in and caught him coming out of the elevator, with a look like he was going to his own funeral. He was surprised to see Clarence, but a few moments later, sitting in his car, he was overjoyed, promising any kind of favor Clarence might ever need.

"I don't need favors, George. I'm glad I could help you. If you ever need a lawyer again, please give me a call."

"I will, Mr. Keaton. Believe me. Send me a bill for this."

"I will, Mr. Mayor. Believe me."

Walking back to the car, he reflected that as one opportunity went by the way, another generally stopped by. Why that was, he continued to have no idea. He doubted the Mayor would be good for the same money as Highfield had paid him over the years, but jobs lead to jobs, clients to clients. You couldn't predict it. Only your insurance guy and your banker could do that. He drove to the club, went down to the bar, waved to Simon and some others as he headed to the pay-phone in the back of the room, where he called Eddie Two Crows. Kiwi answered. Eddie wasn't home. He explained what had happened, and said he'd bring the contract over on Friday morning, so Eddie and the other Elders would have to be there to sign it. She was skeptical as he explained it.

"Why would they do that, give us money?"

"I convinced them that if they only screwed you out of 97% of what you were entitled to, they'd have something to trade when they got to heaven."

Kiwi laughed. He loved making her laugh.

"Clarence, the ravens were passing overhead today. I felt you at one point, and you were frightened."

"I'm okay, Kiwi. There was a small crisis, but I'm okay now."

"I'm glad. It'll be over soon."

"How do you know?" he asked.

"The wind, the passing of the black birds. The signs are there. You just have to look."

"Tell me something. Did you know Eddie was going to ask you to marry him before he did?"

"Of course, years before. I had a dream and I saw a warrior with the head of a falcon. When I woke up, there was a falcon on top of the black oak outside my window. He looked at me. We knew each other. When I met Eddie, I knew he was the warrior the falcon told me about."

"How long did it take for Eddie to realize it and ask you?"

"For-fucking-ever."

Clarence laughed so hard the whole room stopped drinking and stared at him. It didn't stop him, though. Laughter was the only truly natural reaction he allowed himself in public, so he howled a week's worth of anxiety out in unmeasured guffaws. Then he said goodbye to Kiwi and hung up the phone. Everyone in the bar was still staring at him. From the far corner, Simon finally called out.

"You gonna tell us the joke, you son of a bitch?" That got a big laugh, and when it subsided, Clarence shook his head.

"You had to be there." He walked to Simon's table and was going to sit down, but then thought twice about it. It was Wednesday, only Wednesday. If he were to have one or two drinks, the release mechanism could be activated, and that wasn't good. He needed to stay alert. He needed to go home, eat a decent meal and get a good night's sleep, like a regular professional person. He made his excuses to the boys at Simon's table and headed to the parking lot. He didn't expect Frank to be waiting for him in the same place, but he didn't waste any time, either, slipping into the Merc and gunning it out of the lot.

He was mistaken, but still lucky. Frank was waiting in the lot, in a nondescript car. His plan was to come up behind his brother-in-law and knock him senseless, then take him somewhere to sweat the car location out of him, and then kill him. But Clarence coming out again so quickly had bunged up that plan. Frank had figured he'd be in there at least an hour, maybe two or more. And he'd come out drunk, or at least inebriated enough to be easy to handle. When he realized it was Clarence coming out, he ducked his head quickly and banged his chin, already bruised from that lucky punch, into the steering wheel. The pain flamed up and he shut his eyes and clenched his teeth until the fire kaleidoscope subsided. When he opened his eyes again, Clarence and the Merc were gone. His anger and hatred, now nearly two decades old, made him slam the steering wheel with his hands several times. He decided to go to the house and watch for the son of a bitch there.

Clarence drove the usual way home, but then remembered his promise to Paula, so five blocks from his place, he turned the other way and headed for police headquarters. It was after six, so he didn't expect to find Mike or Louise working, but he decided that getting an update and leaving a message about his encounter with Frank couldn't hurt. At the main desk, he asked for Mike Ross, the desk sergeant called, and Mike came. He wasn't exactly pleased to see Clarence, but he took him downstairs to the cops' smoking room, which was deserted just after the six o'clock shift change. Clarence lit a smoke, offered Mike one, which was politely refused.

"What's on your mind, counselor?"

"You get a line on Frank Walsh yet, Mike?"

"We're not even sure he's in town."

"He's in town."

"You've seen him?"

"He attacked me with a knife in the parking lot of the golf club this afternoon." Mike gave him a sneer.

"You're full of shit, Keaton."

Clarence dropped his suit jacket on a chair and pulled out his shirttail to show the knife scar. Mike scoffed.

"You could have gotten that shaving your balls." Which prompted a cannonball of a laugh from Clarence, which took Mike by surprise, and he laughed as well. It might have been the first unguarded moment they'd ever shared, but they both recovered fast.

"You've got Walsh for the murder of Elliot, Mike," Clarence said.

"We don't know who killed Elliot, and even if we did, why should we care when criminals slaughter each other? It saves money."

"There's an eyewitness."

"Really? Some Indian kid, right? And you're representing him?"

Clarence was impressed, but he wasn't going to give anything away.

"I represent someone who saw the crime take place, and they will testify. If you're not interested in clearing a murder case, Mike, that's totally up to you."

"And the same guy attacked you today, right? How'd you get away? No offense, counselor, but you and an ex-con in a fight, I'd pick him."

"Well, Frank isn't the world's smartest guy, he just thinks he is. He always has. And I got lucky." It was a moment before Clarence understood he'd made a real mistake. Mike, who hadn't made detective by being an idiot, copped to it right away.

"Always has? You *know* this guy?"

"That's not relevant, Mike…"

"So you repped a guy who robbed everybody in town, and he gets murdered, and you're trying to pin it on some guy you know from way back? Have I got that right, Keaton?"

"Goddamnit, Mike, I'm not trying to pin anything on anyone. The guy killed my client. There's a witness. The rest is up to you." He stubbed out his cigarette and turned to leave. Detective Ross stopped him.

"Keaton, don't feed me bullshit. How do you know this guy, Walsh? Louise looked him up. He's from the U.P. and he's done time all over the damn state."

"I knew him a long time ago. Okay?"

"Not okay. *Tell* me."

"I grew up in the U.P., Mike. I started my law practice there."

"So you knew him. Did you defend him back then?"

"Yeah. I defended him." Clarence had hesitated just a hair while he decided to lie, and Mike picked it up.

"You just lied to a cop. That's a crime."

"How do you know I lied?"

"Keaton, I've known you more than fifteen years. And that's the first time you've ever lied to me. And you're a shitty liar." Mike was smiling. *It's not the first time,* Clarence thought. *Just the first time you've caught me.* He lit a second smoke.

"All right, Detective, you've got me. The guy is…was…my brother-in-law."

"What? You're related to a scumbag? I am shocked, Keaton." He couldn't stop smiling.

"We're not related, you horse's ass. I married his sister."

"I think I'm getting the gist here. Hell, if you'd married my sister I'd probably want to kill you."

"Well I didn't marry your fucking sister, I married his."

"How come you're not married to her now, Keaton? Did you beat her? She file a restraining order against your ass?"

"No, Mike , she died." That stopped him for a second. But only a second.

"When did she die?"

"1957."

"Jeez, how long were you two hitched up?"

"Two years and a bit."

"Well, then if he's holding onto it this long, he must think you…" he stopped again. He didn't have to say it. Clarence caught himself starting to nod and held his head as still as he could.

"I know he killed Elliot, Mike."

"Yeah, and you'd still defend him, knowing that, wouldn't you?"

"Mike, I don't normally defend people who assault me and try to kill me. But let me ask you, do you even understand the system you work under? The law states clearly: Everyone is entitled to a defense. *Entitled. Everyone.* Not just the people you like. I provide the defense. That's my goddamn *job*. Whether they did it or not isn't a part of my job. You know the percentage of people who are charged with crimes who get convicted, Mike? Do you? It's almost ninety-nine percent. Yes, I would defend Frank if he hired me. It's what I do. But I won't be able to defend him if *he kills me* first. Okay?"

"Jesus, counselor, you have a hard day or something?" Mike's smile now had a tint of self-satisfaction. Clarence cleared his throat and chuckled.

"Yeah, it was. Days when someone comes at me with a knife are always difficult. What about you?"

"Hey, I get that. Makes for a long report-writing session at the end of it."

"Is that why I caught you still here?"

"No. Since my wife and I split, I've got a little apartment with hardly any furniture in it. Who the hell wants to go home to that?"

"I'm sorry to hear it, Mike. I really am." Clarence resisted saying *if you need a lawyer for the divorce*, and was proud of himself.

"I'll put out an APB on Walsh," Mike said.

"Thanks, Mike."

"You see him, you call me."

"I will."

They headed for the stairs. But before they went up, Mike had another question.

"By the way, Keaton, I drove Louise home yesterday and she seemed weird to me. You know anything about that?"

"Well, I might know something about it, Mike."

"She has a new shotgun. It was in the kitchen. Who the hell keeps a shotgun in the kitchen?"

"You'd have to ask her."

"The locks were all new, as well. She even has a damn padlock on the garage. Is that asshole she married still coming around and threatening her?"

"Mike, I can neither confirm nor deny..."

"Yeah, yeah, I know."

"...that it might be *exactly* what's going on. But I can't confirm it and you can't tell anyone." Mike nodded. It was what he'd figured.

"Thanks, counselor. I appreciate it. How's your eye?"

"It's been better," Clarence laughed a little. "But I'll survive. Have a good night." He turned to go and was halfway down the hall when Mike called after him.

"Hey, Keaton!" He turned and saw Mike coming after him.

"What's up?"

"How did she die?"

"How did who die?"

"Your wife. Between you and me."

"Car accident. October 14th, 1957." Clarence knew Mike would look it up. Probably call Marquette PD. He was a thorough guy.

"That's only a couple of weeks away."

"Yeah," said Clarence. "It is."

"So you got married in what, July of '55?"

"That's right."

"So July would have been your twentieth anniversary."

"Yep." Clarence had passed that day, a Friday, calling in sick when he wasn't and getting blackout drunk in his apartment.

"China," said Mike.

"What?"

"China's the traditional gift for the 20th."

"I believe you're right again, Detective," said Clarence. "Thanks for seeing me." He turned and headed down the hall toward the main doors. Mike watched him until he was out of sight.

Clarence walked to his car and then sat in it for a while, smoking and remembering. He and Rosalie been married for almost a year when she'd noticed he didn't really enjoy sex that much. It took her another three or four months to actually bring it up, but he deflected it away with the fact that he was a young lawyer trying to make it in a firm. Trying to get on the partner track meant a lot of hours and a lot of pressure to win cases. That satisfied her for a short time, but she redoubled her efforts to get him interested, trying to engage him at odd times and in odd places. He tried harder, too, for a while. He really hoped she'd get pregnant and that might settle the issue down a bit. But she didn't. She had an appointment with her doctor a week or so before she died. The doctor had called, and Clarence went in to hear the results of the tests she'd taken. She was perfectly capable of having children, as it turned out. He was the problem. *In more ways than one*, he thought.

He finally started the car, but instead of going home, he drove over to Paula's house. He parked outside and walked up her driveway to check the Studebaker. It was safe inside her garage, looking beautiful. He knew he couldn't drive it until Frank was gone, but he was so tired of having to wait for the things he wanted.

Paula noticed his Merc drive up and wondered why he'd come, but watching from her living room window, she figured it out. He just wanted to check on the car. She watched him until he went back to the Merc and drove away. Neither of them realized that the extra time he took at the cop shop and her place that night saved his life.

THURSDAY

C larence awoke feeling well. He gotten home cold sober and eaten something innocuous that wouldn't make the acid rise while he was asleep to burn his esophagus. He'd slept hard and well, so the morning shower, shave and dressing rituals were performed easily. He took a look at the street from his window before he left, and saw no one. It was weird, since he had no doubt Frank knew where he lived. He walked out to the Merc feeling better than usual. The resolving of the blackmail and the oilfield matters made him imagine that he was a pretty damn good attorney. There would be lots of time later to remember what a lazy, stupid, screw-up he normally was.

He'd made coffee and was smoking his second cigarette when the phone rang. It was Louise Merwin.

"Clarence, we got him."

"Got who?"

"Who? Who were we looking for? Frank Walsh?"

"What? When?"

"Last night. An officer pulled him over for speeding and he was such an asshole the guy brought him in and saw the APB, which went out about ten minutes after they got him. So he's here."

"Has he said anything?"

"No, but we need the witness to come down and do a lineup."

"Of course. I'll bring h—the witness. Give me an hour."

"Great. See you then – what? Oh, Mike says hello."

"Hello back."

"What, you guys are buddies now?"

"Complicated. You okay, Louise?"

"Sure. A little insomnia. I'm fine. Get that witness here ASAP, okay?"

"Okay."

Paula came in just after he hung up, and he told her he had an errand. The book had the morning free and two clients and the notary in the afternoon. He reminded her that the contract would come in from Bayne at some point and she should guard it with her life. She made her usual assurances and he was off to the rez.

He pulled up to Eddie and Kiwi's house a little before nine a.m. and knocked on the door. Kiwi answered.

"I need to get Jimmy," Clarence said.

"He's not here," she answered."

"I know that, Kiwi. I need to know where he lives."

"Why?"

"They caught the guy who killed Elliot. They need Jimmy to identify him."

She looked weird when he said that.

"Kiwi, what is it?"

"Jimmy's gone, Clarence."

"Gone where?"

"Eddie put him on the train yesterday. We have friends in the Seneca nation so Eddie sent him to Buffalo to lay low until this storm passes."

"For Christ's sake. Can we get him back?"

"He's on the train. Eddie can call his friend tonight, or maybe tomorrow."

"Tonight's too late. Where is Eddie?"

"He's laying traplines today."

Clarence sat heavily in a kitchen chair. He was so close to being out of this. With Frank identified and convicted, he would go away forever, and it would be over. *Shit.* Kiwi put her hands on his shoulders.

"It's going to be okay, Clarence," she said. "You're going to hurt yourself stressing over it."

"I wish one of you had told me you were going to do this."

"Eddie was afraid Jimmy would tell someone."

"I understand." They had done the right thing. He was being selfish and he knew it. He got up and went to the door.

"It will be all right, Clarence," she repeated. "You're safe."

"Of course," he smiled, not wanting to worry her. "I'll be fine."

"Remember everything," she said. "Everything is useful."

"I'll remember that," he said, and they both laughed a little.

He drove back to town in a foul mood. Not only would this screw the case against Frank, unless he was dumb enough to still have the gun in his possession when they caught him, but it was going to make Clarence look foolish in front of cops. And of all the places one could look foolish, the three you didn't want were in front of judges, D.A.'s, and cops. As a lawyer, your leverage was in always having your predictions come true. *If you arrest my client, here's how it's going to go...* Now he was going to go in and not have what he *said* he would have. Very bad. And there was no avoiding it.

He met Louise and Mike at the jail. Toni Gallo was with them, and they all looked surprised when he walked in alone.

"Where's your witness, Keaton?" Mike asked. Clarence shook his head.

"I'm sorry, guys. He was sent away for his own safety."

"Who sent him away?" Toni asked.

"I can't say."

"Okay," said Louise, "Where did they send him?"

"I can't say."

"Well, fuck, Keaton," Mike was disgusted. "You say you've got the witness, and now he's gone. Fuckin' great."

"I don't suppose you have the gun, do you?" Clarence asked.

"No," Louise shook her head. "Haven't found anything else that incriminates him."

"Did you tell him there was a witness?"

"You think we don't know our jobs, Keaton? Yeah, we told him."

"It's okay, Mike," Louise tried to calm him a little.

"He got a lawyer before we told him about the witness, Clarence," said Toni, "but it didn't faze him at all."

"Who's his lawyer?"

"Robert Flacco." Clarence had a moment of residual envy, but he stopped himself from pursuing it.

"Okay. I guess there's nothing to be done," he said. "I'm really sorry. They didn't tell me they were sending him away. He's just a kid."

"We got a search warrant for Walsh's place and we'll keep looking for the gun," Mike said, not sounding really confident. "But if we don't find anything we're probably going to have to kick him later today." Louise and Toni Gallo nodded.

"Watch yourself, Clarence," Louise warned him.

"Yeah. Don't worry."

He drove back to the office and went in looking a little hangdog and saggy. Paula noticed and followed him into his office with her notepad. He sat in his chair and opened the drawer for an Egyptian cigarette. They were normally congratulatory reward smokes, but today he was making an exception. He lit it and noticed Paula was sitting in one of the Wing chairs.

"Hey, Slim."

"You don't look like anything good happened this morning," she said.

"Nothing did. The witness to Elliot's murder was sent away for safety and nobody told me, so the guy who sliced me is going to get out of jail in a few hours."

"What does he want from you?"

"He wants the Studebaker. And…some satisfaction, I guess."

"Well, I have some news. There were two checks in the mail this morning."

"Excellent."

"They were both small." She paused. After a moment, Clarence spoke.

"I assume that's the good news."

"It is."

"And the bad?"

"Justin Highfield called and said the contract would be here by noon, and that he would be retaining new counsel for all his legal work from now on." She waited for him to be angry, and was surprised when he wasn't. "I guess you expected that?"

"More or less. They were doing some really awful things and I forced them to do something they didn't want to. I figured it would be the end. Good riddance."

"So my raise is canceled?"

"What? No. You earned it. You get it. We may have to move the office to your garage in a few months, but we'll be okay."

"Will we? Highfield was fully a third of our receivables the last few years."

"Yeah and he paid on time, too. Something will come up."

"You don't sound sure of that."

"I'm not. That's the beauty of this job. We might have to scrimp a little for a few months."

"In what way? Should I switch to one-ply toilet paper in the bathroom?"

"Certainly not. We're not heathens. Anything else?" He took a drag on the cigarette and realized he was almost done smoking it and he hadn't enjoyed a second of it. *Goddamnit, Paula.*

"I called Melman to see if he could get here earlier, but he can't. He'll be here at four. Which means…"

"I know. I'll have to stay late. No problem. Send Highfield our final bill for services. Four thousand. Put a thank you note in. The standard one."

"Okay. Do you think he'll pay it?"

"I think he will. Send a bill for three thousand to the Mayor as well."

"Didn't we already bill him three grand?"

"I did him an extra favor. He told me to send another bill. Whatever the client wants. That's my motto."

"No it isn't," she smiled.

"No. It isn't." *Business is business and Christmas is bullshit,* he thought. *That's my motto.*

"Well, I guess we'll be okay for a couple of months," she said.

"Possibly. And Desmond Ivey thinks I'm a solid guy now because he saw me doing business with Highfield and Hay. That should make my next hat-in-hand visit for a large overdraft much easier. I'd say we're okay for six months. What do I have in court next week?"

"Two motions on Monday, one for the Klein lawsuit, and a change of venue motion for Johnson. Tuesday you have a traffic court DUI and that nutbag who likes to fight speeding tickets as well. Wednesday the real estate thing is supposed to close, and Thursday you start the Clevinger trial."

"God, like a dog who works for people, that's me. I could win the Clevinger trial."

"He blew his wife's head off with a rifle in their own bedroom. How do you win that?"

"He didn't know the gun was loaded. It is the most innocent 'I-shot-my-wife-in-the-head-but-I-didn't-mean-to' ever." Paula laughed.

"Oh, I forgot. Your tailor called. Something about shirts."

"Right, thanks. Bring in the real estate stuff and the Clevinger files. I've got the Klein and Johnson stuff here. I guess I'll have to do some real work today."

"I guess so," she said, getting up and heading out. Clarence decided to have a second Egyptian smoke before he started the work. This one he savored every lungful. Then he called Benny.

"Hey, favorite customer!"

"Hey, Benny. You started making my suit yet?"

"No, sorry, Clare. Still swamped up here."

"I'm a little swamped myself, but I might be able to sneak up tomorrow night."

"That'd be great man. I'd love to see you."

"Barring acts of God or other calamities, I'll be there. I'll keep you posted on my arrival time."

"Okay. Looking forward to it." Benny sounded a little rushed, as though there was someone in the shop with him. But he never wasted time on small talk, even within their little codes.

He started with the Klein motion, finishing that in just under an hour. Then the Johnson change of venue request, which he knew he would lose. It was a stalling tactic, anyway. That took about twenty-five minutes. Then the real estate contracts got their perusal. Everything looked okay, but he made a note to call the house inspector, whose name he didn't know, and have a chat with him. Then he dove into Clevinger, calling his doctor witness to have him come in to go over the testimony, and tweaking the draft of his opening statement, which was pretty good, he decided. Then he went over the police evidence reports again, item by item. He made notes on what he would ask the officers and detectives on cross-examination. He was glad the detectives on the case weren't Mike and Louise, because he was going to have to try and make them look sloppy and foolish, which he was fairly confident he could pull off.

When he looked up from finishing the Clevinger stuff it was almost one-thirty, and he decided to go to the club. He was putting on his suit jacket when the phone rang. Paula said it was Mike Ross.

"Counselor, we didn't find anything on the search, other than a file on you."

"On me?"

"Yeah, he's got a file of stuff. The newspaper reports on the car accident, the death and funeral notices, articles where you're mentioned as the lawyer, some photos of you, that sort of shit. It's a little creepy, I gotta tell you."

"You should feel it from my side," said Clarence. Mike laughed.

"We're going to try and keep him another day or two on a parole violation. He threatened you, right?"

"He assaulted me."

"All right, come in and swear out a complaint for assault and we'll be able to keep him until you can get hold of your witness. That work?"

"Sure, Mike. I'll be in this afternoon. Thanks."

"No problem. It's possible I owe you one. But just one. We won't be making a habit of this, right?"

"Never. I'll see you in a little while."

He stopped by Paula's desk and told her he'd be back at three thirty.

"Hey," he said, as he started down the stairs, "Did the contract come from Bayne Oil?"

"It's here," she said. "Delivered a little after twelve."

"Okay, I'll be back."

He drove to the cop shop, swore out the complaint, signed it, and headed to the club. He really wanted a drink, but it was only two o'clock when he got there, and he had at least two hours or more with Melman to go over the contract, which wasn't exactly hard work, but it was meticulous and he just couldn't justify the beer he was craving. Besides, no one at a bar who saw him drinking at two in the afternoon on a Thursday would ever hire him. Other than maybe Simon Roche, who offered him a beer as soon as he sat down. He demurred, and ordered a coke when the waitress came around.

"What's the word, Simon?"

"The word is caution today."

"Caution?"

"Yeah. We've had a good week, right? Made overhead and then some. So let's be cautious and not blow the wad this weekend."

"How many games you looking at?"

"Ahh, let's see now…seven college games Saturday, and I'll probably bet all the NFL games on Sunday."

"How is that being cautious?"

"I'm staying away from the horses today and tomorrow so I can study and make my picks for the weekend. Besides, you bet all the games, you're going to break even at least fifty percent of the time."

"That's bullshit and you know it."

"Hush. I'm *studying*." He had newspapers, tout sheets and handwritten pages covered in statistics in front of him."

"The bar should charge you rent," said Clarence. "What's the line on the Lions?"

"They are…favored….that can't be right…over the Vikings by three."

"They never beat the Vikings."

"You are correct, almost. I think they beat them once a few years ago. But they will beat them again at some point, and the man who correctly predicts that win will make some real money."

"He certainly will."

"But not this week. I've got two hundred on the Vikes taking the three points."

"Very cautious of you."

"My horoscope this morning said that animals would disappoint me today."

"So that's why no horses."

"Exactly. Or Lions. You can't buck the stars."

"I never do."

"Who do you like in the Denver-Dallas game?"

By three-twenty the two of them had figured out exactly how to bet every football game on the board for Sunday, and Clarence had given his opinion on four of the college games as well. Simon was concentrating so hard he barely noticed Clarence left as the bar began to fill with the regular late-afternoon bunch. Driving the Merc back to the office to meet Melman, Clarence had a couple of moments of real peace and satisfaction. Knowing Frank wouldn't be out for a while, and anticipating heading to Lansing as soon as noon on Friday, he allowed himself some breathing without concern, which was delicious. It was so good he got frightened after a minute and forced himself to worry again, which was easier as a default position.

Melman arrived punctually at four, a pinched little man who had no vices and few friends. He played golf at the club, and was known for the fact that he hit virtually every club in his bag the exact same distance. Paula ushered him in and then said goodbye. They got right to it without chitchat. Melman couldn't stand cigarette smoke so Clarence had to abstain for as long as it took, which he did. Together they went over the contract, all twenty-four pages of it, line by line. Clarence would ask questions, and Melman would either answer them or click his teeth to suggest they were irrelevant. After more than three hours, he pronounced the agreement free of mistakes or loopholes. He showed Clarence where to sign as Lawyer of record, and where the Tribal elders had to sign. Clarence thanked him and gave him a check. Melman produced a receipt book and filled one out, exchanging it for the check. *Business is business* was also his motto. Clarence relaxed when he heard the downstairs door shut, and had the smoke he was craving. He poured himself a glass of scotch, too. Neat.

The combination was powerfully addictive. He finished the smoke, and lay back on the couch, closing his eyes for just a moment. When he opened them it was after eight.

He was clearing the desk and putting the contract into its own envelope when he noticed the other envelope. It said *Barnett* on it. He checked inside to make sure it was what he thought, and then wondered what to do. He couldn't take it to the post office and have it shredded until tomorrow, and he certainly wasn't going to keep it overnight, for any reason. He went down the hall toward the bathroom to the utility closet and got the metal bucket the cleaning lady used. He went into the bathroom and opened the window as wide as it would go. Then he lit the bottom of the envelope on fire with his lighter and held it until he was sure it was going to burn well. Then he dropped it into the bucket and stood there for the two or three minutes it took to let it become nothing but ash, waving his arms to encourage the smoke out the window. Then he turned on the tap and put an inch or two of water in the bucket, sloshed it around, poured it into the toilet and flushed it down.

He put on his jacket and coat and left the office by the front door for the first time in a few days. His feet crunched on the gravel heading around back to the lot and the Merc. He loved the sound of his oxfords on the gravel. *His* gravel, his office, his massage parlor.... he laughed to himself. Upstairs the phone rang, but he didn't hear it.

He decided to go to the club. Normally he wouldn't have showed up after eight, but he wanted a drink and a laugh. *Just one*, he thought. There would be a good group on a Thursday night, celebrating an early weekend. All the doctors who took Fridays off would be there, dispensing medical advice that got more and more bizarre the drunker they became. But first, he drove to the reservation and Eddie's house. Kiwi let him in and warmed up a wonderful meal for him to eat. He showed them the contract. They were stunned by it. Eddie mentioned that he'd come home from the council meeting feeling pretty low because they were being completely screwed and there was nothing to be done about it.

"Well," said Clarence, "tomorrow, you can take this to the Elders and have them sign it. Then bring it to my office. If I'm not there, give it to Paula."

"How much money will it be?" Kiwi asked.

"Total? Impossible to say. But they've already spent real money getting the ordinance to get the land and they're going to spend more on the equipment to get started. I think the oil will bring them in the neighborhood of between one and three billion dollars, over, say ten years. That's just an estimate. But if it brings in a billion, that's 30 million for the tribe."

"This is unbelievable," said Kiwi, shaking her head and turning to Eddie. "We can build a new school and hire good teachers." Eddie laughed. "What's funny about that?" she asked.

"Nothing," he replied. "I was thinking I could get new traps." They looked at each other and started laughing harder.

Clarence got back to Elder around ten p.m. and wrestled his conscience to the best of three falls, winning easily and heading home. He would have a delicious glass of The Balvenie and a last cigarette and not wake up tomorrow with a hangover. He had done a good thing, hell, *several* good things this week and felt appropriately righteous. It was such a good feeling that his brain didn't even mention that it could all change in a single moment, as it normally did whenever he allowed himself to feel happiness.

He walked up the steps to his apartment, hung up his jacket, got out the scotch and poured three fat fingers, put the scotch away and was opening a new pack of smokes when he felt a presence in the room. He hadn't turned on the living room light, and now he did, revealing Frank Walsh sitting in his easy chair pointing a small gun at him. A Beretta. He wondered why the cops hadn't found it. He didn't act startled or drop the smokes, but he roiled inside and started to seriously perspire. Death being near did that to him.

"Hi, Frank," he managed, though his breath was a little short. He opened the pack and punched one out, got it in his mouth and lit it. He offered the pack to Frank.

"Fuck off, Keaton. I want my car."

"Of course. How much were you planning to pay me?" The first drag had helped Clarence's composure and he'd gotten his breath back. It was amazing how something that would eventually take away your ability to breathe would often restore it in a crisis.

"I'm not paying you shit. I'm gonna get my car and then kill your stupid ass. And I'm gonna enjoy it. I know you killed Rosalie."

"Forgive me, Frank, but you don't know sheep-shit from cherry stones."

"Why was she driving to Big Bay that night?"

"Why do you think? We had a fight. She was really upset. She was leaving me."

"Yeah, no shit. But *why*? What was the fight about?"

"Sex, Frank. It was about sex."

"You wanted her to do something kinky, right? You sick bastard."

"No…" Clarence was surprised as the truth rose through his chest and found its way into his mouth. He was watching it and couldn't impede the progress. "It wasn't anything kinky. I didn't like having sex with her."

"What?" Frank's comprehension skills were less than average, going all the way back to second grade. "What are you, Keaton? A fucking homo?"

"Yeah, Frank. That's what I am." Clarence felt another surge of flop sweat as he said it. Frank stood up, still pointing the gun.

"You know, I thought about that once, but I decided it just wasn't possible."

"Well, it was. It is. And now you know."

"Why'd you fucking marry her then?"

"I didn't want to be a fag, who would? Who would pick this stupid life? I thought she would, god help me, cure me. And…"

"And…you are so full of shit."

"I loved her. She was the best person I'd ever known. That night she told me it didn't matter what the problem was. All I had to do was tell her and we would work it out. She promised me it would be okay. And I believed her."

"So you told her…" Frank had been truly muted by finally hearing the truth. The gun hand was down by his side, and Clarence wondered if he could take one big leap-step and bowl him over. He doubted it. He'd been lucky once, but that kind of physical luck wasn't likely a second time. He decided to try and keep him talking. It didn't matter, anyway. Either he'd be killed or Frank would be caught and the whole town would know and his career would be over.

"So I told her I was gay. And it was probably the one thing that she didn't expect. And it didn't just shock her, it horrified her. She went to our bedroom and packed a little bag and got in the car and left."

"What'd she say?"

"That's the thing, she never said *anything*. She didn't say goodbye, or you fucking bastard or anything. She didn't even look at me. She just filled a bag with clothes and took her coat and keys and left."

"And she crashed the car."

"There was ice on the road that night. She was probably crying. I don't know."

"You killed her."

"Yes, she died because of me. If I hadn't married her she'd still be alive. If I wasn't gay, she'd still be alive. If I'd never told her, she'd still be alive. Don't you think that tortures me, for Christ's sake?"

"Well, it's not going to torture you much longer, Keaton." He raised the gun. "Let's go."

"Go where?"

"Where's my car?"

"It's locked in my secretary's garage."

"What's the address?"

"I'll drive you over there."

"Fuck that. Tell me the address."

"Look, Frank, you can shoot me right now, and leave town. Take my Mercury," he offered the keys, "You might get all the way to Chicago before they catch you and bring you back and put you away for life. But if you want the Starlight, I'm going to have to take you to where it is."

"Why? Why can't you just tell me? You're going to die tonight anyway. Wouldn't you rather die here?"

"Frank, you fire that gun, my landlady calls the cops. They'll be here in under four minutes. The station's eight fucking blocks away. You'll never make it out of my neighborhood. Be smart. I'll take you to the Studebaker."

Frank's eyes flickered as a slew of thoughts invaded his normally uncrowded brain. He made his decision fairly quickly, as he had all his life.

"Let's go," he said. "I'll have this on you the whole way."

"I would expect nothing less," said Clarence, amazed at the reprieve that made chance possible as well as his continuing ability to form sentences. They went down the stairs, quietly, Frank going first. They got into the Merc and pulled away.

"Who's got the keys to the Starlight?" Frank asked.

"They're in the car, Frank."

"That's very dangerous, Keaton," he laughed. "Someone could steal the fucking thing."

"The garage is padlocked."

"So you'll have to wake her up and get the key to that, right?"

"Yes, but I can do that alone. She doesn't have to see you."

"Well, that's just tough fucking luck for her, isn't it? You really think I'm that stupid? You go in, get the key, tell her to call the cops, sure, that's going to happen."

"You're not going to hurt her, Frank."

"No, Keaton. I'm going to kill her. And you." Clarence hit the brakes and pulled the car over.

"Shoot me now," he said.

"Goddamnit, Keaton, take me to my fucking car!"

"I go to the door alone and get the padlock key or forget it, Frank. You can kill me right here and dump me on the street and get out of town. I'm not getting anyone else killed."

Frank sighed and figured the angles again.

"All right, Keaton. You go to the door alone, you get the key. I'll have the gun pointed at your head."

"Your word on it?"

"My word on it."

Clarence checked his mirrors and pulled away. He had been hoping to see a cop car passing by but there was almost no traffic. He drove silently into a quiet neighborhood and parked the car in front of a modest, two story clapboard house with a detached garage. They both got out and Frank pointed to the garage.

"Let's see if it's open," he whispered.

"It's locked, Frank."

"Maybe she left it open. Move." He put the gun into Clarence's back and shoved him ahead. The garage had a large padlock on it, secured.

"This looks new," said Frank.

"She had it put on when I gave her the car for safekeeping," said Clarence.

"That was smart," said Frank, peering into the window of the dark garage, trying to make out the silhouette of his beautiful car. "It is a car to die for."

"I'll go to the door," said Clarence.

"Yeah, I'll go with you."

"What? You said – ..." Frank hit him in the stomach with the butt of the gun. Clarence went down, huffing and sucking wind, wondering if he'd throw up. While he was down, Frank slapped him really hard across the face.

"Get your fucking ass up and go get the key to this fucking garage. I'll be behind you. You try anything and I'll kill her first."

Clarence managed to get up and they headed for the door. He had a look around as they did and saw no lights on in any of the surrounding houses. So the cops probably weren't coming. He went up the steps to the front door a little louder than he should have, and before Frank could get there he lifted his fist and pounded on the door several times as hard as he could.

"OPEN THIS FUCKING DOOR, YOU FUCKING BITCH!" he screamed.

"What the fuck, are you nuts?" said Frank, literally pushing Clarence aside. Clarence went down to the floor again and there was a really long second while Frank stared at him, incredulous.

Then the door exploded. The sound of the shotgun came right after. Two solid loads of double-aught buckshot blew a perfect round hole through the top of it and shredded Frank Walsh's head like it was paper. He was blown backwards fifteen feet and died before his body hit the sidewalk. Clarence crawled to the far end of the porch, his ears ringing. The lights went on all over the neighborhood, including the porchlight that came on above him.

The door was pushed outward slowly by a hand, and the shotgun appeared, then behind it, Louise Merwin. She saw Clarence's shape in her peripheral vision and swung the shotgun around. Clarence put his hands up and tried to say something, but he had no breath to make sound. She stopped, clearly confused, and lowered the gun.

"Clarence?" she said. He nodded. "Are you okay? I didn't shoot you, did I?"

He managed a very croaky "I'm fine," and tried to get up, but he didn't have enough breath and he sank back down, his back against the wrought-iron railing, trying to find enough oxygen to remain alive. Louise turned and saw Frank's body stretched out on the sidewalk, blood pooling around his head.

"Who the hell is that?" she asked. And then they heard sirens.

FRIDAY

He got home at eight a.m., the interviews and reports at the police station finished. He was advised to get a lawyer, but declined, since he didn't want to get Flacco out of bed and pay him a retainer for nothing. Plus it had been Flacco's diligence that got Frank Walsh bailed out in the first place. Mike Ross said they'd called his home and his office to warn him, and Shorty confirmed when he arrived at the apartment that his phone had been ringing "all goddamn night". He called Paula and asked her to bring the Starlight over when she could.

"Just park it behind the Merc and leave the keys in my mailbox."

"You all right, boss? You sound like you were up all night."

"I was. We'll talk about it another time."

"Okay."

He fell asleep at about eight thirty and the phone woke him a little after ten. It felt like a regular night's sleep rather than only 90 minutes. He managed to garble a *'hello'* before the coughing fit started, and when he recovered, it was Mr. Crocker from Marquette.

192

"I do regret to inform you, Mr. Keaton, that your father passed away last night."

In any other state of mind, the news would have hit much harder. But he'd been pre-trauma'ed by the previous night's adventure, so he didn't cry or feel the pain or the hole such a loss leaves.

"What time?"

"I'm sorry, Mr. Keaton? Oh, what time did he pass on? Yes, I have it here…he departed at 11:48 p.m."

"Thank you, Mr. Crocker."

"The body was taken to Mallon's funeral home, as per your instructions."

"Thank you again."

"If there's anything else we can do…" Crocker began, but Clarence had hung up the phone. He dialed Paula at the office.

"Hello?"

"My father died."

"Oh. I'm so sorry, boss."

"So you need to switch the motions on Monday to Wednesday, okay? And reschedule any clients who were coming on Monday. Eddie Two Crows will probably bring in the signed contract for Bayne Oil on Monday. Have it delivered to Justin Highfield – Eyes Only."

"Got it." He could hear her making notes. "Anything else?"

"Oh God, yes. You have to come here on Sunday at 3:30 and take Shorty to see 3 Days Of The Condor at the Odeon. Show at 4:00."

"Seriously?"

"Yes. If you don't, she'll up my rent and you'll lose your raise."

"Okay. I'll take the money out of petty cash."

"Fine. I'll be back for Tuesday morning."

"See you then."

"Thanks for bringing the car."

"You're welcome, boss. Drive safe."

After packing a bag, Clarence phoned the funeral home and arranged for a viewing of the body for Sunday afternoon, which would be followed by cremation. He said he would drop by on Saturday to settle the bill. Then he phoned Mike Ross at the police station and told him he was going to the U.P. to bury his father. If they needed him for anything, he'd be back in the office Tuesday. Then he put his stuff in the Starlight and started that perfect engine, listened to it for a moment and headed out of town.

He went to Lansing first, figuring he'd get a night with Benny. He got to the tailor shop in the mid-afternoon and was surprised, going in the front door, to see a FOR SALE sign in the window. Benny owned the building and rented out the three other units. It was an inkling of something amiss, but Benny was happy to see him and he closed the shop early and they went to his house. After they'd made love, Clarence lit a smoke and waited for Benny to tell him the news. After a shower, Benny came into the bedroom and sat next to him.

"I met someone," he said. Which Clarence had known as soon as he saw the sign in the window.

"Where does he live?" Clarence asked.

"San Francisco," said Benny. 'He's got a tailor shop out there and he needs another tailor. Offered me a partnership."

"In more ways than one."

"Yeah, that's true, too. You and I were never exclusive, Clarence."

"I know. It's fine. I knew it would come. I always thought I was lucky to know you this long."

"I thought the same. I got offered an excellent price for the building this morning. And the real estate guy thinks my house will sell high, too."

"It's a nice house."

"San Francisco is *the* place for gay people right now. Very open city. Welcoming. Warm, too." He almost said *you should come*, but he knew not to.

"Yeah." *Lawyers don't move,* he thought. *Lawyers don't retire. They die at their desks.* "Well, I'd better get going."

"Oh, come on. Stay the night." Clarence looked into his friend's eyes. He'd never said '*I love you*' to him, something he now regretted. He had always been afraid of this day and at the same time known it would come. He had sometimes practiced his part of their inevitable break-up conversation, but now, in the moment of it, he had no words. He started to get dressed. Benny just watched him.

His shoes went on last and he picked up his bag, but then put it down and went over and kissed Benny, mouth open, arms around, tasting him a long time so he might remember. They broke the kiss, and he put a small one on his cheek too, turned, took the bag and left. He was putting the bag in the trunk of the car when Benny came out, but he didn't say anything. He just watched Clarence shut the trunk, get in the Starlight, start it, and take off. He started to wave, but Clarence didn't even glance in the rear view for a last look.

He got to the highway, and pointed the Starlight towards Marquette, four hundred miles away. About twenty minutes later, he started to cry, and kept doing that, in intervals, for the whole drive.

THE END

JOHN WING Jr

Born in Sarnia, Ontario, John started as a standup comedian in Toronto in 1980, moving on to Los Angeles in 1988. He has over 300 television appearances to his credit, including six *Tonight Shows*, with both Johnny Carson and Jay Leno. A regular performer at comedy festivals, John has headlined at the Montreal *Just For Laughs Festival* as well as the Winnipeg, Vancouver, Edmonton, Niagara Falls, Toronto, and Halifax Comedy Festivals, racking up over fifty in his long career. In 2013, John was a semi-finalist on *America's Got Talent*, performing three times at *Radio City Music Hall*. For many years, he's performed his comedy on cruise ships around the world, *including Holland America, Royal Caribbean, Norwegian, Carnival,* and *Celebrity Cruise Lines.*

He published his first book of poems in 1998. *The Last Coherent Thing* is his tenth collection. *A Car To Die For* is his first novel. Since April of 2020, John has written and performed the podcast *The Bad Piano Player,* now with more than fifty episodes available for download. Married for 32 years to Dawn Greene, with two grown daughters, John lives in Los Angeles, California.

Books by John Wing Jr

Poetry

A Cup Of Nevermind (Mosaic Press) 1998
...And The Fear Makes Us Special (Mosaic Press) 2000
Ventriloquism For Dummies (Black Moss Press) 2002
None Of This Is Probably True (Mosaic Press) 2003
Excuses (Mosaic Press) 2005
The Winter Palace (Mosaic Press) 2007
When The Red Light Goes On, Get Off (Black Moss Press) 2008
So Recently Ancient (Mosaic Press) 2010
Almost Somewhere Else (Mosaic Press) 2012
Why-Shaped Scars (Black Moss Press) 2014
I'll Be There Soon (Black Moss Press) 2016
The Last Coherent Thing (Mosaic Press) 2021

Fiction

A Car To Die For (Mosaic Press) 2021